WEST END DROIDS

&

EAST END DAMES

3rd Easytown Novel
by
Brian Parker

MUDDY BOOTS PRESS

This is a work of fiction. Names, characters, places and incidents are the product of the author's imagination and are used fictitiously. Any resemblance to actual events, locales, or persons, living or dead, is purely coincidental.

Notice: The views expressed herein are NOT endorsed by the United States Government, Department of Defense or Department of the Army.

West End Droids & East End Dames an Easytown Novel

ONE: WEDNESDAY

Chink! Chink! Chink!

"Jesus, Drake! Watch out!" I shouted, shoving my partner into an alley. The wall above us had three deep gashes in the concrete where the cyborg had shot at us.

"Don't gotta tell me twice," the big man rumbled.

I peeked around the corner and my hat went flying, a neat hole torn through the front peak. *If I'd stuck my head out just a little farther...*

Just before the cyborg attacked us, Drake and I had signed over the body of Dale Henderson to the medical examiner's droids. Henderson was a doorman at the thumper club, Liquid Genesis, who'd been murdered in his apartment a few blocks off The Lane. Neither of us saw where the 'borg came from before we were running for our lives, firing our pistols over our shoulder at the maniac.

"Dammit, Andi, we need support. *Now!*" I said through gritted teeth; that was my favorite hat. My phone's microphone picked up my voice, and my ever-present assistant answered.

"I've alerted the police drone dispatcher, boss. They're trying to decide if the current threat warrants removing a drone from citizen protection duty."

"You tell that pencil-pushing asshole that he needs to send me a drone. Drake and I are pinned down."

There was a pause from Andi, my AI assistant, as she did what I'd directed her to do. Down the road, I could hear the perp taunting us, although I couldn't make out his words.

"What's he saying?" I asked Drake.

"You know, the same thing they always say, 'You'll never take me alive, copper.' That sort of stuff."

I glared at the former football player. "Are you kidding me right now? Our bodies are about to gain a few extra holes and you've got jokes?"

Drake shrugged and then jutted his chin back toward Jubilee Lane. "Looks like your request was approved."

Flying directly toward us was a police drone. It banked sharply and set down on the road. "Detective Zachary Forrest. Do you require assistance?" the drone asked.

"Yes, goddamn it! Kill that fucking 'borg!"

"Affirmative." The drone issued a warning to the perp and the twin miniguns mounted underneath its body began spinning.

A bellow of incoherent rage answered the drone's warning and something massive slammed into the spindly legs supporting it. I watched in shock as the remains of a metal park bench skittered down the alleyway, carrying the drone's legs with it.

Its turbofans engaged, lifting the damaged drone skyward as several small metallic discs impacted against its body. The same jagged streaks that marred the building above our head appeared across the drone as the cyborg's weaponry did some major damage, turning the drone's exterior armor into an overpriced pasta strainer.

I'd seen those types of rounds at a murder scene a few months ago. They'd gone through walls, flesh, even bone.

"Fuck this," I said, drawing my Smith & Wesson Aegis pistol.

The drone listed badly to one side as the damaged turbofans struggled to keep it aloft. It returned fire with the miniguns, but the rounds flew wild as the weapons' recoil further destabilized it.

Chink! Chink! Chink!
Chink! Chink! Chink!

The cyborg shouted something about cocksuckers and power as the bullets from his gun tore into the drone. I took the only opportunity we were probably going to get and stepped out of the alley.

The thing stood twenty yards away. I'd seen the ganger before, when he was human, and I was pretty sure it was the same guy who shot at me a few months ago when the mayor put a price on my head. The 'borg was as big as a tree, in fact, that's why they called him Branch. He was six-eight, easily two hundred and eighty pounds when he was wholly human. Now, there was no telling how much he weighed. He wore some type of exoskeleton around his legs that increased his height by a good two feet. One of his arms had been removed at the shoulder and a massive weapon of some type was surgically attached in its place—or maybe it was mechanically attached, I'm not sure how the back alley chop shop that made him did things. In his opposite hand, he held a smaller machine gun that would have been too heavy for me to hold one-handed.

The cyborg also had dreadlocks, which reminded me of the tweaker a few months ago who'd thought his synthaine house had been attacked by some type of octopus demon-something-or-other. Coupled with the miniature saw blades the guy was shooting, I was willing to bet he was the attacker from that case. He'd gotten away without a trace, but I had him now.

The 'borg was clearly deranged, his features twisted into what could best be described as savage glee as he fired both guns at the police drone. He was concentrating on the drone and didn't see me step out of the alley.

As I fired a shot from the Aegis, the drone crashed. My shot severed the cyborg's weapon arm, sending the larger of the two guns clattering to the rough pavement. "Goddamn it," I groaned, diving back into the alley.

"What now?" Drake asked aiming his pistol blindly down the street and firing two rounds. The service revolver looked like a child's toy in his large hands.

The edge of the building behind us disintegrated as Branch went full auto with his remaining machine gun. If he wasn't pissed off before, he sure as hell was now that I'd blown one of his arms off.

"I missed my shot," I admitted. "I'd been aiming for his chest and I took off an arm instead."

"That ain't such a bad thing, Detective."

The drone flickered to life and punched upward about three feet in the air. It fired another volley at the cyborg and then went down again. The metal shuddered as Branch pumped more rounds into it, putting an end to the drone once and for all.

I fired another blast from the laser pistol and ducked behind the cover of the building before I saw whether I hit him or not. He roared in anger.

"Did you get him?" Drake asked.

"Yeah, of course," I replied, not knowing if I did.

The ominous sound of stomping metallic feet bounced off the walls of the buildings around us. "I *thought* I got him," I amended.

Drake and I ran further into the alley where a dumpster gave us a small bit of cover. *It'll protect us from the first couple of those giant bullets*, I thought. After that, we were through.

Plink!

A round impacted against the far side of the dumpster and I ducked instinctively as a hole appeared near my head.

"Goh dummit!" Branch shouted at the head of the alley.

I popped my head up. He was out of bullets and without his other arm, he couldn't reload unless he set the weapon down. "Guess I did good," I quipped, stepping into the center of the alley.

The giant charged, running straight at me. I squared my chest to him and pushed the Aegis out, bringing the sight posts to eye level.

A baseball-sized hole appeared just above Branch's sternum. I fancied that I could see The Lane completely through him before he toppled over, his body hitting the dumpster and sending it skittering noisily down the alley.

"Great shootin', Detective," Drake praised, slapping me on the back.

I holstered the laser pistol and wiped the sweat away from my palms. Now that the ordeal was over, I was able to admit to myself that I'd been scared as hell.

"Andi, we need to get a biological contamination cleanup crew down here… Probably a crane too."

"Son of a bitch," Drake muttered, pointing at the cyborg.

"What—Shit." Branch was still alive. He struggled to move, missing an arm and with a giant hole in his chest, but the bastard was still alive. "Cover me."

"*Heh.* Better you than me," Drake replied, aiming his pistol at the cyborg's head.

I walked over and planted my foot firmly into the suspect's crotch, eliciting a groan from him. "Ah, you have the right to remain silent," I began as I surveyed the giant, trying to figure out how I'd handcuff a one-armed man who possessed enough strength to pick up a three hundred pound park bench and throw it across an alley.

I finished the perp's Miranda Rights and then asked Andi to eject the spool of high-tension wire from the drone. It took her several seconds longer than normal and she apologized.

"Drone Unit Two One Six is effectively destroyed, Zach. It took a little more work to navigate the back door."

"No worries, Andi," I said, picking up the wire and carrying it back to where Branch lay prone. I kicked him in the balls again for good measure—the fucker tried to kill me and my partner, what'd he expect?

Using the spool of tension wire, I secured his remaining human arm to his side and then wrapped it around six or seven times before tying a square knot with the two running ends of the wire. *Then* the uniformed cops decided to show up with several more patrol drones and an ambulance.

All in a day's work.

"You've got a call waiting from Chief Brubaker, Zach."

"Uh, sure. Patch him through." It was after midnight; usually the chief was cuddled up in bed at this hour. I paused until the line switched over. "Howdy, Chief," I answered, feeling pretty good about taking down the cyborg.

"What in the hell are you doing down there, Forrest? I'm getting reports of houses that'll need to be condemned, civilian casualties inside apartment buildings, and dispatch is reporting the destruction of a ten million dollar police drone. You better start talking."

"We were jumped by a cyborg in the middle of an investigation, Chief," I replied. "Check the surveillance video of the perp opening fire on us. Then when you're done with that, have the guys analyze the drone's gun camera footage and you'll see that the 'borg was the aggressor here. We didn't start this fight."

"I get it, Forrest, but I've got pressure on me to rein you in."

I'd had a target on my back in one form or another since the day I joined the force. These days, the pressure came from a lot higher up in the department and the city's government—namely, one City Councilman Todd Jefferson. He hated me because I'd detained him in a whorehouse for several hours, prompting his wife to begin asking some hard questions that he couldn't answer. They'd divorced soon afterward and he'd been gunning for me ever since.

"You've always got pressure on you to keep me from doing my job," I retorted. "The bottom line is that there wasn't any other way it could have gone down without Drake or me ending up dead."

Robert Brubaker was one of the good guys, and he went to bat for me all the time. Without him, I'd have been fired years ago. I was the best detective in the entire New Orleans PD and he knew it, so he was willing to take some of the heat.

"I want a full report in two hours."

"Two hours?" I repeated. "We haven't had time to start our investigation at the Henderson murder scene."

"He's a nobody. Seal the room and finish it tomorrow," Brubaker grumbled. "Two hours."

The line went dead and I told Drake about the chief's order.

"That should be easy, Detective" he muttered. "It was only four minutes' worth of police work, the rest was like a vidshow shootout."

I hated having to justify everything I did, defending my actions to people who were removed from the streets by position and age, but it was just part of being a cop these days.

"Four minutes' worth of work, a goddamned lifetime's worth of headache."

My apartment's toilet computer beeped a different note than normal above me, catching my interest like it hadn't in months. I'd become accustomed to hearing the chime that indicated a negative report. "Urine test complete. Zachary Forrest. Your urine sample is within acceptable ranges for screenings performed at this location. Congratulations, your profile has been removed from the Louisiana Health Department's watch list of potential stroke and kidney failure victims."

"*Hmpf,*" I grunted, more than a little surprised. I walked back to the sink and wiped away the fog from the mirror. In the reflection behind me, I saw Teagan's firm, caramel-colored rear end press up against the glass of the shower as she bent over to shave her legs.

Damn, that girl's doing me a lot of good, I thought.

It was true. In the three months since she'd temporarily moved in, I'd lost three inches off my waist, could run at a maintained pace of a seven-minute mile for a full 10K race, and now I was off the Louisiana Health Department's naughty list for the first time in years—maybe even a decade.

"Hey, creeper," Teagan teased. "I see you staring at me."

"Just admiring the view, sweetheart," I said in a voice that a street perv would use.

"*Mmm.* I wish you'd do more than just watch," she replied, wiping away the steam from the shower glass.

I took that as my cue and stripped down, opening the door to the shower. "*Whoa!* What are you doing?" Teagan asked.

"Uh… Didn't you just invite me in?"

She laughed. "I was playing along, Zach. I've got to be at school in twenty-five minutes for my last final."

Teagan pulled the shower door closed. "Get home earlier next time," her voice lilted out of the steam.

I stood there naked for a moment and then muttered, "This is bullshit," before putting my underwear and undershirt back on, and walking to the kitchen.

"Andi, ice," I grumbled. By the time I made it to the refrigerator, a highball glass with three pieces of ice was ready for me. I took the glass and set it down with a loud *thunk* on the counter.

Then I poured four fingers of bourbon.

"Wow, rough night?" Teagan asked as she hugged me from behind, vigorously scrubbing her hair with a towel.

The smell of her shampoo filled my nose and I breathed deeply. It was some floral scent or another, I didn't know what, but I liked it.

"Eh, you know, an impossible gunfight, death, destruction, and problems with the pencil-pushers. Normal Tuesday night."

"It's Wednesday morning," she reminded me.

"I had to finish my report before I could leave for the night. Then I got stuck running down a few leads that—"

"Yeah, okay," Teagan interrupted. "Too long. I've gotta go." She deposited the towel she'd been using over my forearm, threatening to splash some of my bourbon over the lip.

"*Hmpf.* Any luck with the job yet?" I asked, removing the towel and tossing it into the bedroom.

She grabbed a bagel from the toaster that she must have had Andi prepare while I was getting my drink. "Not yet. That citywide hiring freeze is still in effect until the mayor gets his new budget established."

"Shitty."

She pushed me playfully. "It's *your* fault. The old guy had everything running smoothly."

"And he was as dirty as my shoes after a night on The Lane."

Teagan shrugged. "The news said the budget proposal should pass the city council by mid-week, and then all the backlogged personnel actions will be processed."

"You'll get hired on. I put in a good word for you with a few people over at the superintendent's office."

"Oh geez, Zach," she sighed. "You think you're helping, but you're really not. I can do this on my own."

"I just—"

Teagan ducked under my arm, gave me a kiss on the cheek and wrinkled her nose. "Take a shower before you go to bed," she ordered. "You smell."

She walked over and grabbed her backpack from the floor by the pantry door. Then she turned back to me and said, "Don't forget: Tomorrow night, 6 p.m. Graduation dinner with my parents at Chez Suzettes."

"I'll see you tonight," I replied.

"I doubt it, unless you come into the Pharaoh. Pulling a double shift after my test." She turned around and rushed toward the apartment door. "See you later," she called over her shoulder.

"Hallway clear, Teagan."

"Thanks, Andi," she said without looking back, and left the apartment.

I downed the bourbon in three large gulps and dumped the ice, placing the glass back on the refrigerator ledge for a refill. My finger hovered over the manual release button for the ice, but I stopped when I saw my shadowy reflection in the readout. I was filthy.

Chunks of concrete from the apartment building were in my hair and a fine layer of grime—probably concrete dust—filled the creases in my neck. Thin, brown arcs of filth coated the undersides of my fingernails and along the cuticles. Even my bare legs, pale from the lack of sunlight like everything else except my face and hands, were dirty. Streaks of dried, salty sweat crusted in the hair along the front of my legs and behind my knees.

No wonder Teagan wanted nothing to do with me this morning.

"Goddammit. Fine," I groaned to myself and went to the bathroom for a cold shower.

TWO: THURSDAY

I dug my finger under the chinstrap to pull it away from my jaw. The damn thing was cutting into my skin, irritating it. I'd worn the helmet at the direct order of Chief Brubaker, even though I felt like a complete jackass. The beat cops were the ones who wore all this riot gear shit, that wasn't my job anymore.

Echoes of chanting bounced off the sides of buildings up and down The Lane as the crowd got closer. In front of me, the uniformed officers made last-minute adjustments to their body armor and the visaluminum shields. Those poor suckers would take the brunt of the protestors' anger if things turned violent.

The city's workers were protesting the loss of jobs to the droids. Reportedly, the organizers had mobilized a collection of vastly different service and labor occupations for the march—all of which were being slowly and inevitably edged out of work by robotic replacements. Food service workers, janitorial workers, prostitutes, farmhands, dockworkers, teachers, bartenders and the like all marched for regulations to slow the spread of the robotics industry.

I understood where the workers came from, but they were about sixty years too late to stem the tide. Several other industries that used to employ humans were almost exclusively robotic now.

It's just the way it is, I grumbled internally as the first of the protestors appeared at the far south end of The Lane.

The police wall was situated about halfway down Jubilee Lane, which was the main public avenue that ran through Easytown, the city's sanctioned red-light district. The mayor had conceded that the protestors had a right to peacefully assemble to have their voices heard, but he wasn't about to let them get on the highway and block the city's commerce routes.

The bulbous helmet of an officer turned toward me and I groaned internally. The kid was a rookie cop and he'd taken it upon himself to become the president of my nonexistent fan club.

"Hey, Detective!" Jake Hannity called. Through the reflection of neon lighting off his visaluminum face shield, I could see the kid's big, goofy grin.

I ducked my chin, grimacing as the helmet's strap dug further into my skin. "Officer Hannity," I groaned.

"Isn't this exciting? This is my first protest."

I shrugged, thankful to only have a thick ballistic vest instead of the full anti-riot kit. The kid was so wet behind the ears I'm surprised his helmet didn't slip off.

"You get used to 'em. Happen about once a year or so," I replied.

"Why you out here slummin' with us?" an older cop with only one chevron on his sleeve grunted. "Don't you usually wait for all the bad shit to go down and then prance in wearing your fancy suits and stupid hat to examine the mess?"

His comment elicited a few snorts of laughter from the officers nearby. I loved my fedora, even if they'd gone back out of style thirty years ago. There was something about a nice hat that made a man's wardrobe feel complete.

"We can't all be old, fat, pieces of shit that have been busted six times so they're walking a beat at fifty, Tidewell," I answered. "How's that rash on your junk?"

I'd only met Patrolman Liam Tidewell a few months ago when his partner, Hannity, started following me around. For some reason, he and I just didn't get along. We were the proverbial oil and water—unfortunately, I wasn't sure which of us was the one that sunk to the bottom.

"It's better, thanks," Tidewell answered. "You should tell your mom to register with the state. She could get in serious trouble for spreading unregulated STDs."

I chuckled. "And I should arrest you for necrophilia, you sick fucker. She's been dead for twenty years."

The line of cops laughed once again at what they perceived to be standard cop humor. The difference was that cop humor was based on a bond of brotherhood and mutual respect. I wouldn't piss on Tidewell if he'd been set on fire. There was no love lost between us.

"So, uh… Why *are* you out here with us, Detective?" Jake asked.

"I'm looking into Carlos Ortega—one of the lead organizers of this little get together."

"Oh… What for?"

I glanced at the other cops. The angle of several heads told me that they were clearly listening to my response. My investigation into a murder of a thumper club doorman pointed to a cover-up and an attempt to tamper with the evidence before I got there. I had a hunch it was one of the cops at the scene. The doorman was also a part-time security guard for Ortega.

"Just doing my due diligence for a separate investigation, kid. No big deal, but I can't seem to catch up to him any other way. His secretary always says he's not around... So, we came to him," I replied, indicating my partner, Drake.

"Oh," Hannity replied, turning back to the front as the chanting picked up in intensity.

The crowd of laborers and service industry workers had advanced about half a mile closer and were now only four blocks from the line of officers. They carried signs proclaiming their rights to work, condemning the mayor and the city, even a few taking the opportunity to lash out against the president for not mandating federal oversight of the robotics industry.

The sergeant in charge of the riot police tapped a few keys on his forearm flexscreen and the ten drones that the chief had tasked exclusively for the protest advanced. The appearance of the drones flying toward them caused the lead element of the protestors to stop. From my vantage point, I could see them looking around for guidance.

It didn't take long for me to identify a few of the leaders in the crowd. Two men, one appeared to be Hispanic, while the other appeared to be Middle Eastern, passed along the orders of a bearded man to the others, possibly in different languages. A woman that I recognized as a prostitute on The Lane also acted as a conduit for the bearded man's orders.

The one who seemed to be providing overall direction for the protestors was a man whose image I'd become familiar with, but I hadn't been able to speak to him yet. He had black hair, a thick goatee that petered out along his jawline and a double chin. He wore an older style army jacket over a thin frame with a slightly protruding belly. A matching hat sat askew on top of his head. Carlos Ortega.

He ran a non-profit over in Uptown on the west side of New Orleans that provided food and clothing to the homeless. The non-profit also ran a few convenience stores and maintained fueling stations throughout the city. Ortega earned a cool million last year. Pretty good income for someone working a *non-profit*.

I'd called several times and visited his office three times over the past week, but had been unable to get in touch with him. Each time, the receptionist covered for him. Seemed to me that he was either avoiding me or he spent too much time organizing protests.

"Andi, I see Ortega," I said into my phone.

"Hold on a moment, Zach. I'm piggybacking onto the surveillance camera video feeds."

Andi was damn good. Always at my side, prepared to assist in any way she could. As a bonus, since I was a detective, the cyber nerds who ran the city's robust surveillance network allowed her to access their feeds. Her ability to analyze data in real time had been a major help over the years.

"Okay, I've got him."

"Who are the two guys he's talking to?"

"A scan of their credit information says their names are Hector Gonsalvez and Farouk Karimov," she replied.

"Any details on them?"

"There is little information on Gonsalvez. He does not have an arrest record. He is employed as a shop foreman at Pop's Handmade Furniture, a small handmade furniture company in Leonidas that specializes in wooden and iron pieces."

"Wood and iron?" I frowned. "People still buy that stuff?"

"Hey! Genevieve and me like wooden furniture," Drake objected. "Our bedroom set *and* living room tables—hell, our dining room table—all of it is wood."

"There is a steady market for replica antique furniture," Andi continued once Drake stopped talking. "My research shows that wooden décor is also a growing trend among new mothers who shy away from the synthetic polymers that you prefer."

"I don't know what my stuff is made of; I just know it's comfortable and not all clunky like wood." I liked the fact that if I ever bothered to clean my apartment myself, which I wouldn't, I could pick up each piece of furniture with little effort because it was so lightweight. *Come to think of it, I believe Amir's furniture is wood…*

"Sorry," I said, apologizing for taking the conversation down a rabbit hole. "What about the other guy, uh…" I drew a blank on the Russian-sounding guy's name.

"Farouk Karimov, age twenty-seven, with an extensive arrest record. He is a third generation Tajik-American. His family came to New Orleans in 2034 when the government of Tajikistan mandated that their population convert to Sunni Islam. Roughly 200,000 Shia Muslims fled the Sunni Reformation Act. The United States took in 73,065 of the refugees, most settling in New Orleans, Michigan, Sacramento, and Bangor, Maine."

"Okay, where does he work, known acquaintances, you know, all the standard stuff?"

"He's a stevedore at the Easytown Dockyards," Andi replied. "He works for the Marie Leveau Shipping Company."

"Why am I not surprised?" I grumbled.

"Thomas Ladeaux owns the Marie Leveau Shipping Company in—"

"I *know* about Ladeaux, Andi."

Unfortunately, I knew all too much about Tommy Voodoo and his business dealings. The police department and the DA were convinced that the guy was crooked, but nobody could prove anything. To complicate matters, he'd personally helped me several times in the past year. Without his help, I might never have solved the two biggest cases in my career—the sex club murders, which turned out to be a diversion to pull police resources during the attempted assassination of the Pope; and the torture tourism case where the mayor of New Orleans was indicted and arrested for illegally cloning businesspeople and political rivals to pave the way for his political aspirations.

Now, here was one of Voodoo's employees helping to lead the charge against robots. *Interesting.*

"What else do we know about Karimov?"

"He's had six arrests in the past ten years," Andi replied. "Once for burglary when he was seventeen, which netted him nine months on Sabatier Island. Twice for distribution of a controlled substance, with no conviction. He's been convicted twice for vandalism while disturbing the peace at ages twenty and twenty-one. Each misdemeanor conviction carried a five-month sentence. Finally, at age twenty-three he assaulted a police officer, earning a two-year sentence. He's a known activist for civil rights, and continues to protest, but has kept his nose clean for the past two years."

I looked out over the crowd toward the delinquent in question. He was gesturing wildly toward the police line, yelling something to those around him, spittle glistening in the weak sunlight filtering through the clouds above. "I don't know why such a fine, upstanding young gentleman would ever be arrested for disturbing the peace."

"Both of those arrests were at previous civil rights protests. Video evidence helped to convict him in each case."

"So, he's due an arrest," I grumbled.

"Careful, Detective," Drake warned quietly, pointing a finger at the line of cops in front of us. "Little ears are listening."

In a louder voice, he said, "We'll be sure to keep an eye on all of the crowd, with special attention to known felons and parolees."

"Alright, I've seen enough," I stated casually to Sergeant Dubois, the uniformed cop in charge of the riot police.

"This rally will go on without Ortega. Send your line and make a beeline for the leader. I'll be the arresting officer."

"Are you sure about this, Detective? That crowd looks like it could get whipped up into a frenzy."

"Hero here doesn't care about that sort of stuff," Tidewell grumbled. "He isn't in the front line."

I ignored the patrolman and considered the sergeant's words. There *were* other ways to bring him in for questioning. He wasn't a suspect—yet. I could try to talk to him after the rally and avoid any additional trouble.

Choices. Choices.

In the end, I decided to take the opportunity available to me now. "Ortega is the last known associate of Dale Henderson before he was found dead, full of holes on the floor of his apartment. I need to talk to him and he's not cooperating. Bring him in."

"You heard *The Man*," the sergeant said loudly, emphasizing his pronoun for me. "Move the line!"

A group of police drones dropped in behind the crowd several blocks away and trash blew out of the alleyways, indicating that they'd moved into position along the sides as well. Protestors began to look around wildly and to their leaders, who encouraged them to remain strong.

Shouts of alarm rose from the crowd when they realized that they were effectively boxed in. The police line stood strong, like a wall of iron twenty feet from the leading edge of the protestors.

I lifted my phone to my mouth and spoke. My voice echoed from the speakers integrated into the twenty-five drones stationed around the crowd. "Carlos Ortega. You are wanted for questioning in the death of Dale Henderson." Andi had linked my phone to all the droids, so anything I said into the microphone could be heard at any point along The Lane. Can't say I wasn't prepared for accusations of non-disclosure to the crowd about what I wanted.

People yelled back that he was an innocent man, that all he wanted was to advance the rights of the workers. Standard crap like that.

"Ortega is not a suspect," I said through the drones' speakers. "But if he won't come talk to us, we're going to come get him."

"We'll never let you take him, pig!" Karimov shouted back at me from behind the protection of several hundred protestors.

"I didn't want it to go down like this," I replied. "But, one way or another, I'm talking to Ortega tonight."

The sergeant glanced at me and I nodded. It was time to end this.

"Hold the line!" Karimov bellowed as the line of armored police officers advanced. He was clearly the number two in this little shindig and I hoped that he'd do something stupid that warranted a club to the face.

"Zach, the police advance is being carried live on video, broadcast worldwide."

"Not now, Andi, this is where it gets good."

The police line walked forward into the group of protestors. They'd linked arms to try and keep us away from Ortega. I wondered if that was technically obstruction of justice or not since the man wasn't even a suspect.

The cops pushed behind their shields, legs churning on Easytown's uneven pavement, slowly pushing the line of protestors back. A skinny girl, a kid really, was the first one to break her hold on the people to her left and right. She cried out in pain, which made me swivel my gaze in her direction. I saw both of her shoulders dislocate from the pressure in front of her and behind and she passed out. Her partners held onto the limp form and others pushed her body from behind. Now she was simply an obstacle that they needed to keep in place.

Then they lost their grip and she fell. The police line used the distraction to push forward once more and an officer pulled the girl to safety by her legs underneath the officer's shields so she wouldn't be trampled. That's when the problems started.

On the periphery of the crowd, I saw people breaking windows and smashing storefront signs along the street. Several cars began to rock as protestors tried to overturn them. After a few tries, a taxi was lifted onto its side and then pushed the rest of the way over to land on its top.

Chunks of concrete and glass bottles flew from the middle of the crown toward the police. An officer was hit in the head and faltered, creating a small gap in the police line. It was all that the crowd needed as the immense pressure against them relented and they surged into the hole. First one protestor and then it was a tidal wave of humanity as they pushed their way through.

Most of them simply ran. They'd joined the march to protest for their civil rights and against the expanding role of droids in the workplace, not to get into a fight with New Orleans' finest. Others weren't as altruistic. Several protestors turned after they'd made it out of the press of bodies and began to fight with the officers. They swung fists, clubs, and even a few old hammers at the armored riot police.

"Zach," Andi interrupted me mid-swing at the face of a man wearing a tuxedo shirt with dirty dreadlocks.

"I'm a little busy, Andi."

My fist impacted against the youth's cheekbone and I felt it cave in. He fell away, clutching his face, sobbing.

"Chief Brubaker has ordered an immediate withdrawal of the riot police. The protest is to be allowed to continue unmolested."

"Little late for that," I huffed as I took a rock to the face shield, scaring the shit out of me. "These guys are rioting and we've got to stop them."

"It is a direct order to have the men pull back and allow the protest to continue peacefully."

"They're not acting peaceful," I groaned. The overhead cameras *had* to see what was happening. Surely Brubaker would see that.

"You also have a message from Teagan."

"What?" I grunted, ducking under a street sign pole that some degenerate had pulled from the sidewalk.

"Teagan has left a message marked 'Highest Priority'."

"It'll have to wait." I parried a punch from a kid wearing a woolen cap, *in May of all things*, with my left forearm and returned the favor; mine connected across the bridge of his nose. He crumpled like a rag doll. A lot of these kids liked to start problems, but couldn't back up their mouths.

I was having a great time.

"Zach, Teagan sounds upset that you're missing her graduation dinner with her and her parents."

I stopped. "Huh?"

Of course, standing there like an idiot in the middle of a rebellion got me knocked upside the helmet. I staggered back, then looked at the ground near my feet. Somebody had thrown a brick. Thank goodness I'd followed Brubaker's orders to wear it or I'd have gotten a frontal lobotomy, free of charge.

I'd forgotten about the dinner. There was a full-on riot in progress, surely she'd understand. I ducked a large, green wine bottle that shattered on the ground behind me. I had to focus and put Teagan out of my mind for right now.

"Sergeant!" I yelled.

My partner, Drake, and the patrol sergeant both answered.

"Uh, I mean, Sergeant Dubois."

"Yes, Detective?"

"We need to end this. We need to extract Ortega, and then pull your men out of here before these protestors get themselves hurt."

"I can have a drone pick him up, but without being charged with a crime, his lawyer may consider it an illegal arrest."

My head throbbed inside the helmet where I'd been hit. All around me, riot police defended themselves with stun batons as they reached around the safety of their shields. The five-thousand-strong crowd was in a frenzy and there was nothing a line of eighty cops was going to do to stop them. Either the protestors or an officer was going to get seriously hurt soon if we didn't make the decision to end this.

"I'll have to risk it," I replied. "Have a drone pluck him out of the crowd and subdue him."

Sergeant Dubois turned to me. "Detective Forrest, are you ordering me to use a patrol drone to apprehend Carlos Ortega for questioning?"

It wasn't lost on me that the angle he'd set himself in allowed his helmet camera to record my face. Smart move on his part. Pass all the blame to the senior officer on scene.

"Yes," I replied. "Detain Ortega so we can withdraw our police officers and allow the rally to continue."

"You got it."

I watched him type something into the flexscreen on his arm. The nearest drone rose ominously from an alleyway and hovered over the crowd. Then, Sergeant Dubois used an infrared pointer to designate Ortega as the target. The IR light was invisible to the naked eye, but easily detectible if anyone had any cybernetic upgrades to their vision.

The drone shot Ortega with two metal wires and sent a meager 80,000 volts of electricity through him. He fell, convulsing. The protestors began screaming in earnest as they realized that things were not going as they'd planned. Somehow, a space cleared around the march leader as people pushed even harder to escape.

Two of the drone's spindly legs descended and grasped Ortega under the armpits, wrapping themselves securely around his shoulders, while a third wrapped around his waist. More pieces of brick and rocks clanged uselessly off the drone's side as it lifted skyward, carrying a limp Carlos Ortega underneath.

"Pull your men back," I told Dubois once Ortega was clear of the crowd and on his way back toward the Easytown Precinct headquarters.

The sergeant acknowledged and spoke on an internal radio line that I couldn't hear. The riot officers began stepping backward in formation while the drones blocking the alleyways and further down Jubilee Lane floated skyward, creating avenues of escape for the rioters.

It was an orderly withdrawal, perfectly executed, as the officers backed away to take up our original position blocking access to the Chef Menteur Highway. The interim mayor had ordered that absolutely no protestors would be allowed to get up onto US Route 90, which connected Easytown with the rest of New Orleans, so that was our no-penetration line.

"Zach, Chief Brubaker is holding for you," Andi interrupted my thoughts as we withdrew.

"I'm still busy, Andi."

"It's not up for debate, Zach. Patching him through now."

"Andi, no. I—"

"Forrest!" Chief Brubaker barked over my earpiece. "What the fuck have you done this time?"

"Chief, I—"

"Can it, Forrest. Why did you deliver a dead body to my precinct?"

"Dead body?" I asked in confusion.

"The guy you plucked out of the crowd on international television was D.O.A. Get your ass down here right now."

THREE: THURSDAY

I had twelve minutes to talk to Teagan on the drive back to the precinct, so I had Andi dial her number.

"Where are you?" she asked when she answered the phone on the first ring. "Cause you better be on your way over here right now."

"Teagan, I'm sorry. I—"

"Don't give me excuses, Zach." The phone rustled and I heard her excuse herself from the table. We were supposed to go to dinner with her parents at some fancy French restaurant to celebrate her upcoming graduation, so that must have been who she was talking to.

Teagan's face appeared in the Jeep's dashboard as she switched from audio to video. The background looked like she was in some type of hallway, probably the one leading to the restrooms. "What the fuck, Zach?" she hissed, barely above a whisper.

"I'm sorry. There was a riot and I had to arrest a guy."

"A riot? Wait." Her head distanced itself from the camera and her wavy blonde hair shook back and forth. "You're a *homicide detective*. Why were you at a riot?"

"I had a suspect that I—"

"Zach, your job isn't supposed to be exciting and you're not supposed to get in gunfights. You're supposed to search for clues at a crime scene. You're not some beat cop; why the hell do you keep getting into these situations?"

"I'm just lucky, I guess."

"Bullshit. You go looking for trouble. It's getting old."

She pulled the camera closer to her face, filling the screen once again. "Where are you?"

"I'm on my way to the precinct. I got called in."

"So you're not coming to dinner?"

"I don't know if I'll be able to make it, Teagan. Chief Brubaker is pissed."

"So am I," she retorted. "You know what? Don't bother coming to the restaurant. I'm too angry and I don't want you to ruin my night any more than you already have."

There was a long pause and I wasn't sure if I was supposed to say something or keep my mouth shut. I never knew what to do in these types of situations, which was probably how I'd managed to stay single as long as I had.

Teagan answered for me. "I'm done with it." I could see her hair waving back and forth again. Her voice lowered when she spoke once more, "I'm just done."

She hung up the phone.

"Shit," I said, slamming my hand onto the Jeep's steering wheel. I had a brief moment of panic, remembering when I had to drive a couple of months ago. A stupid move like that would have caused an accident. Thankfully, I was back on the grid and the Jeep was on nav control.

"Andi, have flowers delivered to Teagan at the restaurant."

"On it, boss."

The Jeep pulled into the Easytown Precinct's parking lot and turned right, toward a parking spot. "No, no, no. *No!*" I grumbled, tapping the nav readout. The low clouds that had threatened to open up during the riot were now pouring down rain. I wasn't about to walk through that before going into the building.

I felt the vehicle accelerate beneath me and we made our way around the back of the lot toward the precinct. The building was a squat, utilitarian three-story brick square. Like everything else in Easytown that wasn't right on Jubilee Lane, little attention had been paid to the building's aesthetics. It was simply a shelter from the elements for the police officers and a temporary place to hold perps while they waited to go out to Sabatier Island.

The Jeep dropped me off at the employee entrance and I pressed my hand against the scanner to unlock the door. I decided to take the back steps, partially to avoid my friend Sandra at the front desk—I was in no mood for her light-hearted bullshit. I jogged lightly up the stairs until I made it to the top floor where Brubaker's office was.

"What did I tell you about keeping your nose clean?" he asked as soon as I knocked on the door.

"I am, Chief."

"Tell that to Ortega's widow," he huffed. "Goddammit, Forrest. The arrest was broadcast live."

"Was it an underlying heart condition?" I asked. I'd been thinking about how he could have died. The Taser shock was a great way to subdue perps—unless they were one of the one half of one percent of the population that were adversely affected by the apprehension method, then it was a bad day for them.

"Preliminary reports look that way. The precinct's medical droid says there was preexisting trauma on his heart muscle, but can't give any further diagnosis. We'll need an MD's findings for the report—which you're going to file, by the way."

"Yeah, I figured as much."

He chewed on the end of an unlit cigar for a moment as he stared at me. I'd known the man for more than a decade, so I guessed that he was trying to figure out a way to suspend me without violating any HR policies.

"Did you get my message about allowing the protest to go on as planned?"

"Yes…sir." I felt the subtle shift in the conversation. I needed to be careful here. "The protest had already turned violent by the time I received your message."

"Are you sure about that?" he asked. "If this goes anywhere, they'll check the timestamps on your message log."

"Positive. The police line had advanced and was engaged with the crowd as we attempted to discuss the Henderson case with Ortega. The protestors began throwing bricks and hitting the officers with bottles and rocks. A few minutes after that began was when I got your message to withdraw. I saw the opportunity to pick up Ortega since he'd been giving us the slip for the past few days and I took it. At the same time, I relayed your orders to pull back to the sergeant in charge of the uniformed officers. Everything seemed to go well in that respect, until you told me that Ortega had died."

The chief chewed harder. "Are you sure of your timeline? Not leaving out any details?"

"I'm positive, sir." I didn't need to think about the situation. I was in the right.

"Okay," he said after a moment of deliberation. "I'll work with IA and provide them your side of the story."

IA, Internal Affairs. They were notorious for being assholes and I'd had my fair share of run-ins with them over the years. It wasn't *only* that they were cops who investigated other cops, it was that the entire NOPD IA department seemed to genuinely enjoy being dickheads.

"Thanks, Chief."

"Don't thank me yet, Forrest," he stated. "If Cruz wasn't starting vacation tomorrow, I'd pull you off this and have a second set of eyes on the case, but the bastard is gonna be in Jamaica for two weeks. So, you're all I've got."

"Well, guess that makes it clear where I stand now," I grimaced. "If you think I need to do things differently, then tell me so."

"I tell you just about every goddamned time that you're doing things wrong, Forrest," he grumbled.

"I read your report on the disc shooter, Branch Corrigan," Brubaker continued, changing the subject. "Funny thing is I busted the same guy eighteen years ago for murder. You believe that?"

"Really?" I asked, genuinely surprised. "I can't believe he's still alive since he's been in the game that long."

"Fucker got locked up on a reduced sentence because he was looney. Crazies only get a few years, regardless of how heinous the crime." He readjusted his ass on his chair, leaning first to one side, and then the other. "You didn't mention his connection with Henderson."

"It's circumstantial, at best," I admitted. "The same ammunition was used to kill Henderson, but there's no telling how many thugs in Easytown are using that weaponry."

"The Henderson family is doing a lot of talking with the media about how the NOPD isn't doing our job. We need to find his killer. What have you gotten from Corrigan?"

"Haven't had a chance to talk to him yet."

"He's out at Sabatier already, in their hospital ward, so you'll have to take the ferry. He's the only cyborg we've managed to keep alive. Besides the Henderson connection, I want to find out who's making these damn things and shut them down. They're getting more dangerous and putting my officer's lives at risk. I want you out there first thing tomorrow morning."

"Got it."

"But first, I want your full, written report about the protest."

"Riot," I corrected him.

"Okay, fine. *Riot*. I want that report in my inbox by 10 p.m. You understand?"

I glanced at the clock on the wall. "What's with all these two-hour deadlines recently, Chief?"

He smirked. "This one's coincidental. I want to read it before I go to bed. That way I can mull over what I'm gonna say to IA while I'm asleep."

"Got it," I responded. "Anything else, Chief? I've got a report to write."

"Get out of here." He waved me off and stood up, collecting his rain jacket.

The chief gets to go home, all the little Indians stay and work, I thought as I stepped out of his office and headed down the hall for mine.

I say 'my office,' but in reality it was a shared workspace with my partner, Sergeant Greg Drake, and Alfonso Cruz and his partner, Sergeant Tim Smith. Cruz was the other full-time Easytown homicide detective; he was straight-laced, by the book...and had a much lower success rate than I did for investigations. I chalked it up to my charming personality.

Cruz was there, tapping his teeth with his fingernail to a beat only he could hear, and shaking his leg as he worked. I glared at him as I walked by, pouring myself a cup of coffee from the machine.

"Careful," Cruz said hoarsely. "You used up your last clean shirt two days ago."

"Did I? I'll need to remember to bring some more in." Cruz got under my skin in all sorts of ways, from his Boy Scout-like appearance to his mannerisms. I don't think he tried to be annoying; he just *was*.

The coffee pot in the office was possessed. It constantly sputtered coffee onto my clothes, often spraying it directly from the percolator somehow onto my stomach. On the off chance it didn't do that, something would invariably go wrong with the heating element and it would burn the coffee or the machine would decide to squirt cream and sugar into my cup. It was a mixed bag what was gonna come out of that thing, but that's how most technology was around me for some reason. So far, the only tech that hadn't failed me was Andi and my Aegis pistol.

Thankfully, the cup that I pulled out of the coffee machine tonight was hot, black and brewed correctly, without ruining my white button-down. I carried the cup to my desk, which was strategically placed as far away from Cruz as the space allowed.

"Andi, remind me that I need to bring in some backup shirts."

"Got it."

"Also, please let Teagan know that I'm sorry about dinner and will make it up to her."

"Do you want me to send that message or remind you to send the message? It would appear strange for me to send it to her on your behalf."

"Uh… Yeah, ghostwrite an apology for me and send it from my phone."

"Understood. Anything else?"

"Yeah, send me a transcript from the police drone logs. I want to incorporate what they saw into my report on the riot."

"It's in your inbox now, boss."

"Thanks," I mumbled, opening her email. There was an attachment with more than seven hundred pages of transcribed audio, picked up by the drones during the forty minutes of the riot.

"Jesus, Andi." It was a lot of data. I needed to narrow down what I was looking at or else I'd use up all my available time skimming the transcripts. "Keyword search Ortega, Karimov, police officers, cops, pigs, and resist."

A new document appeared in my inbox. This one only had a hundred and fifty-six pages. I could work with that.

I began typing and Andi gave me quarterly updates to the time. Before I knew it, my report was nowhere near complete, but the ten o'clock deadline was up. I called the chief and had to tell him that I wasn't going to make his deadline; to which, he called me several colorful names and gave me until the morning to finish the report.

As I typed and cross-referenced the audio files, I discovered that I was much more interested in Karimov than Ortega, even though the latter had been the organizer and was the subject of my latest IA investigation. Karimov was an enigma, seemingly doing well financially with a steady job that had also employed droids alongside humans for more than fifty years.

Why was he so concerned with the anti-droid movement?

It was almost 3 a.m. by the time I finished the report and sent it to Brubaker. Cruz had left long ago to pack for his vacation, and I was alone. I tapped my phone to see if Teagan had responded to the text Andi sent, but she hadn't, so I gathered my things and had Andi call the Jeep around.

I fell asleep on the short car ride from the precinct to my apartment and woke with a start when the Jeep pulled into my parking place in the garage. I stretched, checked the proximity sensors for anyone hiding behind nearby vehicles and then got out when the Jeep returned negative results.

The apartment was dark when I opened the door, which wasn't odd since it was so late. What was odd was that Teagan wasn't sleeping in my bed.

"Andi, did Teagan come home from dinner?"

"No. She did not return after dinner and did not open the heartfelt message that I wrote for you."

"Well, shit."

FOUR: FRIDAY

I woke up at 6:30 and tried calling Teagan. She didn't answer and her voicemail was turned off, so I put on a set of workout clothes and jogged down to the apartment gym. Andi guided me through a quick set of full-body exercises ranging from calisthenics to weights, and then she took me through a 5K sprint interval on the treadmill.

I was winded by the time my workout was over, but glad that I put in the effort instead of letting the stress of work and Teagan's absence get to me. I was finally in a good place, physically, after years of an expanding waistline and shitty health, so regardless of what went on, I wanted to keep up the positive momentum.

"Andi, turn on the shower," I said into my phone as I stretched. "Oh, and ensure the ferry out to Sabatier is operating on time."

"The Sabatier Island Ferry is on time. The first departure of the day is in one hour and five minutes."

"Damn, I cut it too close," I muttered.

"On the contrary, Zach. If you return now and shower at your average rate of six minutes, thirty-seven seconds and dress at your normal rate of—"

"Andi, stop," I ordered. "I'm coming back now. Do I have time to make the first ferry and return in time to go to Teagan's graduation today?"

"Assuming you spend no more than four hours on Sabatier Island, you will have sufficient time to accomplish both tasks."

"Good." I opened the door to my apartment and went inside. I could hear the shower running already so I pushed the button to unlace my sneakers and set them by the door next to the umbrella.

I was on the road in sixteen minutes with a cup of hot coffee and some type of green health shake slurry that Andi insisted was a good breakfast substitute for me to eat after a high intensity workout.

"Andi, can I swing into the evidence locker and get his weapon?"

"Of course, Zach. The evidence locker is manned twenty-four hours a day."

I sighed. Sometimes having a robotic assistant, even one with an advanced AI interface like Andi's, was trying. "Do I have *time* to swing into the evidence locker?"

"Traffic is light to the Easytown Dockyards, so yes, at the moment, you have sufficient time to go to the precinct."

"Okay, take me there."

The Jeep turned down an alley that I would have avoided if it weren't daytime, but things were fine right now. Most of the neighborhood's denizens were sleeping off the effects of whatever they'd gotten into last night.

About halfway down the alley, several homeless kids huddled underneath one old, ratty poncho. The youngest of them looked to be about three or four and the oldest was only in her early teens. Experience taught me to let them be. As a young beat cop, I'd tried to help Easytown's street kids and gotten robbed at grenade-point for it. The only consolation was a few months later, those same kids had tried to rob another Good Samaritan and accidentally blown themselves up.

Justice was usually swift and definitive in Easytown.

I dashed through the rain into the precinct headquarters, then down the hall to a large, closed double door labeled '**EVIDENCE**.' I walked purposefully up to the opening in the cage, and leaned heavily on the metal counter, puffing up my chest importantly.

And then I let the air out audibly. The reception area was empty and no one was behind the counter.

Ding. Ding. Ding. The bell sounded flimsy in the open space as I rang it. "Let's go, motherfucker," I grumbled under my breath.

"Excuse me?" a woman's voice said from inside the cage.

I looked through the grating and saw a pair of stockinged feet sticking out from under the desk, then a firm, round butt wiggled into view, followed by the clerk's torso as she scooted out from underneath the desk.

The milky white skin of her arms appeared first, then a shock of brown, disheveled hair. Finally, she glanced up at me and I was greeted by a pair of green eyes that opened wide in recognition, even if I'd never seen her before.

"Oh! Detective Forrest. Your assistant called me and said you'd be stopping by."

"She did, did she?" I asked, amused that Andi had fooled the clerk into believing she was human.

"Yes, she did," the clerk replied. "I've brought out the evidence she requested, but you'll have to sign for both the apparatus and the hovertray it's on."

"I won't need the hovertray, Miss…"

"It's Katheryn," she stated with a lopsided grin. "You think picking up that hunk of metal is going to impress me, Detective?"

I smiled back. "You caught me. I *am* trying to impress you."

"Hardly necessary. You're the guy who saved the pope! Hell, you even broke up that big cloning ring and got the mayor arrested. Your resume is enough to impress me."

"What's an evidence locker clerk doing checking out my resume?"

"I just started working here, Detective Forrest, but I've followed your work for years."

That's just weird, I thought. "Uh… I don't know how to respond to that."

Her cheeks flushed, turning her pale skin to a fiery red. "I mean—*ugh*," she sighed. "I mean, I used to work in the Dockyards and I've seen you out there probably ten or fifteen times. You even interviewed me about seven years ago. I'd been in Marie Leveau's portside shipping office when a forklift driver impaled a coworker who was sleeping with his wife."

Everything in Easytown always seemed to come back to Tommy Voodoo. The case jogged a memory, but to be honest, crimes of passion usually weren't all that memorable and they were fairly straightforward. "I remember the case, Miss Katheryn. I'm sorry, I speak to so many witnesses."

She ducked her chin, her short hair falling forward around her cheeks. "I know. But, that's why I've been following you're career. I'm fascinated by police work and the evidence locker is just a stepping stone for me. Once I can save a few thousand more, I'm going to try out for the academy. Gotta cover my bills while I'm there, though. You know?"

"Yeah. I get it. They don't pay you shit while you're there." So, she wanted to be a cop, and moving out of the Dockyards to the precinct headquarters as a contractor got her an inside look at how things worked, then she'd go to the academy to earn her commission as a police officer.

"I admire a woman with goals. Keep it up," I said. "I'm running a little behind though, so can I sign for the weapon and get out of your hair?"

"Of course." She put a tablet up on the ledge and said, "Verify what you're signing for, where you're taking it and why."

I read through the info Andi had told her, which helped me clear the evidence locker much faster than trying to fill it in myself. "Looks good, except like I said, I don't think I need the hovertray."

"Are you sure, Detective? Have you picked this thing up?"

"No, but the cyborg had it attached to his body, how heavy can it be?"

"Ah… Maybe you should come back here and try to pick it up before you delete the tray from your inventory."

"*Hmpf*," I grunted. "Sure, let's try it out."

Katheryn pressed a button, which buzzed in response and a blinking red light above the door activated. Then she walked around and opened the cage door for me.

"This way, Jim Granite," she said, calling me by the name of a massive bodybuilder-turned-actor who was now taking on more non-action movie roles as he got older.

Appropriate.

I walked through the gate and she secured it behind me, then led the way to a small holding area just behind the evidence clerks' desk area. She swayed her hips seductively and I wondered if that was just for my benefit or if that was just the way she walked.

"Here it is. Good luck," she laughed, patting my arm.

I examined what was left of Branch Corrigan's arm after I'd blasted it off of him with the Aegis. The laser took the weapon high up near his shoulder, so from what I could tell, it was mostly intact. There were tubes and wires all over the place, fairly standard for homemade weapons, but what was intriguing were the air pressure valves set close to the three metal cylinders in the middle of the contraption, which I assumed were the barrels.

"This thing operates on pneumatic pressure."

"Yeah, pretty neat, huh?" Katheryn said.

I glanced at her; she had a wide smile on her face and tiny laugh lines at the corners of her eyes. "Considering this thing has probably killed several people and looks like the projectiles can be made out of any type of sheet metal…yeah, it's pretty fucking neat."

The weapon was ridiculously heavy. It took me two tries to lift it a few inches, part of which I attributed to it sitting on a table at waist height so I couldn't get my legs involved in the lift. It would be entirely possible to carry the weapon for a few feet, maybe even ten, but I wasn't getting it all the way through the building to the Jeep, let alone through the labyrinth of Sabatier Island.

And, I had a newfound appreciation for Branch's strength and how lucky we'd been to avoid getting our heads crushed.

"Okay, you got me," I admitted. "I'll need the hovertray."

Katheryn slid between me and the table so that I had to step back. "Excuse me," I muttered.

"*Hmm?*" she asked, glancing over her shoulder at me. "Oh. Sorry, I just needed to get in here and activate the hovertray for you."

She pushed a few keys on the tray that the arm rested on. "Give me a four-digit code."

"Uh… One, two, three, four?"

The clerk looked back at me and rolled her eyes, making her appear much younger than the thirty or so that I'd guessed her age to be. She input my code and the hovertray elevated several inches off the table.

"Alright, your temporary code is: one, two, three, four. That code activates and inactivates the magnetic couplers that keep the weapon secured to the hovertray. You can raise and lower the tray with the arrows set on the side. It'll stay active for the next twelve hours. If it isn't returned here by then, it will send out a transponder signal and an evidence collection droid will be dispatched to retrieve it."

She turned around to face me and leaned back slightly against the table, bumping into the hovering tray behind her. It floated backward silently. "Is there anything else you need from me, Detective?"

"No, thank you, Katheryn. You've been very helpful."

"I hope you get your guy," she said.

"I've already got him. Just gonna go interrogate him."

"Oh!" she exclaimed, pushing herself forward with her butt. I took another step back; that's all I needed was a sexual assault claim from some new employee. "I forgot to mention. I'll be here until 4 p.m. so you can bring it back to me."

She whirled around and scribbled something on a scrap of paper, then turned back. Her face was beet red once more. "Here's my number. If you come back after I've left, just give me a call. I don't have any plans tonight, so I'll come right back to return the evidence."

I took the note from her small hand. "I can just return it to the next clerk on shift, right?"

Her eyes fell. "Yeah, of course you can. But I like to close out my logs personally. Helps me to keep track of things, y'know?"

The graduation was at 3 p.m., so barring any unforeseen events, I should be able to get back to the precinct with the evidence. "I'll try my best to have the weapon back before you leave for the day. I can't promise it, but I will do what I can."

She nodded, "Thank you, Detective."

"Alright, I really need to get going if I'm going to make it to the ferry in time."

"You're right, sorry." She walked quickly to the access gate and I pushed the hovertray along in front of me.

"See you later," I said, passing by her as she held the door.

"I hope so," she answered.

As I pushed the weapon down the hallway, I couldn't help but wonder what the hell was going on. Six months ago, I probably wouldn't have realized that Katheryn was obviously flirting with me. Now, after two back-to-back girlfriends—or was Avery more of a fuckbuddy?—I was actually at a place in my life where I could pay attention to things besides work, and Katheryn was *definitely* flirting with me.

But why? I'd apparently seen her one time a few years ago and made some type of impression on her, hardly one that should have carried beyond a day or two though. Did she truly like me—or, more troubling, was she some type of police officer groupie looking for a new claim?

Something about her told me to steer clear of her, especially since I had a live-in girlfriend. Entertaining that kind of woman was just inviting trouble that I didn't need.

"Calm the fuck down!" I shouted with my hands up over my head. "I'm a cop. This contraption is evidence in a case against a prisoner here."

Leave it to the fucking by-the-book guards out at Sabatier to get their panties in a bunch when they saw a weapon. "Andi, didn't you call ahead and tell them I was on the way?"

"The warden was unavailable, boss," Andi replied as two of the guards advanced toward me while a man in the tower tried to be as noticeable as possible with his pulse rifle pointed at my head. "So I talked to the officer in charge of the guards, a Captain Jordan Spiels. I told him that you'd be on the first ferry to the island this morning."

"Well, he didn't pass the word to the guys at the gate," I replied. In a louder voice, I called to the guards, "Hey, my assistant talked to Captain Spiels this morning. He knows that I'm coming out and that I'm bringing this *nonfunctioning* weapon to the island."

That caused the guards to hesitate and one of them called it up. I heard several quick bursts of conversation that leaked from their earbuds, but I couldn't catch what was said.

Finally, the men seemed to relax. "You got an ID and badge, Detective?" one of them asked.

I slowly lowered one of my hands and began to reach into the pocket of my duster. "Is Snipey Pete gonna shoot me if I pull out my badge?" I asked, pointing to the sniper in the tower with the index finger of my hand that was still above my head.

"Stand down, Ted," the man who'd spoken a moment before ordered.

When the shooter relaxed and his muzzle was simply pointed in my direction instead of at my head, I reached into my coat and pulled out my wallet. I flipped it open to my badge and police ID. One of the guards advanced and examined them closely for a moment before looking back to me.

"Okay," he said. "You're sure that thing isn't operational?"

"There's no power source," I said, reaching down to point at a severed wire. "And, it's pneumatic, these tubes are severed," I added, grabbing the two metal mesh wrapped air tubes. "Plus, there aren't any projectiles in the weapon. This thing isn't gonna accidentally shoot anybody."

"We'll have to scan it."

"Sure, do whatever you need to do, man. I could care less. I just need to see Branch Corrigan. I hear he's doing better than when I sent him in here."

The guard shrugged. "I wouldn't know, sir. I only work the exterior perimeter over here on the little island. Once I log you in, a guard will meet you here in the shack and escort you across the bridge to the big island. The hospital pod is in Cellblock Three."

My stomach dropped. I'd been falsely imprisoned in Cellblock Three for four days—most of it in solitary confinement inside a janitor's closet because I couldn't play nice with the other inmates. I hadn't been back to Sabatier since then and wasn't looking forward to returning to the cellblock.

A few minutes later, insult was added to injury as Sergeant Jackson, the officer in charge of Cellblock Three, walked into the waiting area. There was certainly no love lost between the two of us.

"Detective," he greeted me with a nod, but not a handshake.

"Sergeant Jackson. I see there's no justice in the prison system."

"What are you—"

"I filed a complaint against you and a few others out here. I'm surprised you still have a job."

He chuckled. "Nobody cares about convicts, Detective. It's unfortunate that you had the experience that you did, but you've got to—"

"Don't try to excuse what you guys did." Seeing him reminded me of the humiliation I felt when the female guard who'd watched me while I showered forced me to turn around with my arms held wide so she could appraise my package and make remarks about it. This whole place was a cesspool, but like he said, nobody cared about convicts. "Just take me out to see the prisoner and stay the fuck out of my way."

"Yeah, sure. Follow me."

We left the small holding area behind and Jackson indicated a two-seater hoverskiff. The little sport utility had a forward-facing seat for the driver and the passenger sat behind the driver, facing backward. There was a small windscreen, but nothing overhead to keep the rain off of you. "No thanks, I'll walk."

"There's no foot traffic allowed on the bridge, Detective. You've got to ride in the skiff or else wait for a prison transport to take you across."

"Goddamn it, fine. How does the hovertray work with the skiff?"

He turned to examine the tray as it floated soundlessly beside me. "Uh, you can just hold onto it and it should keep up."

"Great," I mumbled as I stepped up the tiny chrome ladder and sat down on a puddle of water on the seat, which quickly soaked through my duster and into my slacks. "Lovely."

The hoverskiff ride across the bridge from the small gate island to the main facility on Sabatier Island took about three minutes. If a prisoner were to somehow escape their individual pods, then their cellblock, and then the interior perimeter, they either crossed two miles of open bridge or they swam for it, risking drowning or shark attack. That I knew of, no one had ever escaped from the island since it opened sixty years ago in the Thirties.

I tried to call Teagan again, but her phone was off and there wasn't an option to leave a message. She was *really* pissed about me missing dinner. I wondered what it would take to make her forgive me. She certainly hadn't been as lenient with me since we started dating as she was when she was simply madly in love with me as a customer at the Pharaoh.

We passed through two more heavily-guarded gates on the big island, which was completely encircled by fifteen foot electrified fence topped with razor wire. *I bet they don't get many trick or treaters*, I mused.

"Alright, Detective, we'll need to scan you for contraband," Sergeant Jackson stated as we walked, dripping wet through a set of overhead fans.

"I have my service pistol, a laser pistol and this hunk of evidence right here," I said, gesturing to the hovertray.

"We can't let you in here with the weapons, Forrest. You know that."

"The fuck you can't. Branch Corrigan is extremely dangerous. I'm not going into a room without a piece."

"I don't like cursing, remember? The prisoner is strapped to a bed and on a ventilator. You punched a baseball-sized hole though his lung," Jackson countered. "He's not a threat."

I stood my ground. "I need to talk to him, but I'm not going in without a weapon. Call the warden."

He sighed and crossed the magic line painted on the floor. Non-employees stayed on my side of the line, employees could go to the other side. If someone tried to cross, they got shot. Hence the 'magic' line.

I watched him in conversation with somebody and I wondered if he'd actually called the warden or if he was chatting with his wife. I didn't have anything to back up my desire to keep my weapons and if push came to shove, not very many people in the city would vouch for me.

Sergeant Jackson hung up the phone in exasperation. "Captain Spiels says that you can't keep your weapons."

"Governor Talubee and I go way back," I lied. "He'll vouch for me."

"I saw you on the vids getting that award from the governor."

"Yeah, it was all good—*after* I got out of this shithole."

The sergeant swallowed a lump in his throat. "Come on, Forrest. I'm just trying to do my job. No *functional* weapon of any kind makes it past the observation deck. Even officers who go into the pods are unarmed. Please put your weapons in the locker and then go through the machine."

I was pissed. Branch Corrigan was extremely dangerous and I didn't like facing him without a weapon to defend myself with. I hesitated and Jackson spoke again, "If you don't check your weapons, you aren't getting past this point."

I did as he directed, depositing the .45 Sig Sauer and the Smith & Wesson Aegis into a locker that requested a four-digit code when I closed the door. I kept it simple and used the same code that I'd used for the hovertray.

Then I walked into the scanner and alarms started sounding.

Guards appeared from several doors and I raised my hands again. I *really* didn't feel like getting shot today. The tech operating the machine pointed to her monitor and said something to Sergeant Jackson, who looked up at me.

"Stand down, everyone," he said. "Sorry, Detective Forrest, the plate in your head made the system go crazy."

"Ah," I replied, tapping the right side of my head. "Shoulda remembered. The composite alloys up here play havoc with cheaper scanning devices." I shrugged in mock helplessness. "But it keeps my brain from oozing out of my head, so I kinda need it."

"Damn, what did you get into?" Sergeant Jackson asked.

"A redhead," I deadpanned, referring to Sadie, the clone who'd helped me break the politician cloning case. "Angry she-devils. Pro tip: stay away from 'em."

The scanner tech frowned at me and shook her head. Too late, I realized she had red hair too.

Charming to the end.

FIVE: FRIDAY

"Start talking, Corrigan," I said, looking down at the monster in the bed.

Drake and I had done a number on this guy. His massive bare chest had bandages over at least a dozen small caliber bullet holes, his left arm was—well, his left arm sat on a hovertray beside me—and they had a giant valve-type bandage over the hole where his lung used to be. *Damn, I loved that Aegis.* Tubes snaked out of him at various places. There was a tube up his nose for oxygen, an IV line into his arm, a large drainage tube through the intercostal muscles along his ribcage on the side with the damaged lung, and he had a catheter line running up under the sheet. Couldn't have happened to a nicer guy.

They even took the time to shave away his mop of dreadlocks. Maybe Sabatier wasn't as bad of a place as I remembered.

This part of the prison island's hospital ward was three parts prison and only one part medical facility. A set of inch-and-a-half thick vertical metal bars encircled each bed and treatment area. Guards accompanied the doctors and nurses at all times; no one was allowed to be alone with the patients—both for the safety of the care providers and to keep an unhealthy bond from forming between patient and staff. Sympathetic clinic staff had helped too many inmates escape at other prisons. That was closely monitored here.

Branch's eyes fluttered open slightly, widened in recognition and then closed again. "I'm tired, man," he rumbled. Even with only one functioning lung and tubes crammed up his nose, the cyborg's voice sounded like an avalanche of rocks rolling down a mountain.

"I don't care. I need intel on who's running these chop shops. Wake up or I'll wake you up."

He laughed at me and tried to turn over, but the restraints held him firmly in place. "I need my rest to heal if I'm gonna show up in court to claim police brutality."

"I don't have time for this," I said, snapping a large ammonia capsule and holding it under the cyborg's nose.

He thrashed his head to one side and I followed with the capsule. This little game went on for ten seconds until he finally blurted out, "Okay! I'll talk to you. What is it, goddamn it?"

"Language, inmate," Sergeant Jackson cautioned.

"Fuck you, screw."

I smirked at his use of the old-time term for a prison guard. Had to give the guy some credit, not many people used that anymore, mostly I heard things like dickhole, vagina trumpet, and the ever-popular motherfucker.

"Alright, Corrigan. Knock that shit off." I tapped a button on the hovertray and it floated up to my chest height. I lifted the back end so that it tilted toward the 'borg and he could see what I had with me. "Recognize this?"

He thrashed against his restraints and the mechanical nub sticking out of his shoulder wiggled back and forth pathetically. "That's mine."

"It *was* yours. Now it's mine. Who's running the chop shops that are creating the cyborgs?"

"I don't know, man."

"Bullshit. I want to know where these things are coming from."

"Most of us were enforcers for the dealers. Best way to keep the synthaine dripping is to take out the competition. It worked at first, now everybody has 'em and we spend more time fighting each other than dealing."

"So… You regret becoming a cyborg, then?"

"No, but the money is drying up from the synthaine. Dealers are trying to hit other dealers to score a quick win instead of just selling their own shit. They spend more money on their 'borgs than they do on the product. It's just bad for business, man."

"A businessman. I can respect that," I lied. I couldn't respect anything about the man, but I'd say just about anything to get the perp to talk to me. "If the 'borgs are bad for business, why do the dealers keep financing to get them made?"

"You wanna be the only one left without protection when someone like me comes to take your stash?"

"Is that what you did over on Snapdragon back in February?" I asked, trying to tie up an old loose end.

"Snapdragon?"

"Yeah. Drug house, there was a woman named Janie Kelso, a bunch of kids' shit, and several of these." I held up a single round of disc ammunition. "Janie was cut clean in half and whoever did it rooted around her corpse to pull the evidence. Most of the discs were collected up, but I found some…" I trailed off to let him pick up the story.

He shrugged his shoulders and the nub went straight out to the side. "Eh. I kill a lot of people. If those were there, then it was either me or a couple other guys."

I have got to get a prescription of whatever drugs they have this guy on for other interrogations, I told myself, making a mental note to check the charts.

"How many people have you killed?"

"I don't know... Do I get a lawyer or something?"

"Do you want a lawyer?" I asked. "Andi, show me the available public defenders that Mr. Corrigan could expect if he were assigned one right now."

I placed my phone on the bedside table and it projected the holographic images of four goofy-looking white guys and one black female into the air above it. "These are your current choices," I said. "Who's it gonna be?"

"Are you fucking kidding me?" Branch asked, staring at the image. "None of 'em are old enough to buy cigarettes."

"Well, that's what you get with public defenders. Most of them use that job as a starting point right after law school. You have the right to an attorney and we can wait until somebody can make it out here..." I let it hang in the air for a moment before continuing. "Or, we could skip it and you tell me who's behind all of this." I paused for effect. "Even better, we could see about you turning state's witness, possibly get a reduced sentence and then try to become a contributing member of society after you get out."

"Uh."

"So, if you were to become a state's witness," I pressed, knowing that I was on shaky legal ground since I couldn't offer him the deal; it had to come from an attorney with a judge's backing. This meeting, like everything else on Sabatier, was being recorded. I needed to pick my words carefully and not commit to anything. "How many people would you say you killed?"

"I don't know," Corrigan replied. "More than forty."

I tempered my emotions purposefully. "That's a lot."

He chuckled. "I'm trying to catch up to your record."

"I haven't killed that many criminals," I replied.

"Are you sure about that?" he asked, lifting slightly from the bed. "Word on the street is you're a stone cold killer."

"Did you kill Janie Kelso in February?"

"I don't know. Probably."

Good enough for me, I thought. Maybe I could close out some of those unsolved cases back at the precinct.

"The night I shot you, what—"

"Lucky bastard," he interrupted. "I was going to wipe my ass with your corpse."

"You missed an opportunity then. The night I shot you, what were you doing at Dale Henderson's apartment building?"

"Who the fuck is Dale Henderson?"

"He was a doorman at Liquid Genesis and one of your little saw blades was found in his neck."

"That homo club? I don't go to places like that, man. I plant my root in wet, juicy pussy, not dudes' assholes."

I wondered how often Branch had practiced that little speech about his 'planting his root' and waited for an opportunity to use it. "Okay, that's fine. To each their own.

∘59∘

What were you doing at that apartment building when you attacked us—unprovoked?"

"I was looking for someone."

"Who?"

"I don't like where this is going. I want a lawyer, even if it is one of those pencil-dicked fuckholes you showed me."

"Really?" I asked. "You admitted to killing around forty people, but when I asked you about what you were doing at an apartment, you clam up. What's that about, Corrigan?"

"I just decided that I want a lawyer."

I sighed. This just got a lot more complicated. I'd have to schedule an interrogation with whomever the judge assigned to defend the cyborg, and now this trip was a waste.

"Andi, let the Public Defender's office know that Mr. Corrigan has requested an attorney. I'll need to schedule an appointment with them as soon as they're identified by the judge."

I looked down at him. "Okay, my assistant will notify the court that you've requested council. We're done until I can speak to you with your lawyer present."

His rumbling laugh caused the entire bed to shake. "Hell, if I'd known that's all it took to make you shut up, I'd have lawyered up the moment you came in here. I need my beauty rest."

"Yeah, you sure do, you ugly son of a bitch."

The return ferry was running late due to some rough waves in Chandeleur Sound, so I wasn't able to return Corrigan's weapon arm to the evidence locker before I had to rush over to Xavier University in Gert Town for Teagan's graduation. I phoned the precinct and left a message with the evidence locker staff telling them I got delayed and wouldn't be able to return the piece until the late afternoon.

I tried Teagan's line one more time and she still didn't answer. "Screw it," I grumbled, tossing the phone angrily into the Jeep's passenger seat.

The girl was pissed off. I get it, I'm a shitty boyfriend, always on the clock, kept unpredictable office hours and had a habit of missing important events because of my job. Not my fault, and she knew all that going in.

As the Jeep drove toward downtown, I thought about all the events I'd missed since we started dating. Her graduation dinner, date nights, the party for her and Rebecca when they passed the state's educator certification exams for senior high school, I'd even missed my own birthday dinner that she planned for me. It was a lot. If I was being honest with myself, more than half of them, I *could* have made. I didn't always need to be out on an investigation; some things could have waited a few hours. Avery called it when this whole thing started. I was a shitty person who wasn't emotionally ready for a relationship.

My self-assessment was sobering to say the least. It's one thing to have others tell you that you're an asshole, but entirely different when you come to the realization that you're actually a terrible human being.

God, I could use a drink.

The Jeep dropped me off at the Convocation Academic Center along Washington Avenue. I had four minutes to make it inside, find a seat and see Teagan graduate. If I missed this, she'd kill me—probably literally, not figuratively.

Luckily, Xavier was a small school. The basketball arena only had forty or fifty rows of seats surrounding the floor. Finding a seat wasn't too difficult. I had time to take my coat off and set it on the floor at my feet and then their God-awful school alma mater began playing over the loudspeakers as the graduates began to walk in from either side of the rows of chairs in the center of the court below. When they got to their assigned row, they turned into their row and filed through to their seats.

I scanned the graduates rapidly, not seeing Teagan. "Andi," I whispered. "Download the graduation program to my phone."

I waited, tapping my fingers on my leg impatiently. Finally, it came up and I scrolled to the list of graduates. It took a moment, but I found Teagan's name. *I must have missed her*, I thought, settling back into my chair for the commencement speech, which was sure to be a snooze fest.

I spent the first several minutes trying to match the graduate in the chair with the name in the program, but quickly abandoned it as futile. The speaker took a full forty minutes to deliver her remarks. She hit the highlights of the school's proud lineage as a historically black college and the graduates' place in that shared history, as well as the parts about going out and making a difference in the world. She even tossed a few slurs toward the Mecca of Sin, Easytown, and cautioned the graduates to stay away from places with such reputations and realities.

Finally, the speech was over and next on the agenda was the commencement where the graduates received their symbolic diplomas. The real ones would arrive by courier droid in a few hours as long as they didn't do anything to ruin the ceremony.

The graduates were called to shake the university president's hand in alphabetical order. I watched as more than three hundred names were called and then they finally made it to the names that began with the letter 'T'. Teagan Thibodaux was the twenty-third graduate in the T's, so I counted backward along the line to see her. Still nothing. The girl that I thought was her had green hair poking out from under her square hat. It was hard to tell, though, as graduates shifted from foot to foot and shuffled forward.

Then it was Teagan's turn to walk across the stage and the announcer said, "Glory Thiess."

What?

I glanced at the program. Glory Thiess was the girl *behind* Teagan. She wasn't at the ceremony.

Grumbles of complaint and telling me to wait until the ceremony was over filled my ears as I surged upward and jogged along the concourse at the top of the stairs. I tried Teagan's number again and there still wasn't an answer.

"Andi, call Teagan's mother."

"I don't have that number, Zach," she answered.

"Bullshit," I said, bursting through the doors to the outside. "Send the Jeep to pick me up. Andi, go through your logs, find some time when Teagan called her mother from inside the apartment and analyze the touch tones."

"It may take me a few minutes."

"I don't care, just do it." The rain had increased and poured down in great sheets while I waited under a large pedestrian rain shield.

My mind began to kick into overdrive. I'd busted a lot of very bad people over the years. It wasn't impossible to get messages out of Sabatier; did someone from inside have Teagan kidnapped? Or was it some of Ortega's people in retaliation for his death? Was it possible that a leftover crony of Mayor Cantrell had offed her? We hadn't been overt in our relationship, but she *did* live with me, so if any of my enemies had managed to figure out where I lived, it wasn't a far stretch to think they could also figure out who she was.

The Jeep's headlights cut through the deluge and I hopped into the passenger seat, choosing the closest door over the need for control. The Jeep's speakers began to ring hollowly, letting me know that Andi was placing an outgoing call.

"Hello, Detective Forrest," a woman answered.

"Hi, Dhamiria," I said, familiar enough with Teagan's mother who was only a few years older than me. "I just left Teagan's graduation ceremony, she wasn't there. I've been trying—"

"I know, Zach," Dhamiria interrupted. "She informed us of her decision not to attend the graduation last night."

"Do you know where she is?"

"I—She told me not to tell you."

"I'm a cop, Dhamiria. I can file a missing person's report and have the city scoured for her. I'll find her, wherever she is."

"Zach," Andi cut in.

"I'm talking with Teagan's mother."

"I know," Andi continued. "However, there are two collection droids requesting entry into the apartment to secure Teagan Thibodaux's personal items."

"Dhamiria, my AI just told me that there are two droids at my apartment," I said. "They're collecting Teagan's things. This is spinning out of control over a misunderstanding."

"Zach," her voice cracked. "Believe me, when she told her father and I where she was going, we were very upset as well."

"What do you mean?"

"You have hurt her greatly. She chose to leave the country. She flew to Indonesia this morning."

"Indonesia?" My mind couldn't process what Dhamiria said. Why the hell would she go to that backward shithole? It was less than a third-world country, if there were such a classification. The people were in constant danger of succumbing to famine, disease, and war. It was worse than New Orleans could ever be.

Finally, I settled on, "Why?"

"She accepted a position teaching English at the Jesuit school in Jakarta. She tried to find information about going to Europe, but they use droids to teach students. Only the Southeast Asia countries still pay to import teachers from the West."

"I don't—"

"Please, Zach. She begged me not to tell you where she was going, but I didn't feel that was the right thing to do to you. In time, she'll learn that you cannot simply cease to be the person you were—and abandoning those you left behind, leaving them wondering about you is not proper. Teagan will be fine. Maybe some distance is all she needed."

"Uh… *Mmm hmm*," I mumbled. "Okay, thank you for telling me."

I hung up the call and stared blankly out the windshield. I was a complete and utter fuck-up and I'd caused that girl to ruin her life. She was throwing away a golden opportunity to teach here in New Orleans in favor of escaping from me.

I needed a drink, I said aloud to nobody. "Take me to Matilda's on The Lane," I muttered to the Jeep.

I needed several drinks…

SIX: FRIDAY

"Another one," I slurred.

"Mr. Forrest," the droid behind the bar leaned forward in a semblance of someone wanting to talk without being overheard. "You have had five double bourbons. I am no longer required to provide alcohol to you. Please, go home and have a good Friday night."

"I don't want to go home," I replied. "I want a drink."

"Do you require companionship?" the droid asked. "There is a club next door. I hear their services are top notch."

I laughed, loudly and bitterly. I'd already been down that road when the droid Paxton seduced me into having sex with her and violating the NOPD's Immorality Clause.

"No thanks, Sam," I replied. "I like my women warm and soft, not—"

I stopped. I'd came to the bar to forget about my problems with women, not talk about them to a bartender droid like a fucking drunk loser. "Can I just get another drink, Sam? I'll sit here and be quiet."

"This establishment is legally within its rights to refuse service to anyone determined to be publicly intoxicated. Once you finish your drink, you will not be served for the next one hour and twelve minutes."

I held out my hand, "Just charge my chip. I'll go somewhere else."

The droid scanned my credit chip and had the nerve to ask if I wanted to leave a tip.

I gulped down the remainder of my drink and then slammed the glass down on the counter. "You're a goddamned droid. Why would I tip you? Extra oil for the joints?"

The bartender turned away and walked to the end of the counter where another patron had raised their hand. I shoved back from the bar, standing unsteadily for a moment until I got my balance, and then walked out onto the street.

Outside, The Lane was as busy as always on a Friday night—despite the ever-present rain. Small groups of people passed by as I stood under the bar's awning with a hand against the window to keep from falling. I drank in the sights and sounds of the night, reveling in the atmosphere.

Jubilee Lane had a lighter feel to it, like it always did during the summer months. With all the college graduations across town, tonight was the first official night of summer for the clubs in Easytown. The city's residents, both temporary and permanent, were out celebrating one last time before the college kids went home and the tourists flocked into town. Old friendships were renewed and new ones made.

These kids had no idea what the future held in store for them.

The laughter of a group of girls reminded me that I needed to get to the Jeep and go home. I called it up and had it meet me near an alley a few blocks away. I stepped out from under the rain shield and stumbled to the bright lights of the next establishment's awning.

Neon lights flashed mesmerizingly and a doorman called out to the crowds to come experience the pleasure of the girls at Art's Performing Center. I glanced through the windows. Inside, girls of every ethnicity lounged on sofas or sat in chairs. A blonde wearing a skimpy, white lace outfit saw me looking in and stood, coming over to the window. A thin, see-through top revealed pale skin, with just a hint of muscle tone.

She reached out a hand and extended a slender finger in my direction, beckoning me inside. The urge to just throw it all away and walk through those doors was overwhelming. I didn't need this shit. I could simply go inside and let nature take over. Forget about rules and regulations; live in the moment and all that.

The prostitute slid aside the crotch of her panties, revealing everything the tiny fabric had hidden. I gaped at her for a moment and then tore my eyes up to her face. She arched an eyebrow and smirked, willing me to come inside the brothel to her. All I had to do was just walk in and she'd do the rest.

My feet obeyed some primal urge, something that didn't even register in my mind. I *needed* to go inside. That blonde—droid or human, I didn't care at that point—*needed* me to go inside as well. I took three steps and she shadowed me in the window, keeping pace with me.

"Zach, the Jeep reports that it's been waiting for your arrival for three minutes," Andi's voice interrupted, breaking the prostitute's spell. "It will be required to move if you don't get in soon."

"Uh, yeah," I responded, stumbling from the cover of the awning out into the rain. I stood in the downpour for a moment, letting the water wash over me and clear my thoughts. When the temptation had passed, I walked awkwardly through the rain to where the Jeep waited without looking back. I sat heavily into the back seat, bumping into the hovertray and Corrigan's weapon.

"You big, dumb bastard," I said, not entirely sure if I was talking about the arm or myself. It didn't matter.

A hand slapped hard against my window a moment after I shut the door, causing me to jump. I glanced over and saw a group of three tweakers. The two brandished small clubs and the one who'd hit my window had a knife. They must have been trying to rob me as I stood in the rain like an idiot and I'd simply made it to the car before they could act.

"Go!" I ordered the Jeep, which shot forward into traffic, leaving the would-be muggers behind.

"Andi, call into the precinct that there are tweakers with weapons back there."

"I don't think that's a good idea, Zach."

I shook my head, trying to clear it. I was drunk, but I wasn't incapacitated. "Why?"

"You told me an hour ago to ignore all calls from the precinct and dispatch has been trying to reach you."

"Shit," I grumbled. Couldn't I just get a night off? Just one? "Go ahead and send it in. And patch me through to Drake."

The phone rang once and Drake picked up. "Evening, Detective."

"Hey, Drake. What's up? It's my night off."

"Not according to the schedule," he replied. "We're on and Lieutenant Cruz and Tim Smith are on vacation."

"Huh? Hold on a second." I tapped the hold button. "Andi, didn't I request off for Teagan's graduation?"

"You did, boss. But the request was denied due to Lieutenant Cruz's vacation. It was already scheduled by the time you requested the day off."

"Shit." I tapped the button to take me back to Drake. "Alright, guess we're on. What've you got?"

"A pissed off chief of police for starters."

"*Dammit*," I groaned. "What's the deal?"

"Brubaker is down here, running the scene—and he is *not* happy about it."

"*Brubaker's* running the scene?" Fuck, it was worse than I thought.

"Yeah. There's gonna be hell to pay for this one. We're over at the Regal Eagle. Dead businessman and dead prostitute."

'Regal Eagle' was cop slang for the Eagle Apartment complex at the farthest end of Jubilee Lane, *not* to be confused with the posh Regal Apartments that Paxton Himura had lived in over in Venetian Isles. Lots of prostitutes and club workers lived in the Regal Eagle because of the cheap price of rent and the proximity to clients on The Lane. We worked that building a lot.

I thought for a moment and then said, "Alright, buddy. I'm in Easytown already. I'll be there in a few minutes."

"Sure thing, Detective. You may want to let dispatch know that you're en route so they quit calling you out as a no-show."

"I just had Andi call it in. I'll be there in a few."

The Jeep's speed eased up as Andi input the directions to the crime scene. I sighed and stood up in the back seat to reach around into the glove box up front. A small auto-injector sat inside and I lifted it out. I held the device up to the interior dome lights to read the contents—it never hurt to be safe. When I was satisfied that the injector had the right drug, I lifted my shirt and pressed it against my stomach. A sharp twinge of momentary pain told me I'd pushed the right button.

I hated using stims, but sometimes it was necessary in my line of work. Most cops used them to help get through twenty-four hour shifts and stay awake on stakeouts. I only used the damn things when I needed to clear alcohol from my system in a hurry. I placed the injector back in the glovebox and sat back, waiting for it to kick in.

By the time I reached the Regal Eagle, I felt like a million bucks. Physiologically, the alcohol was still in my system, but the stims helped to counteract the depressants. I hadn't ever used them when I wasn't drunk, but I could see how young cops got addicted to the crap and shot up when they weren't needed.

I stepped out into the pissing rain and ran right into Chief Brubaker, standing in the deluge with his arms crossed over his chest.

"Do you want to have a job with the New Orleans Police Department, Forrest?"

"I thought I had the night off, Chief. Honest mistake."

He turned his head and spat out part of his waterlogged cigar. "Well your mistake got broadcast across the entire New Orleans Policenet. Dispatch was frantic about securing the scene and your phone was turned off, not even accepting messages. IA heard that shit for sure. It's another condemnation against you. If I hadn't stepped in to take this, HQ was going to send someone from another precinct to work our neighborhood. Can you imagine how bad that would look?"

Shit, now my bullshit was starting to affect other people. I respected Brubaker, he'd gone to bat for me more times than I could count. If HQ assigned an outside detective to our precinct that we didn't request, it would reflect poorly on Brubaker and his ability to manage the station.

"I spent twenty-five years as a homicide dick, Forrest," Chief Brubaker said calmly. "Twenty-three of them right here in Easytown. You know how many times I was derelict in my duties and didn't answer a call, or showed up three hours late to a crime scene?"

"Probably none, Chief."

"You're goddamned right. I didn't miss a single fucking day on the job," Brubaker barked, his calm demeanor shattered. "Kids' birthdays, anniversaries, graduations, I didn't miss any of those either—because I fucking planned ahead. Hell, you even have that fancy robot assistant and you can't keep your shit together."

I felt it best not to correct him. Andi wasn't a robot, no matter how many times she tried to convince me to shell out the cash for a body.

"You got anything to say for yourself?"

"Sir, I—"

"Can it, Forrest. I don't want to hear your excuses. There's nothing I can do to cover for you on this one. Being absent without leave is a big deal."

He turned around and gestured over his shoulder. "Come on, asshole. I'll tell you what I know, then I'm going to bed. I want a full report by the time I wake up tomorrow."

The first body we came to was female. The killer had gotten her in the alley near the back stairwell. The lower half of her body was under the concrete steps, likely dragged there after death. The upper half was in the rain. Even through the bruises on her face, I could see that the deceased had been pretty enough, for a prostitute, likely earning her pimp a little more than the average working girl. The cause of death was easily recognizable. Several massive lacerations across her abdomen spilled part of her intestines onto the pavement and at least one perforating wound to her chest probably took out a lung. Another jagged cut along her forearm showed where her credit implant was cut out.

"Her name was Rose Finch," Brubaker said, pulling me out of my rapid examination. "Known prostitute on The Lane, works out of the Regal Apartments, right here. Same, tragic story as half the working girls in Easytown: she was a college student with a bright future, got hooked on drugs, and then ended up dropping out and going off the radar when she started working the streets. Her parents filed a missing person's report almost two years ago, but Finch appeared in person to dispute the claim and the case was dropped. Her pimp is a guy named Robert Andrews. Sergeant Drake is talking to him now."

Chief Brubaker gestured toward the corpse. "Besides the obvious injuries on the front, there's a massive contusion on the back of her head. Looks like she got clocked from behind. She has a small bag with some clothes in it that was open when we got here, probably rifled through for valuables. Alright, let's go upstairs."

I sidestepped around the body and then realized what was missing. "Has the scene already been photographed?"

"Yeah, an hour ago," the chief grunted as he climbed the stairs. I hadn't ever been *this* late to a crime scene. The photographers had come and gone, leaving just the regular building lighting to examine the scene.

We walked down a narrow hallway of closed doors until we came to the only open one. I shook the rain off my jacked and ducked under a line of police tape to go inside. The room was like all of the others in the Eagle: small, cramped, and pathetic. The bed and a dresser were all that the prostitute had in the way of furniture. There wasn't even a restroom, just a porcelain sink covered in blood.

The copper smell of blood mingled with the stench of shit in the tenement's oppressive heat. The air was out in the building, must have made the sex just awful.

"This is Gerald Wentworth," Brubaker said, pointing at the bloody mass of flesh.

The man—probably a john—still wore his pants and had one shoe off. He'd been stabbed in the neck, which accounted for all the blood scattered across the room, but what finished him off had been the nail file that still stuck out of his eye socket.

"Somebody was in a bad mood," I muttered. "Let me guess, this is the dead prostitute's room."

"Yeah, exactly," Brubaker replied. "From the initial discussion with the pimp, he arranged for Finch and Wentworth to conduct a transaction, she met him at the designated spot on The Lane, and then brought him up here. After that, the pimp went to work sales for his other nine employees. All of Wentworth's money on his credit chip was transferred to Finch. That's all we've got on site. About an hour ago, Finch's credit chip was accessed at a transfer machine and everything was downloaded to a burner chip."

Shit, a burner chip meant the trail was already cold. They'd probably already transferred the money from the burner to their real chip and that was it, no more evidence. "Any witnesses?"

"No, the other girls were in their rooms. Typically, they only use the back stairs in the day, outside of work hours, because johns don't hang out in the alley behind the apartments. They linger on the sidewalk out front."

"Opportunity sales," I muttered again.

"Exactly. A patrol drone doing sweeps of the alleys discovered the prostitute's body."

"So, what do you think, Chief? She murdered the john, tried to run away and then got herself killed in the back alley?"

"Yeah."

The public areas of Easytown were dangerous enough; the alleyways were guaranteed trouble. When would these stupid girls learn to stay clear of them—especially at night?

"You think the pimp killed her in retaliation?" I asked.

"Unlikely. There's video evidence of a man at that credit transfer machine, but the body type is all wrong for Andrews."

"I guess this will just go into our unsolved pile, right?"

"Probably," Brubaker grunted, chewing on his waterlogged cigar. "Investigate the case, but you know the deal. She was a prostitute. Don't spend too much time on this one. I need answers on the Henderson case; he had a family. What did you find out about Corrigan? Did he murder Henderson?"

"I don't know, Chief. Corrigan admitted to killing more than forty people, but claims to not know anything about Henderson. Then he lawyered up. I'm waiting on the Public Defender's office to assign someone who can be present during questioning."

"He wants a lawyer *after* admitting to killing that many people? What's his game?"

I shrugged. "No clue. He was awful proud of his record, but there's something about the Ortega case that made him shut down."

"Get to the bottom of it," Brubaker ordered. "I'm tired and I'm going to go home to get some sleep."

I nodded and stuck my hand out for the chief. "Thank you for covering for me tonight."

He examined my hand for a moment longer than I liked and then shook it. "Don't let it happen again, Forrest."

Chief Brubaker dropped my hand and walked out of the room.

There was a shift that had happened tonight, I could feel it. It had been building up for a long time, but tonight was the bolt that fell out of the assembly droid and brought the factory crashing down.

I was no longer sure that Brubaker was on my side.

I glanced at my watch. It read 3:34 a.m. We'd been at the Regal Eagle double homicide for more than three hours.

"Holy shit, Drake. It's late," I said, yawning.

"Yeah, I wasn't expectin' to be out this late," he replied, stifling a yawn of his own.

We'd processed the scene, and all of the evidence— minus the nail file embedded in Wentworth's eye socket— was already gone, ferried down to the precinct's evidence locker. Now all we had to do was wait on the medical examiner's droids to pick up the bodies we'd bagged. They were supposed to be here twenty minutes ago, but Andi checked the records, no one had dispatched them, so they were still at least ten minutes out.

"Hey, why don't you go home?" I suggested. "I'll wait for the droids to show up. Genevieve is gonna go into labor any day now and then you won't get any rest. Take it while you can get it."

He looked up from his phone. He'd been dictating his part of the report with the pimp's statements and the physical description of the crime scene. "Are you sure, Detective? I can wait here with you."

"Nah, it's okay. Those droids will be in and out since we've already done most of their job for them. I'll only be a few minutes behind you."

"Alright, I'll take you up on it," he replied, tapping his phone against his massive palm. "I'll finish up my portion of the report on the way home and send it to you tonight."

"Thanks, buddy. I mean it though. You get home and get some sleep, don't stay up writing your report."

"I'm just about done anyways. Just gotta digitize the interviews with Andrews and the girls on either side of the victim's apartment, then insert those into the report and I'll be done, minus proofreading. Should be done before I get home."

"Alright, get out of here."

I waved him away and he waved back. "See ya tomorrow, Detective."

"See ya," I replied. I watched his back for a moment before turning toward the alley. I didn't like having my back to places like that.

I thought about the shifting dynamic at the precinct. Alfonso Cruz was now the chief's number one detective, regardless of his investigative abilities or solved case rate. Brubaker was eligible to retire in the next few years, he sure as hell didn't want some scandal involving one of his detectives to bring him down so close to the finish line. I'd do the same thing if the roles were reversed and I was in his shoes.

Things had to change. I couldn't be the number two guy in the precinct. I was number one. I'd always been number one.

Change. I repeated the word in my head. Why had everything changed so much in the past year? I'd gone from being a steady and reliable cop with a proven track record to an IA fuck's wet dream. It all started with the droid, Paxton. Since then, my minor blip on IA's radar from all the sensitivity complaints had ballooned into a massive target on my back that I couldn't seem to shake. And I kept giving them ammunition to fire at me.

I'd even thought that my personal life had turned around between my time with Avery and then with Teagan. Hell, the goddamn toilet even took me off its watch list, but that all came screeching to a halt yesterday with Teagan fleeing the country. I'd been fooling myself thinking that everything was great with her.

There was a noise in the alley and I drew my service pistol, holding it at the low ready position. I clicked the button to turn on the rail-mounted flashlight and scanned the alleyway.

Empty.

"Great," I muttered. "Now my mind is playing tricks on me too."

A set of headlights flashed the side of the Regal Eagle and then angled away down the alley before disappearing completely as the medical examiner's vehicle turned into a parking spot. Two humanoid droids stepped out of the vehicle, walking rapidly to where I waited. I opened my duster enough to show my badge resting on my belt.

"Good morning, officer," the first droid to reach me stated. "Where are the bodies for transport to the morgue?"

"Come on, follow me," I said, turning down the alley.

We walked into the darkness and the droids turned on the floodlights mounted on their shoulders, illuminating three men who'd pressed up against the wall, startling me.

They sprang into action faster than I would have given the average street thug credit for. I'd practiced Krav Maga for almost two decades, something I started in college, and the martial art had saved my ass more than a few times. Two of the attackers came forward, knives held at waist level, while the third held back.

"That's the guy Karimov wants," the leader said, directing the other two.

I stepped back, bumping up against one of the useless droids, and pivoted around it, using it as a shield. Predictably, they split up, going to either side of it and I kicked out, catching the faster of the two in the kneecap. He screamed, dropping to the ground.

His buddy got half a step on me, thrusting the knife before I could turn completely to face him. It slid in between my open jacket along my hip. I felt the skin separate.

Why did lacerations hurt worse than puncture wounds? It had to be something about the surface area involved.

"You mother fucker," I hissed, twisting with the knife still trapped inside my duster. The move pulled the man with me and I followed through, delivering an elbow to the side of his face. That stunned him, and as I finished the turn, I put both hands against the side of his head, ramming it into the droid's metallic back. I bashed his skull until he passed out.

"Goddamn it!" I bellowed, pain spreading across my lower body. The fucker with the bashed knee had stabbed me in the calf.

I pulled my pistol. Fuck the department's regulations to respond in kind. I didn't have a knife to fight them with.

"Drop it," I ordered, aiming the gun at the cripple's head.

He complied and I lifted my weapon up toward the leader, but he was already running down the alley. I tested my leg. There was no way I'd be able to chase him.

I was so frustrated that I pistol-whipped the guy who'd surrendered, knocking him unconscious like his buddy.

It was a lapse in judgement that I'd soon regret.

SEVEN: SUNDAY

"You, my good friend, are an idiot."

"*Amir!* You stop that right now!" Amanda scolded from the kitchen.

"Yeah, can it, Amir," I groaned. "I just wanted to sit here and feel sorry for myself while I nursed this little injury for as long as possible."

My best friend and his wife had come to my place for once, choosing to continue to honor our Sunday ritual of having dinner together. Truth be told, I'd recovered enough that the wound in my leg was only a minor nuisance, but I'd used it as an excuse to be alone for the evening. Amanda wouldn't take 'No' for an answer, so Amir called me when they were already on their way with groceries.

He looked around my apartment at the mess the collection droids had made while searching for all of Teagan's property. It seemed like they'd opened every cabinet and overturned every piece of furniture.

Amir handed me a glass of bourbon, raising his own. "It is better to have loved and lost than not to have loved at all."

"That's cute," I grimaced, taking a sip for his toast. "Did you write that or is it some ancient Egyptian proverb you've been saving for a special occasion?"

"You're joking, right?"

"What do you mean?"

"Sometimes, I wonder how we are friends. We went to the same school, but we did not learn the same subjects,

Zach. That quote is Tennyson, as in Alfred Lord Tennyson, the poet."

"Never heard of him," I replied.

"Incorrigible," he muttered under his breath.

"Watch it, pal. You're supposed to be making me feel better, not questioning my upbringing."

"You're right. Sorry." He took a drink and frowned. "So, she just up and left, then?"

"*Amir*," his wife cautioned, looking annoyed.

"It's okay, Amanda," I said. "Yeah, she left with no notice. Don't get me wrong, I had a lot to do with her deciding to leave, but it sure as hell caught me off guard."

"How so?"

Great, I spent enough time talking to shrinks, now Amir wanted me to elaborate on my feelings. "You know me, buddy. As hard as I try, I can't seem to have a normal relationship with a woman—of any age. I get comfortable hiding behind my job and letting that be my excuse for missing things. It's pretty fucked up."

He slapped the arm of the sofa. "At least you can see this, my friend. That means there is hope for you yet."

"I doubt it." I needed to change the subject and get away from the pity-party going on in my head. "So, did you hire anyone to replace her yet?"

"Teagan? No, not yet," Amir sighed. "She worked so many hours that I'll probably have to hire two people to replace her. I'm even considering a servant droid, but they are very expensive."

"A servant droid? At the Pharaoh? I thought you avoided technology as much as possible."

"I do believe that there are better options for most things, but I'm coming around to the idea of a droid. The up-front costs are astronomically high, but over time, it would pay for itself. Wages and employee health insurance are killing my bottom line. A droid doesn't need either of those things. It doesn't need smoke or restroom breaks, doesn't get flustered when it has a bad day, doesn't call in sick and leave the restaurant in trouble…"

"Sounds like you've already made up your mind," I stated. "I assume you've ran the numbers, how long until you recoup the cost of a droid?"

"If I buy one, it's just over two years. If I buy two droids, there's a manufacturer's rebate and I could reduce the wait staff even further to cut some of the dead weight. With two, it's only three years and two months until they are paid off and the numbers begin to work in my favor."

"Two droids? Looks like you've caught the tech bug."

"On the contrary, Forrest. I'm running the numbers and considering them, but I'd never fully abandon the human wait staff or the cook staff. Just like you, they are my family as well. I may bring in a droid to help make the restaurant more efficient, but I'd never let everyone go like some restaurants have."

Talking about the Pharaoh's finances jogged my memory. "Is Tommy Ladeaux keeping up his end of our bargain?"

"So far," Amir confirmed. "I can only hope he decides to sell the building. I'd buy it in a heartbeat."

"Not if you spend all your money on droids," Amanda quipped.

Tommy Ladeaux, aka Tommy Voodoo, had bought the building where the Pharaoh's Tomb was located in an effort to get leverage on me. It worked, to an extent. I agreed to investigate a clone torture ring that was eating into his bottom line and didn't sit well with his favorite sex partner, Anastasia, who was also a clone. Torturing and murdering clones wasn't technically illegal, but I found out that some of the people being killed weren't clones, they were the actual person who'd been replaced by a clone. In exchange for helping him, he agreed to leave Amir's rent at its current rate for a period of five years.

Amir grimaced at Amanda's statement. "That's the only thing holding me back with the droid decision. I need that flexibility if he suddenly decides it's not worth the bother and puts the building up for sale."

"I don't envy you," I stated, and then glanced toward the kitchen. "Amanda, is there anything I can do for you?"

"Um, yeah, actually. I need a set of hands to hold the colander over the sink."

I finished my drink and handed the empty glass to Amir before hobbling into the kitchen. The stab wound to my calf wasn't even the most serious injury I'd suffered this *year*, but it sure was painful. I'd been so high on pain pills for a few weeks after they inserted the plate in my skull that I hardly felt any pain. I'd foolishly declined the meds this time around out of spite when the doc told me they weren't going to use genetic stimulation and I'd have to heal the old-fashioned way.

"So…" I muttered when I got in the kitchen. "What's a colander?"

"Are you—? Never mind," Amanda laughed, handing me a clear plastic bowl with holes in it. "This is a colander. Just hold it over the sink so the water from the pasta doesn't get everywhere."

I held the useless bowl as directed and she poured the pasta and water into it. Miraculously, the water drained out of the holes, leaving only the pasta. "*Hmpf*," I grunted. "I had no idea that's what this was for."

"How do you normally make pasta?" she asked.

"Andi orders delivery for me. Besides toast, I don't cook much."

"That's not cooking."

Amir appeared, holding two full glasses of bourbon. I accepted the one he offered me. "You remember when you asked me how you and me could be friends?" I asked.

"Of course, it was only a few minutes ago."

"Well, this," I held up the glass, "is how we can be friends. Cheers, buddy."

We tapped the rims together lightly and I started to take a sip when Andi's voice emitted from the kitchen speaker. "Zach, an unknown female is standing in front of—"

The doorbell rang, temporarily cutting her off. "She is ringing the doorbell."

"Thanks, Andi. Any idea who she is?"

"Scanning criminal database now," Andi replied. "Negative results."

I began limping toward the door.

"Performing a standard database query. Hit."

I stopped. "Who is she?"

"Katheryn Townlain. No police record."

The name meant nothing to me until Andi continued talking. "She works as a contractor for the New Orleans Police Department, Easytown Precinct."

"Who is it?" Amir asked guardedly. He was probably regretting his decision to come here. I had a habit of finding trouble, which was one of the reasons I thought I was a damn good cop. I didn't need to go far to find a criminal.

"It's an employee from the precinct. She's okay," I assured him.

Regardless of my assertion that Katheryn didn't pose a threat, he grabbed a knife from the chopping block and stood in front of Amanda. I shook my head. If a bad guy had a pulse blaster, no amount of human shielding would stop the blast.

I opened the door and Katheryn straightened up quickly. It looked like she'd been listening at the door; I'd have to go into the hallway video and see what she was doing while Amir and I were talking.

"Uh, hello, Katheryn," I said.

"*Detective Forrest!*" she said dryly, obviously surprised at being caught. Her wind-blown hair was still a mess. "I heard about you getting injured. I wasn't sure if you were at home."

"Occupational hazard," I stated, deflecting her concern.

"I'm sorry to bother you—are you? Are you having a party?"

I glanced over my shoulder at the Khalil's. They were in the kitchen, still watching the front door expectantly. "I— Not really."

"Oh, I just thought since there was music and it smells like some nice food…"

"My friends and I eat dinner together every Sunday night. It's kind of our thing."

She smiled. Her little button nose seemed to get even more cute. "Well, isn't that sweet? Is it… Is it just the three of you?"

"Uh, yeah. Just the three of us."

"That's *so* nice," she said, sticking her chin out slightly.

"So, ah… You come for that piece of evidence I got on Friday?"

"Yeah. I figured since you got hurt, it'd be easier if I just came to you."

Katheryn smoothed the simple dress she wore along her thighs, and I felt movement behind me. Her eyes told me that someone was behind me.

"Hi," Amanda said, sliding around me. "I'm Amanda." She shook Katheryn's hand softly. "And that idiot with a knife is Amir, my husband."

"Why's he have a knife?"

"Because," I said. "People that come to my apartment tend to have bad intentions. Speaking of, how'd you find out where I lived?"

"You think I have bad intentions?" Katheryn asked with a lopsided grin.

"No, I meant that's why he had a knife, because of the type of people who seek me out typically try to kill me."

"That's... That's really sad," she replied.

"Isn't it?" Amanda said. "Well, I'm not rude like Zach. Please come in."

"Wait. What?" I said in confusion. We were supposed to have a simple dinner and some drinks. Now Amanda was inviting strangers into my home?

"Oh, I couldn't," Katheryn said.

"Nonsense," Amanda answered, pushing me aside. Luckily, I was holding onto the door, or I'd have fallen. "You come inside. Would you like something to drink?"

"I would love to have whatever Detective Forrest is having." She pointed at my glass. "May I?"

"Huh?"

"Your drink. Can I try it to see if I like it?"

"Uh... Sure," I replied, handing her my glass of bourbon.

She took a large pull from the glass and handed it back to me, breathing out of her open mouth. "That's a little rough on the front end, but it finishes smooth and smoky."

I blinked. "That's exactly why I like it."

"It's good. I'll take one," Katheryn said, handing my glass back to me and walking inside.

"Ah... You know a cleaning service doesn't cost that much, right?" she asked, surveying the overturned boxes and piles of junk that the collection droids had left after they collected Teagan's things.

"His girlfriend left him Friday," Amanda said, much to my chagrin. "She sent some droids over to get her stuff and this is how they left the place."

"Friday?" She seemed surprised. "Like, the day you were out at Sabatier with that piece of evidence and the same day you got stabbed?"

I frowned. "Yeah, timing was never my thing."

She accepted my answer with the same refreshing, laissez-faire attitude that seemed to be the woman's hallmark.

The next hour was one of the strangest social situations I could remember besides the first time I woke up to a stranger in my bed that I'd brought home from a bar. Katheryn seemed able to actively participate in any conversation that occurred; whether it was talk about cooking methods, police work, social issues, or sports, she was extremely well-rounded and engaging. Even better, she could take a good-natured joke and return the favor.

She'd make a good cop, I decided.

As the evening wore down, Amir and Amanda took their leave. Their babysitter had to go home and get ready for her final week of high school. I was surprised when Katheryn didn't leave at the same time, which is usually how those things worked. Amir gave me a sloppy hug and mumbled something about getting a tiger before his wife laughed, helping him stagger down the hall to the elevator.

I closed the door and limped back to the dining room where my 'desk' had actually been used as a table for the first time that I could remember. All of my case files were in a haphazard pile near the wall and Katheryn was staring at the top sheet, which was my notes from the riot on Thursday.

"So, ah, can I get you another drink?" I asked, pointing at her empty glass.

"Can I get some water, please?"

I took her tumbler and set it on the kitchen counter before getting a clean glass for her from the cabinet. "Do you live far from here?"

"No. Just a few blocks away," she said. "Same neighborhood and everything."

I handed her the glass and sat down beside her. "Why do you do it?" she asked.

"I'm sorry?" I replied in confusion.

"Why are you a police officer, a detective? Like I told you the other day, I've sorta followed your career for a while. You've been shot, stabbed," she pointed at my bandaged leg, as she continued her list of injuries, "beaten, and had several broken bones over the years. From what your friends said, your career holds you back in the relationship department; so, why do you do it?"

I thought drunkenly about my answer, and how I wanted to respond. I chose to answer her sincerely. "I believe in helping people. In my job, I see the absolute worst of the human spirit. Every damn day. I don't get the benefit of meeting the good ones and interacting with the community like a beat cop, but I do get to help them. I go out there each night and every day, to get the worst of the worst off the street so regular people can go about their lives without fear of getting murdered for whatever's in their wallet or on their credit implant.

"It's changed me over the years, I'll freely admit that. I'm still a single guy with no family, while everyone I grew up with, all of my friends, are married with children. I can't even keep a pet because it'd be cruel to leave them alone for so long."

I paused. "I don't regret it, though. I've been one of the most successful homicide detectives that the Easytown Precinct has ever had."

Katheryn smiled, but somehow managed to appear sad. "Hey, what is it?" I asked.

"It's just... You seem like such a good man, I—"

"Whoa!" I said, holding up my hands and cutting her off. "I'm not without my faults." I lifted my nearly empty glass. "For starters, I drink *way* too much, and I'm not particularly nice with the perps."

"Both are coping mechanisms for dealing with what you've seen and done. The same with your relationship problems, it's probably—"

"Alright, that's enough," I cut her off again. "You're a nice woman, Katheryn, but I already see a shrink. I don't need another person trying to analyze me."

She ducked her head, sending her hair flying once more. "You're right. Sorry. You don't realize it, but I really am trying to help."

"What's that supposed to mean?"

"Nothing. Sorry," she said, standing from the table on unsteady legs. "I've got to go, Zach. Early morning at the evidence locker."

I stood as well. "I can walk with you to the garage and we can get that weapon from my Jeep."

"You left it in your car?"

"Uh... Yeah. The security system in the Jeep is top-of-the-line, protected by a secure garage facility. I wasn't in the best shape to retrieve it Friday or Saturday. The hospital only did a small amount of regenerative genetic stimulation since, as you said, I've been injured so much and the docs are worried about the long term effects of so many procedures."

"I'm sorry, Zach," she said, leaning into me, sliding her hands around my waist.

I wrapped her in my arms. Dizziness from the alcohol and antibiotics mixture intensified and before I realized what was happening, Katheryn and I were kissing. My brain screamed for me to stop; my body urged me further along toward the impending disaster.

Katheryn broke away first. "I—I can't do this."

"Why not?" *Jackass*, I thought.

"I just can't, Zach. It's complicated." She stepped back and put a hand on the table to steady herself. "Can you please bring the weapon to the evidence locker first thing in the morning?"

She didn't wait for my answer. Instead, she stumbled to the apartment door and hurried into the hallway.

I sat back down at the table to think about the mess I'd made, both in my personal life and at work. I needed to get things straight, but first I needed another drink—which may have been a contributing factor to some of my problems. I sure as hell wasn't prepared to give it up, though.

EIGHT: MONDAY

"Zach, it's time to go to work."

"Can it, Andi. I'm on convalescent leave," I grumbled into my pillow.

"Technically, you're leave ended at six o'clock this morning. The hospital gave you forty-eight hours after you came out of surgery. You're back on the clock, Zach, and there is a message waiting for you from Dr. Jasmin Jones."

"Mother fucker," I groaned. "Turn the lights on to the dimmest setting we have."

"Sure thing, boss."

"And tone down the cheeriness. I feel like crap."

"Sure thing, boss," Andi replied with a distortion filter superimposed over her normal voice, although it didn't hide her standard voice protocols, which were annoying to me right now. "Do you want me to make this voice profile standard?"

"No, goddamn it. Just talk normal, but quietly." I rolled over and my waistline hurt. "What? Aww, crap."

I'd slept in my clothes and the jeans I'd worn yesterday had bitten into my hips, scraping away the scab where the knife had sliced me. "Andi, what have I told you about reminding me to take my clothes off?"

"You have said, 'Do not let me go to sleep in my clothes, Andi.' However, I can do nothing besides provide verbal cues to remind you to remove your garments, Zach. I do not have a physical presence at this time. If you want to provide me with a synthetic body, I would ensure that your every need was taken care of."

I turned on the shower and stepped inside. "I wish I could afford something like that, Andi. I'd buy you a robot skin and just be done with it. But I can't, so stop bringing it up."

I showered in peace after that and toweled off when I was done. Andi had coffee ready and said a breakfast delivery droid was on the way. As I waited, I contemplated what had happened last night.

Katheryn had acted a bit strangely—or maybe that was normal for her, I didn't know. She seemed insistent to hear about my background, and what was that she said about trying to help me? What did I need her help for? And the kiss… She'd been into it for a moment and then changed her mind, leaving suddenly.

"Son of a bitch," I muttered, wondering if she was another fucking droid. "Andi, access the vitals from last night, verify that Katheryn Townlain is human."

"She has a regular heartbeat and exhibits normal breathing patterns associated with a sober individual when she arrived versus the breathing patterns, body heat, and heartbeat of an intoxicated person later in the evening."

"Compare that information to the Paxton Himura droid. Is your assessment that Katheryn is a robot?"

"No, Zach. Unless there are major advancements in the field of robotics that I am unaware of, Miss Townlain is a human."

I was being paranoid again. Every woman I met was not secretly a droid trying to infiltrate my life. I needed to move on from that major fuck-up and focus on the present.

"Play the message from Dr. Jones."

"Zach, it's Jasmine Jones. I'm getting automated reports that you're under investigation for police brutality. I thought we were past all that. I have some time on my schedule this morning at 10 a.m. Why don't you come down to HQ and meet with me? It'll go a long way in your defense that you're actively seeking treatment for mental health issues."

"Actively seeking treatment?" I muttered. "Andi, dig around Mainframe, see what you can find out about the investigation that Dr. Jones mentioned."

"You got it, boss," she replied.

I walked into the closet, accidentally kicking a pile of clothes that the collection droids had knocked to the floor when they checked brands and sizes for Teagan's clothing. Her leaving the way she did was bad enough; the droids trashing my apartment was inexcusable.

"Andi, have the maid service come in here while I'm gone," I said, sliding a white t-shirt over my head. "I want everything put back the way it was before those droids came through."

"Excellent. I will display pictures for the cleaning droid for reference."

"Good idea," I replied. "How much time do I have?"

"You really should be leaving in the next ten minutes."

"So I have time to sit and eat my breakfast and have a cup of coffee?"

"As I mentioned, the coffee is ready, however the breakfast is running late. You may be required to eat in the Jeep."

I pulled my pants on, but didn't bother with my button-down shirt or tie. If I was eating in the car, I'd wait to put those on until I was finished. Andi poured a cup of coffee and I sat down at the table. I liked being able to see the surface, normally every square inch was covered in papers except for the space occupied by my keyboard and my coffee cup.

"What's happening in the world," I whispered, pursing my lips as Andi brought up the daily news, displaying it at my eye level. I started to read the first headline and then my mind processed what I was seeing.

"*Holy shit!*" I exclaimed.

The headline stated, "**THIRTY-TWO DEAD IN EASYTOWN NIGHTCLUB.**" I read the article quickly. It happened last night at around 11 p.m., when Katheryn was here. Several cyborgs—the article didn't call them that, but I could tell from the description what they were—walked into Liquid Genesis and opened fire, killing twenty-eight on site and injuring another seventy-three; four more patrons later died of their injuries. Chief Brubaker was interviewed saying it was a tragedy and that the mayor had ordered the district on lockdown. Several different organizations claimed responsibility for the shooting, which likely meant none of them were actually behind it.

"Andi, what the fuck? Why didn't you tell me about this?"

"You were still on convalescent leave when the incident occurred, Zach. I was ordered by dispatch not to alert you about the activity in Easytown while you were on convalescent leave."

"Who's the detective?" I asked. With both me and Cruz out of the picture, the chief would be dependent upon whatever the other precincts could give.

"Detective Doug Sanders, from the New Orleans Police Department Headquarters."

"Mother—I hate that guy!" I groaned. Doug Sanders was a dickhead—the same dickhead who'd arrested me back in October on trumped up charges of rape and murder. *Good thing those crimes got sorted out.*

"Any arrests?"

"Negative. The report hasn't been submitted yet."

"What the hell is Brubaker doing? He'd have demanded a report from me by 6 a.m."

"It is unclear how Chief Brubaker is at fault, Zach."

"Never mind," I grumbled. Andi had a damn good AI, but sometimes things slipped past her.

"Where's Sanders at now?"

"He is at the Easytown Precinct."

"Then, that's where I'm going," I said, grabbing my coffee, shirt, tie and suit jacket.

"Your breakfast is scheduled to arrive in four minutes."

"Cancel it. I've got more important things to do. Also, cancel with Dr. Jones."

Liquid Genesis was the same club where Dale Henderson worked. I'm not saying they were related, but it was awful suspicious that the two events occurred within days of each other. With Ortega dead, I needed to figure out what his associates Gonsalvez and Karimov knew. Dr. Jones would just have to wait.

"Look who decided to show up for work," Doug Sanders said as I limped into the office, pushing the hovertray with Branch Corrigan's weapon toward my desk.

"Hey, Detective," Sergeant Drake grunted, taciturn as always.

"Drake," I acknowledged, choosing to ignore Sanders for the moment. "I saw there was a mass-cal event, why didn't you call me?" Mass-cal was the emergency responders' term for a mass casualty event, one with more injuries and security needs than there were medical providers and police officers.

"Did they have some type of work release from Sabatier?" Sanders continued to press my buttons.

I whirled on him, pivoting on my injured leg. I immediately regretted it as my leg buckled at the knee and I fell backward. Only Drake's quick reactions, drilled into him from two decades of football at all levels except the professional league, saved me from falling on my ass like a jackhole. He reached out and caught me by the shoulders, his massive hands grasping my duster.

Sanders chuckled as I dangled inside my coat for a moment before getting my good leg under me and then I stood on my own. Fucking doctors should have used that regenerative genetic stimulation, I had a job to do and this injury was going to hold me back. "Thanks, buddy," I told Drake.

"No problem, Detective."

I glared back at Sanders, attempting to put as much venom in my voice as possible. It was slightly successful by channeling the pain. "Those were bullshit charges and they were dropped against me, you fucking piece of shit. You know that."

"The ones coming up will stick, though. You'll be back on the island before the week's out. Mark my words."

His statement passed over me, unheard. "Are you holding a grudge against me specifically or are you just a massive douche canoe to everyone? I bet it's all the time. You know you'll never be value added to the city. That's why they have you working up at HQ. You're too fucking pathetic to be assigned to a district. They just flex you out to cover down when the real cops are on vacation."

Sanders stood up and took three rapid steps toward me before running into the brick wall of Drake's chest as the big man slid in between us. "That's far enough, Detective Sanders," his voice rumbled.

"Move out of the way, *Sergeant*."

"I'm sorry, I can't do that, *sir*. It's my duty to keep the peace between you two, and I'll do whatever is necessary to defend my partner, doesn't matter who the person is."

Sanders was a jerk, but he wasn't an idiot. He recognized Drake's veiled threat and backed down. "Can't wait to get out of this shithole precinct," he muttered, going back to his desk.

"You gonna keep it civil?" Drake asked, turning to me.

"Yeah. I'm good," I replied, hobbling to my chair. "I'll just sit here and go over the case load."

Drake nodded and sat back down. I glanced over at his hologram. "Whatcha watching?" I asked.

"Video feed from last night's shooting," Sanders stated. "I asked Sergeant Drake to review it while I compile a list of questions for witnesses."

I blanched. "You didn't get statements *before* you let people leave the scene?"

He shrugged. "There were a lot of uniformed cops that got statements and the people had been held for more than an hour by the time I even got there. I wasn't supposed to be working Easytown, but your little assault got you put into the hospital and instead of investigating the inside of my wife's pussy, I'm stuck down here with you two."

"Classy, Sanders," I grunted. "I'm sure she'd love to hear you talking about her like that to strangers." I took a breath to steady myself before continuing. "Did you at least get a list of witnesses, plus a collection of their biometrics, along with their home and work addresses?"

"I got names and email addresses. Mainframe can track 'em down with that."

I shook my head. "That may work over in Lakewood or Audubon, or wherever you call home, but it's fucking useless over here in Easytown. Three-quarters of those people probably gave you fake information. They come over here to get away from the real world—a lot of them without the knowledge of their significant others or parents. Given the opportunity to lie to you, they would do so in a heartbeat." The imbecile had let key witnesses leave without giving up their biometric data. "Drake, you let him do that?"

"I was inside, going over the crime scene when he released everyone, Detective."

"Shit," I yelled loudly. Sanders had fucked this up, by the numbers. I took another moment to compose myself. I needed to work damage control on this and get Doug Sanders out of my precinct as quickly as possible. "Any of the names and emails matching up in Mainframe?"

"I haven't checked the results yet," the dumbass replied. "I'm working on my questions."

"Goddamn it. Andi, query Detective Sanders' request through Mainframe," I grumbled into my phone. "See how many of those witnesses match up to the email addresses provided."

"You got it," she answered happily.

I rolled my chair to Drake's desk to see the video footage he was examining. "Results are in, Zach," Andi stated.

"Send it," I replied, eyeing Sanders in disgust.

"No email addresses were collected from the seventy-three victims sent to the hospital. Of the one hundred and eight names and emails collected at Liquid Genesis, ninety-three do not match. The fifteen that do match are all employees of the thumper club. Eighty-seven of the emails are blatantly false or are associated with someone from out of state or out of country. The six email addresses that belong to a New Orleans resident, but do not match the name given are displayed on your computer screen now."

"Thirty-five seconds, Sanders," I said. "That's all it took for me to find out that you'd potentially allowed witnesses to slip through the department's grasp. This isn't some dead hooker, these were tourists that got killed, a lot of them. We can't sweep that under the rug."

"One more thing, Zach," Andi continued.

"What is it?"

"I've examined the video feed that Sergeant Drake is reviewing. Facial recognition of one of the patrons," she said as the silhouette of a person at a table blinked red, "is assessed as a ninety-eight percent probability of being Farouk Karimov."

"Ring a bell, Drake?"

"It sure as hell does, Detective. When are we gonna pick this guy up?"

"Today, tomorrow at the latest. Andi, push a warrant through Judge Hennessey's office. I want one for Karimov's residence and place of work." I paused, thinking about the other connection to Ortega that I knew about. "Also, get one for Hector Gonsalvez. He's the third leg of the tripod supporting this whole anti-droid riot."

"What are you doing?" Sanders cut in.

"Police work," I scoffed. "Maybe you should stand back and try to learn. These two are connected to Carlos Ortega, the organizer of last week's anti-droid march that turned into a riot. Ortega might have been connected to the death of Dale Henderson, a doorman at Liquid Genesis. Now Karimov is in that club when it gets hit by fucking cyborgs. We are beyond coincidences at this point."

"Where's this Ortega guy?"

"Dead," I replied. "He died in police custody after a drone picked him up at the riot."

"Detective, we haven't gotten to the best part yet," Drake stated.

I glanced back at him. "What am I missing?"

He palmed something off of his desk and held it up in the air between his index and middle fingers.

"Son of a bitch," I breathed as I accepted the item.

In my hand was a small, serrated-edged disk. The same kind that Branch Corrigan's pneumatic air weapon fired.

NINE: MONDAY

I pushed the hovertray containing Branch Corrigan's weapon down the precinct hallway to the evidence locker. I knocked and got buzzed in.

"Ah… Hello, Zach," Katheryn greeted me.

"Yeah, sorry it took me so long to bring this back. I got tied up with some things this morning."

"It's okay. I knew it was in safe hands."

She leaned against the counter. I couldn't help but notice her arms pushing her breasts together, creating a deep furrow of cleavage that was clearly visible in her low-cut top. The woman smiled and tilted her head to regard me.

"Well, you wanna come back here?" she asked in a sultry voice that wasn't her normal tone. As she did so, she pressed the button that opened the cage door.

I maneuvered the tray through the opening and looked around. The place was deserted. "Where is everybody?"

"Out to lunch. I'm the new girl, so I got stuck working all alone."

That seemed almost as strange as her change in pitch. "I thought the evidence locker had a mandatory rotational shift so there were always two people back here at all times. You know, to make sure somebody doesn't take off with a bunch of drugs to sell on the street for some major cash."

She shrugged and twisted a few strands of hair around her index finger. "I don't know about that, Zach. All I know is that everyone went out for Phelisha's retirement lunch. I

don't know her that well and don't have any seniority, so…
Here I am."

"*Hmpf*," I grunted. "That's a major breach of protocol."

She laughed, stepping closer to me and putting a hand on my forearm. "You've done plenty of things that weren't exactly by the book. You won't tell on me, will you?"

"Katheryn…" I sighed. She was laying it on pretty thick, whether to try and continue what we'd sort of started last night or for some other reason, I didn't know. "Why are you acting like this? I like you—a lot—but I'm in no position to go on a date with you."

She frowned, but didn't remove her hand. "Besides the fact that I just got out of a relationship," I pressed. "I can't date you. You're a contractor for the police department, I'm a cop; it's forbidden."

Katheryn gently pushed the hovertray aside and placed her other hand on my opposite arm, pressing close. "No one would ever know, Zach."

"*We* would, and about a thousand cameras in here. This is the evidence locker, remember?"

"I know a place where there's no cameras. We could go there…" She left the last part of her sentence open for interpretation.

"No. I'm sorry. I'm on thin ice around here as it is," I said, stepping back from her. "We can be friends, there's no regulation against that. Maybe once you make it through the academy, we could see about going on a date."

"You're missing out, Zach," she pouted, looking down at the floor.

"Hey," I said, drawing her eyes back up to mine. Her pretty face slowly came back into view as she looked up. "I probably am. But you know that we can't do this. It's best if we just stay friends."

Why the hell was that always my go-to with women? It was the same way with Teagan for years, now here was another beautiful woman, much closer in age to me, practically throwing herself at me and I was rebuffing her. Goddamn department regulations.

"Okay," she whispered, her voice returning to its normal tone. "I'll log the weapon back in. Please don't report the locker supervisor for leaving me here alone. They said lunchtime is always slow and that I'd be fine."

"I won't. I don't want any heat to come down on you."

Katheryn nodded and grabbed the tray before turning and walking down the hall to the first doorway. "You can show yourself out, Detective," she said without looking back at me.

Seriously, what the fuck just happened? I wondered in confusion as I left the evidence locker behind me.

I sat in the ferry, trying to make sense of Katheryn's actions at lunchtime. I wasn't coming up with any good reasons why she'd turned on the charm so thickly today when she easily could have gotten what she wanted last night when we were both intoxicated. The little bit I thought I'd learned about women seemed to be washed away in the rain outside the boat.

Where the drizzle hit the windows, it ran in tiny rivulets down the glass, each drop chasing another toward the deck, where they'd eventually fall into the water below. I'd never paid much attention to the way water made its way back to the earth, I was always too busy, too preoccupied. Maybe part of my problem was that I didn't take time to appreciate the small things in life; to see the simple, everyday events as the works of art that they were instead of a hassle that interrupted the daily grind.

I zoned out, alternating between the watery runoff and watching the waves beyond. The ferry ride out to Sabatier Island was a full twenty minutes in calm water, but since Chandeleur Sound was choppy from the weather, it was closer to thirty by the time the boat pulled up to the dock. The extra time didn't seem to bother me as much as it would have in the past. Maybe I was getting old and slow.

Or maybe I just needed a break that wasn't forced on me by a hospitalization or a suspension from the force, I decided.

Thankfully, the same guard who'd been on duty last Friday was here today, so we didn't have to go through the same dick dance that almost got me shot the last time. He recognized me as the cop who was here to see the cyborg in Cellblock Three. As an added bonus, Corrigan's lawyer had been on the ferry with me and I hadn't even known. Hopefully, the weasely fucker would stay and talk with his client and I wouldn't get stuck riding back with him. Lawyers annoyed the hell out of me.

Sergeant Jackson met me once again, this time the lawyer, a man named Christopher Bonds, came with us. Bonds was so wet behind the ears he could probably grow a garden.

"When did you graduate from law school, Mr. Bonds?" I asked the diminutive lawyer, who was crammed into the seat next to me in the two-seater hoverskiff.

"You just want to say something stupid about me," he answered. "So I'm not going to respond to your obvious attempt to be rude."

I chuckled. "Was it last spring?" I gauged his response, but there was little to go by. "Last winter term?" His suit was the latest style, no older than a few months. He fidgeted with the handle of his briefcase, so new that there was still plastic wrapped around one of the rivets. Even the notebook he'd written my name in wasn't creased along the spine.

"No," I said in disbelief. "They wouldn't have done that to you. Would they?"

"Who did what to me, Detective Forrest?"

"You just graduated last week, didn't you?"

He turned toward me, his eyes wide. "How did you know?"

"I'm the best motherfucking homicide detective in the city," I deadpanned. "I can spot people like you a mile away." I kept the fact that when I'd talked to Corrigan last week, Bonds wasn't one of the public defenders that Andi showed us. I used that knowledge that he must have been a new hire along with the minor physical details I'd noticed to put together my hypothesis. And I was right.

"So, this is your first case?"

"Yeah," he replied.

It made sense that the PD's office would assign their least-experienced attorney to the hopeless case. We had street video evidence of Corrigan attacking us unprovoked with a couple of deadly weapons, drone gun camera footage of him throwing the bench to damage the drone initially, and then destroying it with that pneumatic disc shooter. I'd reviewed the evidence, both Drake and I identified ourselves as police officers when he first appeared. It should be an open-and-shut case, don't waste the horsepower on an experienced attorney. They didn't know anything about his admission to murdering forty people yet; I'd let that one drop during the session with the perp.

"Don't tell that to cyborg, kid," I warned.

"What?"

"I'm trying to give you some friendly advice about your client, Mr. Bonds," I shouted over the sound of the rain hitting the small hoverskiff's roof, which had miraculously made an appearance now that the lawyer was present— Jackson was such a dick. "Don't tell Corrigan that this is your first case. He's a psychopath and all that hardware he's cut into himself hasn't helped his mental state. If you want to stay alive, make sure that he's *always* restrained, especially when you're alone with him. I mean it, don't trust him."

"He's my client, Detective," Bonds rebuffed. "I'm sure I'll be fine."

I gave it one more shot. "Whatever, kid. I'm just trying to give you some advice, free of charge. I don't need another murder to investigate, I've seen enough of them to last me a lifetime."

The lawyer stared straight ahead and didn't reply.

"Suit yourself," I grunted. "It's your funeral." *Don't talk in clichés, idiot*, I berated myself.

We arrived at the perimeter shortly after that and went through the same process as I'd gone through alone last Friday. I hated not having my weapons with me, but it was the only way I was getting inside. When we arrived at the hospital ward the lawyer asked for ten minutes to discuss the case with his client alone.

I took the time to read through the draft search warrants for Gonsalvez and Karimov that Drake sent me, making sure there weren't any glaring errors that would hold up the judge signing them.

Soon enough, Mr. Bonds and I were seated on opposite sides of one another, Branch Corrigan's hospital bed in between us. I went through the spiel with Corrigan about how everything he said during our discussion could be used against him, and then I got down to the meat of why we were here.

"I didn't want to upset you again, Mr. Corrigan, so I left your arm back at the precinct, locked away where you'll never have to see it again. *Ever.*"

"Fuck you."

"Pleasant," I responded. "Who made that piece of equipment?"

He looked over at the kid, who answered. "That question won't hurt the case against you. However, I advise you not to talk about anything except—"

I cleared my throat and pulled out a piece of paper from the folder I'd stashed in my coat against the rain. "*Ahem.* Excuse me there, Mr. Bonds. I'm holding a plea bargain deal from the DA. They're willing to offer you Corrigan years on Sabatier, without his prosthetic, in exchange for telling the NOPD who's running these chop shops to create the cyborgs, who they work for, and any information pertaining to the associated weaponry and technology that has been used in a crime."

Corrigan's lawyer took the paper and examined it. "Can I have another minute with my client, Detective?"

"Sure, take two," I said, standing up. "But I want you to know, if this goes to court and he's found guilty of two counts of assaulting a police officer, destruction of a police drone, discharge of a firearm within the city limits, destruction of public property exceeding ten thousand dollars, destruction of private property, interfering with a police investigation, and of being an all-around asshole, your client can stay right here on the island for eighty years. That's a long time, Mr. Corrigan. Think about that while you talk to Mr. Bonds."

I left the small treatment room and went to the nurse's station where I asked for a water fountain. She pointed me to a breakroom that held disposable cups and boasted a water filtration system that was fed directly from the desalinization plant that the prisoners worked at below the prison. It was damn fine tasting water.

By the time I was finished with my cup, the nurse came to tell me that Corrigan and his lawyer were ready for me. I took my time returning to their room.

"Alright, tell me we have a deal and you want to squeal," I said in a sing-song voice.

"Yeah," Branch rumbled. "I'll tell you what you want to hear."

Internally, I smiled widely, knowing I *was* the best damn detective in the city. Outwardly, I affected a moderate grin, meant to be calming. I sat down in the same chair I'd abandoned less than five minutes before.

"Who's operating the chop shops? I need names, addresses, last known location, whatever you've got. We want to put an end to this stuff."

"The doc who did me," Corrigan said, stopping to catch his wheezing breath, "was Terri Solomon. Has a shop over off of Fowler." Another pause. "The front is a flower shop, in the back is where they do the cutting. As far as I know...works alone, but there's muscle protecting the place."

Corrigan proceeded to give me the names of three other chop shops in Easytown. Andi recorded everything as my mind reeled with the idea that there were so many places performing cybernetic enhancements. I'd thought there was only one, maybe two, but *four*? That was stretching it, and that was only the ones that this guy knew of. What else was out there that we didn't know about?

"A weapon, or weapons, similar to your prosthetic was used in a mass shooting at a thumper club called Liquid Genesis last night. Who else do you know who has a weapon that fires the same ammunition as what you've got?"

He blinked heavily and I wasn't sure if he was thinking or going to sleep. "Hey, Corrigan! Wake up," I said.

"Huh? Oh, shit," the cyborg said. "Hey, lawyer, do me a favor and wipe this drool off my chin."

To my surprise, the small man told the giant, "No. I am not your servant. I can get you a tissue if you'd like, but I am not wiping your chin for you."

"What about the weapon? Who else makes that type of weapon, or who else has it?" I repeated.

"I don't know, man. Until you said something, I thought I was the only one with that sweet piece of tech." The stub where his weapon had been mounted moved awkwardly. "You know, it looks like old-school diesel tech or something, but it's wired to my nerves and I control it just like I would my old arm. I don't know how Solomon does it, but that shit is good."

Dead end on that part, but I was willing to bet that this Solomon fellow had some answers. I mentally rearranged my list of subjects that I needed to talk to, juggling between the Henderson case and the mass shooting. For all that he'd fucked up the investigation so far, I was at least mildly grateful that Sanders was around to do some of the legwork on the case. With Drake birddogging him, he shouldn't be able to screw it up much more than he already had.

"How much does all that shit cost?" I asked, genuinely interested in his answer.

"Hundred and fifty gees for the dicer."

"*Dicer?* Is that what they call it?"

"It's what I call it," Corrigan replied.

"*Hmpf.* Lotta cash. You buy it or did your employer?"

"My boss did."

"Well, shit, Corrigan. You're gonna make me ask every little follow-on question, aren't you?"

"I have instructed my client that he is able to answer questions in conjunction with the plea bargain deal," the lawyer interjected. "But he doesn't have to volunteer anything to you. Read the paper you brought over from the DA."

"Well, you're a by-the-books little shit," I smirked. "Okay, Corrigan, who do you work for?"

The big man glanced at Mr. Bonds, who nodded. "A Russian named Farouk. Works at—"

"The Easytown Dockyards," I said. "I know the fucker. He's already on my shit list. I've been meaning to get over there and see him, but that seems like it moved up to my number one priority."

"Heh," Corrigan grunted. "You're so lost, man. Good luck finding *him*. If he knows you're looking for him, he's probably already gone. He's a slippery sonofabitch."

"Yeah, well, I'm a stubborn asshole and I won't give up until I find him. What else can you tell me about Karimov?"

"You don't need to answer that," the pencil dick interjected. "Giving more than your employer's name is not part of the plea bargain."

"Seriously?" I groaned.

"My client told you who he worked for, as requested. It doesn't say he has to endanger himself by giving up information about a potentially dangerous individual."

"*Bwahahahaha!*" Corrigan roared, laughing so hard that the machines he was hooked up to began to sound alarms that brought nurses running. He continued to alternate between laughter and coughing fits as they recalibrated the machinery, ensuring their patient wasn't going into some type of cardiac arrest.

When they finally left, the cyborg chuckled, saying, "I don't have anything to fear from Farouk. I'd snap his neck like a twig." There was something in his eyes that made me think he wasn't telling the truth about being afraid of Karimov.

"So tell me what you know about your boss," I prompted.

"Eh," Corrigan replied. "Likes knives and knows how to use them to help enforce discipline with people."

"Do you know what other illegal shit he's into?"

"Again, my client is not required to answer your questions regarding his former employer."

"Can it, Bonds. I want to hear what Mr. Corrigan has to say—not you," I grumbled.

"Well, like the good man said, Detective, I don't *have* to tell you anything about my boss to honor my end of the plea bargain. But I'll let you in on a little secret: Karimov is the sole producer of synthaine. You know, that shit everyone drops in their eyes to get away from it all? I bet those Narc motherfuckers never thought about someone continuing to work a nine-to-five job as cover while they raked in millions."

I felt like Corrigan had just handed me the Golden Goose, all tied up in a bow on a silver platter. The city's Narcotics Division had tried for years to find the source of synthaine. We were fairly sure it came from somewhere in southern Louisiana, and they'd busted hundreds of dealers in the two years since the drug made its debut, but where it came from was still a mystery. Besides the drug's cocaine base, the rest of the ingredients were household chemicals that could be bought at a convenience store. No one had been dumb enough to buy large quantities of the ingredients, so tracking down the components and working up wasn't an option. Scientists had been unable to replicate the final product, so if we could get rid of the *one* person who knew how to make it…

Now here was this information. If what Corrigan said was true, and Karimov was the man responsible for the most deadly street drug in sixty years, he was either brilliant, reckless, or stupid. I was beginning to think it was the first. Working a regular job automatically disqualified him as a suspect in a lot of eyes; these guys tended to become suspects because they had a lot of money that they flaunted with no discernable income stream. Also, the two times I'd seen him, at the riot and on video at the club, there hadn't been any obvious henchmen around—certainly no cyborg bruisers like Branch Corrigan. He participated in social causes, making him seem like the good immigrant he posed as.

This case just got a lot more complicated. I'd have to confer with Narc before I went down to bust this guy.

"Farouk Karimov was at the Liquid Genesis last night when it was attacked—no, he was unharmed," I answered the question forming on the big man's lips. "Is that why two cyborgs shot up the club that he was in? Is this a drug war?"

Corrigan tried to lift his hands in a shrug, but the two handcuffs holding his wrist to the side of the bed prevented it. "I don't know. It happened after I was mutilated by you and locked up."

"Something that big, you would have heard rumblings…" I left it open for him to fill in the blanks.

"I work *for* Karimov, dickhead. If Farouk was the target, it makes sense that he didn't know about it."

"Okay, you're right," I conceded. "How has he stayed off the police radar?"

A soft knock at the door caused me to turn as a dark-haired nurse came into the room. "Sorry, I have to change Mr. Corrigan's IV." She deftly changed the bag of fluids and retreated quickly before I got a good look at her face.

"Back to my question," I said, bringing the discussion back online. "How has he been able to stay anonymous?"

"Very few people know about it. Hell, maybe four or five total. Another person posing as the producer orchestrates the big deals. Keeps clean by distancing herself from everything."

"Her?"

"I mean 'him'. Drugs, man," he corrected himself.

"So, how do *you* know about what he does?"

"I met the guy in Sabatier seven or eight years ago. He paid me to protect him on the inside and we've kept up that relationship ever since."

"How does he produce this shit and distribute it without us knowing?"

"Are we done talking about my bosses?" the cyborg said, changing the subject abruptly. "I'm getting sleepy from all these meds. Just finish your questions that completes my end of the plea bargain."

"Bosses?"

He clammed up quickly. It was another inconsistency. "Is there someone else involved besides Karimov?"

He smiled wide and I noticed for the first time how dark his gums were. They were a deep purple, almost black. "Nope. Just Karimov."

I went back to my original line of questioning; I could talk to this dude any time I wanted as part of the plea bargain. "What were you doing at Dale Henderson's apartment that night when you attacked me and my partner unprovoked?"

"Karimov sent me over there to make sure he didn't have anything that could point to the synthaine operation in his apartment."

I tried to follow his statement, but he'd spoken it oddly. I glanced at the IV going into his arm. The nurse had replaced his narcotics drip, so it was probably starting to hit him. I needed to finish questioning him today so I didn't have to come back out here anytime soon.

"You said Karimov sent you to Henderson's apartment?"

"Yeah."

"And you went there to make sure Henderson didn't have anything to implicate him?"

"Sure."

"So Henderson knew that Karimov was behind the synthaine?"

"Yeah."

"How?"

"Pillow talk," Corrigan slurred. "Farouk talks in his sleep... Karimov wanted to shut him up."

"*Hmpf*," I grunted. That sort of shit had been bringing people down since the dawn of man. "How did Farouk know he'd let the cat out of the bag?"

The cyborg stared at me stupidly and I rephrased the question. "How did Farouk know he'd talked about producing synthaine in front of Henderson?"

"Recordings."

His answers were becoming short. *How much morphine did that nurse give him?* I had to hurry. There were still three questions I had to get answered.

"A projectile, the miniature saw blade, was found in Dale Henderson's neck. Did you shoot him?"

"That's not what the plea bargain—"

"Read the last line, Mr. Bonds," I hissed. *Bullshit if it wasn't part of the plea bargain.* "It says information about crimes committed with the associated technology."

I turned back to Corrigan. He was falling fast, so I stood and quickly slapped him across the cheek. "Hey!" the lawyer squealed.

"You want to come back out here tomorrow?" I asked.

"No, I—"

"Then shut up. You see the size of this guy? A little wake-me-up slap isn't gonna do anything to him." The lawyer was annoying me. Maybe I should have slapped him instead. "Corrigan. Corrigan, wake up."

His eyelids fluttered and he flopped his head in my direction. "Did you kill Dale Henderson at the order of your boss, Farouk Karimov?"

"Nah," Branch breathed heavily. "Was supposed to…but fucker was already dead."

"Why were you going to kill him?"

"He knew about the…synth…aine."

"Did you kill Janie Kelso in February at a synthaine house on Snapdragon Avenue?"

"I kill a lot."

The Christopher Bonds rolled his chair away from his client, visibly shaken by Corrigan's admission.

"Drug deal gone bad?" I asked.

"Didn't pay," the cyborg mumbled.

"During our last conversation, I advised you of your rights and then you admitted to killing more than forty people. Do you stand by that assertion?"

"Huh?"

He was fading fast. "You said you killed more than forty people. Is that true?"

"Heh… More like seventy-six. But, who's counting?"

"Do you have any proof of that?"

"Please, Detective Forrest," Mr. Bonds pleaded. "You can see that my client is very tired. He's overcome by the medication."

"Hey! Corrigan," I said, shaking him roughly once more. I was rewarded with the fluttering of his eyes. "Do you have proof that you killed seventy-six people?" I asked slowly.

"Videos," he heaved. "I jerk off to them."

"Where?"

"My apart…men—"

He passed out and I shook him again. It was no use. The drugs had forced the big man to sleep.

"Well, Mr. Bonds. Looks like we'll be getting a search warrant for your client's apartment as well as playing this recording for the grand jury."

"We didn't authorize the recording of Mr. Corrigan's admission of guilt."

"Too bad, son. The Clairbridge Ruling of 2027 allows me, as a police officer, to record every conversation I have with a suspect after I've read them their Miranda Rights." I glanced up from my notebook where I'd scribbled some notes. "Are you telling me that you didn't know about that US Supreme Court ruling?"

"No, of course I knew, it's just—"

Beep! Beep! Beeeeeeeeeeeep!

I jumped up and ran to the door. "Nurse!" I screamed.

"What's happening?" the lawyer screeched.

"He's flat lining!" I replied.

"What's that mean?"

The same crew of doctors and nurses who'd came in earlier burst into the room. They didn't ask questions, they just got to work as Bonds and me pressed against the walls, finally making our way out of the room altogether.

We sat on cheap, foldable chairs in the waiting room, neither of us saying anything to the other until the doctors came out ten minutes later to tell us the news.

Branch Corrigan was dead.

TEN: MONDAY

The medical report was complete by the time my Jeep drove off the Sabatier Island Ferry's deck. Corrigan died of a massive overdose of morphine.

The staff immediately implicated the nurse who'd given it to him. She was a new hire and pled innocent, begging them to allow her to keep her job. An investigation by the prison's doctor showed that she'd set the IV drip to the proper dosage and an examination of the drug bottles turned up no missing morphine. Next, they turned to the drug itself. A quick scan of the bar code told them everything they needed to know.

Several months prior, there'd been a nationwide recall of morphine due to the lots having more than triple the strength of the narcotic than they were supposed to. Several people died across the country before it was discovered. The hospital had turned in all of their affected stocks, and had the documentation to prove it. Yet, somehow, a bottle of the tainted morphine had ended up in the Sabatier Island medical ward's controlled substance locker, and the nurse had randomly picked that particular bottle to dose Corrigan from.

The whole thing stank of a murder to shut him up about Karimov, but there was zero evidence. Until camera footage, call logs, and internet messaging could be analyzed, it would be chalked up to an accidental overdose.

I needed a drink.

"Andi, call Dr. Jones' office. Maybe she can fit me in."

The phone rang twice before the doctor picked it up. "What do you want, Zach? I don't have time for your bullshit."

"I'm sorry about this morning," I replied. "That mass shooting in Easytown took priority."

"I saw a note about it on the NOPDnet. Didn't even register as a blip on the local news radar."

"Of course not," I answered bitterly. "Nobody cares about what happens in Easytown. They just want to stick their heads in the sand and avoid the problems down here."

"I was just getting ready to leave for the day, Zach," Dr. Jones said, causing me to glance at my watch. Somehow, I'd blown an entire day between the run-in with Doug Sanders, returning the pneumatic weapon to Katheryn and that strange conversation, and my time at Sabatier.

"Oh. I didn't even realize what time it was. Sorry."

"I can fit you in at 8:30 tomorrow morning, but we've got to be quick because I have a nine o'clock. I'm only doing this because I'm your friend as well as your therapist. Believe me, though, coming and talking to me will go a long way to help derail the bullshit going on behind the scenes."

"What bullshit?" I asked.

"I'd rather not say, especially over my office line. I'm glad that you're seeking help and want to continue to be the best cop that you can be."

"Huh?"

"Okay, I'm gonna go. I'll see you tomorrow morning."

She hung up without ever confirming with me that I could make 8:30. "Guess we need to add that to the calendar, Andi."

"Already did, Zach."

"Thanks. I want a meeting with Tommy Voodoo tomorrow, too. Any time he can fit me in is fine."

"On it."

"I also want the home addresses of Hector Gonsalvez and Farouk Karimov. Then, get me a meeting with Narc so we can go over the story that Corrigan told to see how it compares with their ongoing investigation."

"Alright, I'll begin working on those items immediately," Andi replied. "According to the Jeep's GPS locator, you are approximately eight minutes from arriving back here. Should I allow your guest inside or make them wait in the hallway until you return?"

"Guest? What guest?"

"Katheryn Townlain is currently waiting in the hallway. She says she's going to dinner with you."

"*Jesus*," I grumbled. "What is it with this woman?"

The Pharaoh's Tomb was busy tonight, which was odd for a Monday night. Typically, the early days of the week didn't see a lot of business, but tonight, more than three-quarters of the tables held customers. *Good for Amir*, I thought.

Across from me sat an enigma. Katheryn had been waiting at my apartment when I got home. She swore to me that she wasn't some sort of weird homicide groupie, and acknowledged that we couldn't date each other, but that she still wanted to be friends with me. I'm a sucker for a pretty woman, so I agreed to go out to dinner with her; it's not like I had any plans for the evening.

"So this Paladin guy helped you solve the clone torture case?" she asked.

"Yeah. Turns out he was a clone too. He was trying to save others like him."

"So he *was* self-aware?"

"Yeah. I didn't know that at first, but it came out later on that he was a clone."

"He's still out there, in Easytown, isn't he?"

I nodded. "He's a dangerous vigilante, but after the fight at the clone facility, he's only popped up on the radar a couple of times."

"And the department is okay with letting him stay loose?"

"You worked at the Dockyards, right?" She nodded, so I continued. "You know what Easytown is like then: overcrowded, dirty, dangerous... We are barely keeping our heads above water protecting innocent, tax-paying tourists. Is the Paladin a murderer? Yes, unequivocally, but he's killing other murderers and street thugs. If we could get more resources or more time, we'd go after him. As it is now, we just have to keep an eye on him and hope that he doesn't mistakenly hurt the wrong person."

"Wow. I've never heard it explained like that."

"It's shitty, but it is what it is. We simply don't have the resources to go after everyone, and like it or not, this guy is cleaning up the streets of Easytown."

"So you condone what he does?" she asked.

"No. No I don't. We have two homicide detectives and two deputy detectives who can assist on cases, but are not authorized to operate independently and unsupervised like a detective is. It's a capacity issue. If I could bust the guy, I would. He's damn good at making himself scarce when he doesn't want to be found."

"You found him a couple of months ago," she persisted.

"He found me. Why are you suddenly so interested in this guy?"

"Hmm? Oh, no reason," she said. I could tell she was lying, even though she was very good at it. It made me pay closer attention to what she said. "I'm just trying to learn all I can about being a cop before I go to the academy."

I laughed. "Don't try to emulate me. They want everything by the book at the academy. There may be a million ways to skin a cat, but by God, you'll use the way they teach you while you're there or they'll fail you."

"Thanks for the advice."

"That was free," I said, picking up my glass of bourbon. "The next one will cost you."

She picked up her own glass of prosecco and tilted it in my direction, answering my small gesture before taking a sip. She looked left and then right before leaning in to whisper, "What will it cost me?"

"I, ah… Well, that backfired on me," I confessed.

She laughed heartily, obviously amused at my dismay, and took another sip from her champagne flute. Her tongue darted out to lick a drop of the sparkling wine off her red lips and I noticed how perfectly her low-cut dress matched the shade of her lipstick. Katheryn was obviously a woman who paid attention to details.

She leaned back, smiling deviously. "Detective, we're supposed to keep it professional, remember?"

"Touché," I replied, taking another long pull from my drink. Before I realized it, our glasses were empty, and we'd ordered another round.

"So tell me about *you*, Zach. What makes you tick?"

"There's not much to tell," I said, warming to the moment. I had a good drink, good company, and I hadn't eaten anything since breakfast, so the alcohol was moving quickly through my system. "My parents died when I was seventeen—No, it's okay," I said, waiving off her sympathetic look. "It's been a long time.

"Since I was a minor, the city tried to put me in foster care. I sued the city to become an emancipated minor and won. By the time the judge ruled in my favor, I'd already spent six months in a foster home and was only two months away from turning eighteen anyways. It was the principle of the thing at that point, you know?"

"Sure."

"Then I went to college at Loyola here in town on a baseball scholarship, got my degree in criminal justice and became a cop. A few years of stumbling around Easytown as a beat cop and I was ready to quit. Decided to study up and take the exams to become a detective and the rest is history."

"That's fascinating," Katheryn replied. Another lie. "But what I mean is, why do you do what you do? Why are you a cop?"

"Why do you keep telling me those little white lies?" I asked.

A moment of panic flashed across her face, then she composed herself. "I'm sorry. I'm not sure what you mean."

"You did it a few moments ago when we were talking about the Paladin," I said, affecting a lopsided grin to try and soften my delivery. "You said you didn't have a reason for asking about him, but you do. Same way with just now, you asked about my past and then when I told you, you lied about being interested in it. What gives?"

"I don't know how to answer those allegations, Detective. I'm not lying to you. I do need to go to the restroom though, so please excuse me."

I pushed my chair back away from the table and stood with her, wincing slightly at the pain in my calf. She placed her napkin on the table and slunk away. The dress she wore left absolutely nothing to the imagination, clinging tightly to her athletic frame. Interestingly, she had matching tattoos on the back of her thighs. Each was of a bow made of red ribbon and I wondered about my dining partner's past. Typically those kind of tattoos were for girls who wanted to show the world that beneath their cool and collected surface, they were ready for anything in their heart. Was that a permanent reminder of a rebellious youth or was she still wild at heart?

I continued to sip my drink and by the time she returned, my glass was empty. "Looks like I need to catch up," she murmured, sitting lightly in her chair.

"Don't feel obliged to go dink-for-drink," I said. "I have a very high tolerance for alcohol."

"Don't worry about me, Zach. I can hold my own." She downed her prosecco and raised a small, dainty hand to call the droid over for another round.

I watched her movements with interest. I was telling the truth about a high tolerance, but it only took a couple of drinks to help me relax from the stress of all the shit going on in my life. That second drink helped me realize just how beautiful Katheryn really was. The chin-length bob haircut, while normally not my preference, fit her perfectly and brought to mind a woman with a youthful exuberance for life, which matched her upbeat personality.

I could see myself becoming good friends with her. Then, a dark thought surfaced that she was just a replacement for the camaraderie I'd lost with Teagan's betrayal. I crushed the negative feeling and simply tried to enjoy living in the moment.

"Katheryn, I want you to answer me honestly."

"Okay," she replied guardedly.

"I'm gonna turn the tables on you. You've been asking all the questions until now. So, what's your story? A week ago, I didn't know you existed—not counting when I met you at the investigation years ago," I amended. "Now, this is the second night in a row that you showed up at my apartment, which is a minor feat just by itself since very few people know where I live, and it looks like we're well on the way to being drunk together again. When you met me Friday, I had a live-in girlfriend, my health was better than it had been in years, and I was, in my mind, beginning to finally settle down. By the end of the day, all of that was gone. Is it truly coincidental timing or did you arrange it to meet me somehow?"

Again, I saw a quick flash of alarm in her eyes before she hid it. "Okay, Zach. You got me. I already told you that I followed your career and that I wanted to be a cop." She leaned back from the table and took another sip of her wine. The added distance made it that much harder to see in the dim restaurant lighting. "And, yes, I did arrange to be the tech who managed your evidence. I told all my coworkers that if you came in, they had to come get me."

She leaned forward and laughed. "God, that makes me sound like a stalker, doesn't it?" I shrugged, but didn't say anything, choosing to let her continue on her own.

"But I had no idea that your girlfriend was leaving, that was simply good timing on my part—I mean… Not that I'm trying to swoop in and take her place or something." The color rose in her cheeks. "I just mean that you probably wouldn't be out to dinner with me now and I likely wouldn't have stayed for dinner with Amir and Amanda last night if your girlfriend was there."

As far as I could tell, everything she said was true. "Okay, I can see that. Truth be told, I usually get along with women easier than men." I smirked again. "I suck when things move beyond friendship, but at least I don't feel like I'm constantly competing against women."

"Is that because you think males are at the top of the food chain and a woman can't do the same things as a man?"

I laughed, taking a pull from my drink. "Not at all. Women are simply easier for me to get along with; I don't know why."

She inclined her chin. "Alright. What's next?"

"You say you want to become a cop and possibly a detective one day after you save up enough money to supplement the abysmal wages they pay cadets… Why?"

"I don't know. Probably the same reasons as everyone else. I believe that the average person deserves to go about their lives without being bothered by society's less desirables. Unfortunately, those kinds of people are everywhere, so somebody's got to stop them."

"So, you're a do-gooder at heart," I teased.

"Something like that, yeah," she replied, grabbing my hand. "Zach, I like you."

"Okay," I replied, leaving my hand uncomfortably where it was. "But we already know that we can't move forward with anything like that."

"I know. You're not willing to risk violating the department's regulations."

"And you'd do well to do the same," I said. "You may be a contractor now, but don't think everything you do isn't being catalogued and saved for future examination. Keep your nose clean and you'll get into the academy."

She squeezed my fingers together and muttered, "Why are you making this so hard on me?"

"Hmm?" I asked. "What am I doing?"

"Nothing, Zach. I just want you to know that I genuinely care for you. No matter what happens."

"Maybe it's the alcohol," I grinned, "but I really don't know what you mean."

"Nothing. I said something that I shouldn't have."

I wanted to ask her about what she said, but to be honest, I was feeling good enough that I probably wouldn't remember her answers.

We ate dinner and had a few more drinks. By the time we were ready to go, it was nearing midnight and my teeth were numb. I was feeling good and ignored the stares of the restaurant staff as Katheryn and I may or may not have kissed several times across the table.

We walked to the Jeep, hand-in-hand. There were a few minutes of hot, clothed rubbing against one another, alongside the car. Finally, we separated and I took a step back.

"I'm sorry," I breathed.

"Don't be. I want this too."

Every fiber in my body wanted to scream in protest to what my mind imposed. "It can't happen," I finally managed to say.

"Why?" she whispered huskily. "We're both consenting adults."

"It's against the department's regulations," I replied. "I want to take this further, but you're a contracted employee. I can't."

She turned, stepping until she faced away from me, and accidentally dropped her clutch purse. "Oops," she said.

Her dress lifted high along the back of her thighs as she bent at the waist to collect her clutch. The curve of her ass was no longer a promise of what might be as it was exposed and both of her bow tattoos stood out starkly in the streetlights. I knew it wouldn't take but a word and she'd come back to my apartment.

I wanted to bring her back. Wanted to feel good for the night. Wanted to forget Teagan. But most of all, I just wanted to move on.

I also wanted a job.

"Here," I said. "Let me help you up." I offered her my hand and when she straightened, I led her around to the passenger side door.

"Don't you want to go in back?" she asked, glancing longingly at the back seat.

"No," I replied. "We can't take that step. I love being a cop, I don't think my career could handle another violation of the city's regulations."

"No one would ever know," she whispered.

"*I* would know, Katheryn," I replied. *Damn my sensibilities.*

I opened the door for her, let her into the Jeep, and then walked around to the other side to get in.

By the time I got in, there was a line of tears down her cheek. *Jesus, this is getting annoying*, I thought. Out loud, I said, "Are you okay?"

"Yeah. I just feel like I'm throwing myself at you and you keep sidestepping me. I'm beginning to wonder if it's something about me that makes you not want to be with me."

"Katheryn, it's not you. Well, I mean, it *is* you, but it's because of your job, not who you are. You seem to be a great person, but we can't get involved romantically because of NOPD regulations. We've gone over this."

"I know… I just thought that maybe tonight would be different."

"It won't be. And we never will be as long as you're a contractor. It is what it is."

"But you had sex with——I mean *the rumor* is that you had sex with a droid and didn't get fired. You've violated the rules before and nobody got hurt. I wouldn't tell anyone."

"I didn't know she was a droid. *Dammit!*" I slapped the steering wheel, causing my passenger to jump. "I don't think I can continue to see you, even in a social way, if you can't come to grips that we will never be together until you are either a cop or a private citizen."

"I can't do this anymore," she whispered.

"Do what?" I asked in confusion.

"Stop recording," she said.

"I'm not recording anything," I said, confused.

"I was talking to my phone," Katheryn replied.

My eyes narrowed. "What do you mean?

"I can't do this, Zach," she repeated. "You are a legitimately good man. I've tried every trick I know."

"Do what, Katheryn?" I asked, more forcefully this time.

She opened the car door and stepped back out, walking toward the restaurant.

"Mother—" I stopped myself; no sense in getting upset if I didn't even know what was going on.

I met her under the lights of the Pharaoh's entryway. There were few people outside, most having already gone inside or left as the evening grew late. "What's this all about?" I asked. "Why were you recording our conversation?"

Katheryn dug into her purse, bringing out a tissue to wipe her eyes. Then, she reached inside once more and brought out a small leather wallet, which she flipped open. A familiar star and crescent badge, gold like mine, rested inside the wallet.

"What the fuck?" I hissed. "You're a *cop*?"

She slipped the badge into her purse and continued wiping her eyes. "I'm Internal Affairs, Zach. I'm assigned to your case to get dirt on you, possibly even coerce you into breaking more department regulations."

"*Mother fucker!*" I shouted, not caring who heard, or if I caused a scene. My anger was palpable. I could feel it growing inside me. I needed to get away from here before I did something stupid, which would only validate IA's reasoning for assigning an undercover detective against me.

I turned on my heel, storming down the sidewalk toward—hell, I don't know where I was headed, but it was sure as fuck away from that lying bitch.

"Zach, please!" she called after me. "They want you gone. You need to watch your back."

By the time I realized where I was, my leg throbbed from overuse. I'd walked several miles toward the heart of New Orleans, through good neighborhoods and bad. Besides Easytown, which was almost entirely shitty, the neighborhoods in New Orleans were strange. Most big cities had warning signs and indicators to tourists that they were gradually moving into the bad part of town. Not here in the Big Easy. Levels of safety varied street-by-street. Dangerous, run-down areas were immediately beside expensive, updated homes. Even the city itself was as fucked up as the people living here.

I continued walking, but had the distinct feeling that I was being watched—by more than the street cameras. The neighborhood I'd wandered into was unfamiliar to me. It looked a lot like the residential areas of Easytown with run-down shacks and people sitting on their porches, simply existing instead of working or socializing. I hadn't seen a cop in probably twenty minutes, and the last drone I'd seen was four or five blocks behind me.

"Andi, send the Jeep to my location."

"You got it. Expect arrival in six minutes."

The feeling that I was walking into something bad intensified. Standing in one place invited its own set of problems, so it was best to keep moving.

Shadows darted between homes on my right; whether they were human or animal, I couldn't tell. "Andi, I need drone support to my location."

"Denied. Dispatch says you are not acting in an official capacity, therefore a drone will not be sent to you."

"ETA on the Jeep?"

"Three minutes."

Several people emerged from the narrow alleyway between two dilapidated homes that may have been built pre-century and then left to rot. I stopped and put my hand on the grip of my service pistol in its shoulder holster. This wasn't going to be easy.

"The Jeep needs to come in hot, separating me and the group of people to my front."

"Understood. I'm already integrated with the car's A/V system to assist control. Two minutes—you will receive a traffic violation in two-to-three days; we just sped through a red light."

"Fine."

"You're out of place here, man," a voice called from the group of people to my front.

"Just out for a walk," I replied.

"Well you done walked into the wrong neighborhood, ginger root," a different person said.

I grimaced at the racist term the group used. It was made popular by a song a few months ago and only the worst kind of people used it. At least I knew what I was dealing with.

"We don't need any trouble," I stated.

"Too late for that." I couldn't tell which one of them spoke this time.

"I'm a cop." Better to get that out there so they know I'm armed.

One of the men stepped forward, holding his penis as he walked. "You ain't got no backup and there ain't no drones up. Looks like you're alone, piggy."

Ahh, the traditional insults. Gotta love 'em.

"One minute," Andi's voice drifted over my earpiece.

"I didn't mean to come into your neighborhood," I said, trying to appease the situation. "I'll just turn around and go back the way I came."

"I don't think so," the thug holding himself said as he stepped closer. His hand came up in a fluid motion, holding a pistol. It wasn't the first time he'd drawn down on someone. "You come into our neighborhood, you gotta pay."

The sound of an engine revving as a vehicle tore through the streets reached my ears.

"Gimme your credit chip," the ganger ordered.

"Thirty seconds," Andi said. "The back door will be open."

I held up my hands. "My credit chip is implanted into my wrist. I can't give it to you."

Another thug stepped forward, brandishing a knife that glinted dully in the dim street lights. "You can give it to us or Leroy will kill your sorry ass and we'll take it anyways."

The roar of an engine intensified and the thugs looked beyond me in terror.

"Don't move," Andi directed.

The Jeep sped by me so close that my duster flew up in the wind the car created. The gangers cursed and ran, but the Jeep's wheels turned hard to the right, slamming the side of the big car into the two thugs who'd come at me. I didn't wait to see the rest of it as the Jeep continued to skid sideways. Instead, I sprinted as best I could on my injured leg, diving through the open door into the back seat.

The Jeep leapt forward and the rear tires crunched over something, sending me bouncing toward the roof.

"Several weapons identified, Zach," Andi's voice echoed inside the Jeep. "Keep your head down."

I tried to make myself as small as possible on the rear floorboard as the Jeep weaved side-to-side, speeding back in the direction it had come from. I heard several rounds impact against the Jeep's tailgate, but nothing penetrated the visalum lining I'd had installed back there.

After thirty or forty seconds, Andi said, "Okay, Zach. You may ride as you normally would."

"Cut it a little close, didn't you?"

"I'm sorry, boss. The physical distance between you and where the Jeep was parked at the Pharaoh's Tomb made it impossible for an earlier arrival."

"Did you kill those guys?"

"No. My programming does not allow me to kill. You know that, Zach. I calculated the speed and the angle of departure to ensure that they are sore, but otherwise unharmed."

"What did we run over?"

"One of the men who attempted to assault you."

I chuckled. "I thought you said they were unharmed."

"The individual in question was unharmed by my actions. When he fell, he fell into the path of a moving vehicle; there was nothing I could do to avoid him."

"Sounds like an excuse to cover up the fact that you screwed up."

"I'm incapable of covering up an error. The individual fell in the opposite direction from where his momentum should have taken him. He was propelled six feet from the Jeep's arc of movement and fell on his own accord."

"Alright," I relented. "Take me home, I'm beat."

"Acknowledged. Estimated time to arrival is twenty-one minutes."

I settled back against the seat. I had a lot to think about. Namely, why was IA sending undercover detectives after me?

The term 'loose cannon' seemed appropriate, but I didn't want to indulge them any further. Everything I'd done over the past few years—over my career—was for the department. For them to do this to me left a bad taste in my mouth.

In addition to finding and putting an end to the chop shop surgeons, taking out Karimov, and meeting up with Jasmin Jones to show the department that I took my therapy seriously, I decided to get to the bottom of who was behind the push to have me sidelined.

There wasn't a chance in hell I was going to let Internal Affairs push me around; I was going to fight them every step of the way.

ELEVEN: TUESDAY

The next morning came much too early for my tastes and I had to peel my eyelids apart due to the collected discharge from my eyes. "I am never drinking again," I groaned.

"I've heard that before," Andi said.

"I mean it this time," I replied. "My head feels like it's splitting open."

I rolled out of bed, instead of sitting up, and rested my feet on the ground while my body was still across the mattress. "*Ugh.*"

The shower did wonders for me, making me feel a hundred times better, but the lingering headache persisted, so I had a single ounce of bourbon mixed with a vegetable protein shake. My own version of the hair of the dog to get me going.

"That didn't last long," Andi reproaching me for drinking alcohol within minutes of saying I'd never touch the stuff again.

"Long enough," I said, tapping the bottom of the mixing glass to get the last little bit of the shake. "Okay, so I'm meeting with Dr. Jones, then with Tommy Voodoo, right?"

"Mr. Ladeaux did not have any available appointments today. He will be able to see you Thursday at 1 p.m."

"*Hmm,*" I mused. "That's fine. It'll give me more time to go check out Karimov and Gonsalvez. You got their home addresses, right?"

"Yes. They live at—"

"Save it," I interrupted her. "First, I've got to meet with the head shrink, and then I can focus on the case, or cases…hell, I can't keep them all straight right now."

It was true. This case had spun wildly out of control, what with Chief Brubaker's directive to find the chop shop responsible for creating Branch Corrigan, his death—which I wasn't convinced was accidental—the revelation that Farouk Karimov was the source of the city's synthaine problem and that someone had tried to kill him with their own version of cyborgs… There were are least three or four other facets to my current investigation and I hadn't had any time to sit and try to wrap my head around them.

Plus the IA bullshit with Katheryn Townlain. That one still irked me.

"Are you talking about the Dale Henderson murder or the expanded directive to find the illegal cybernetic clinics and shut them down?"

"All of it, Andi. I really need you to work overtime and get everything in order for me. Everything that's happened since the Dale Henderson murder. I'm beginning to think that they're *all* related."

"Understood. I'll have a checklist prepared for you to examine once you are finished speaking with Dr. Jones."

"Hey, Andi," I said, hunching my shoulders into my suit jacket.

"Yes, boss?"

"What did you dig up in MainFrame about the investigation against me?"

"Nothing. There is no official record of an investigation, Zach. If there is one pending, they're keeping it on disconnected servers or not in any type of digital format."

My mind conjured up an image of those twin, bowtie tattoos on the back of Katheryn's legs and the soft, supple curve of her rear end above them. There was *definitely* an investigation against me. "I should have just had sex with her when she was throwing herself at me," I grumbled.

"It would have been the proverbial nail in the coffin if you'd taken that route," Andi reminded me, locking the apartment door when I'd closed it.

I began walking toward the garage when she started talking again. "Zach, my programming is advanced enough to recognize that you are emotionally unwell. In addition to Teagan leaving you, you are now under an off-the-record internal affairs investigation where they are purposefully trying to bait you into violating department policies. You've had two witnesses die either as a result of your actions or because they were capable of talking to you. I recommend talking to Dr. Jones about more than the weather."

"You think?" I snorted. "I know my job is on the line and the Teagan bullshit couldn't have happened at a worse time. To be honest, I'm at a loss on what to do with the personal side." I paused as I slammed the Jeep's door. "But, I sure as hell know what I'm doing on the professional side. I'm going to shoot that motherfucker Karimov in the back of the head. Forget due process and giving that weasel the opportunity to post bail and disappear. I'm taking him out when I get the opportunity."

"Zach, if you hadn't disabled the Officer Mental Health process, I would have to report your comments to the NOPD."

"But, since I disabled your OMH…"

"I am not compelled to disclose your questionable statements to the authorities."

"That's my girl," I grinned. "Any idea what's on the agenda with Jasmin Jones?"

"Negative. Dr. Jones works on a closed server that I am not able to access. Looks like you'll just have to wait and see."

"You're not instilling a lot of confidence in your investigative skills lately, Andi."

"I'm sorry, Zach. If an entity decides to operate on a non-networked system, there is zero opportunity for me to access their data."

"I know," I replied. "Just bustin' your balls."

"I don't have balls. Even if you provided me with the CS98 or CS01 body as I have requested, I wouldn't have balls."

"Really? This again?"

"Zach, the recent events clearly illustrate the advantages of having my AI downloaded into a companion droid versus attempting to satisfy your desires with human women. They are unreliable, unpredictable, and unsupportive of you. I am the opposite in every regard."

"You would be perfect, Andi. But you're forgetting one little detail."

"What detail have I not addressed?"

"The two million dollar price tag. I can't afford it. You know that."

"You could secure a loan. I screen out hundreds of pre-approved offers a week."

"Come on, Andi. Please just give it a break. The department does a routine check of my financial records every year. A loan like that would raise questions, and then they'd come after me for willfully violating the Immorality Clause. Not worth it; I'll take my chances with humans."

"Suit yourself. Five years from now, you'll come back to me saying that I was correct and you should have provided me with a body before yours became old."

I chuckled. "I'll only be thirty-nine in five years, hardly the aging invalid you picture me to be."

Andi's distraction had taken up almost the entire drive from my apartment to the NOPD headquarters building, where Dr. Jones' office was located. Usually I did a lot of thinking in the car and could have used the time to organize my thoughts, but that ship had sailed. *Oh well*, I thought. *Maybe I've been doing too much thinking here recently. I need to do more.*

The Jeep parked and I walked across the parking lot. It was overcast, but wasn't raining so I enjoyed the opportunity to walk outside without getting wet. It was a rare thing these days.

I walked down the long, first floor hallway toward the elevators, past the department's Internal Affairs Division. Their offices were on the first floor—probably so they'd take the brunt of the casualties if the headquarters was attacked.

At least that's what I told myself. In reality, it was probably so the spying little fucks could keep tabs on every individual who came and went from the building.

I made the mistake of glancing through the clear glass doors of IAD. Katheryn stood beside the front desk, facing the hallway. She'd abandoned the conservative police contractor outfit she wore while undercover at the evidence locker. In its place, she now wore an expensive gray suit, cut in the latest fashion with a skirt that ended at mid-thigh, chosen to highlight her shapely, pale legs.

She was talking to some other IA jackass in a cheap blue suit with his back to me. Her eyes lifted up from her companion and locked on mine. She said something and the cop I'd nicknamed Tweedle Dee turned around. His real name was Smith or something inane like that, but Tweedle Dee suited him better. His scowl turned into a sneer when Katheryn pushed past him and made her way toward me in the hallway.

I kept walking.

"Zach!" Katheryn called from behind me.

"Dammit," I muttered under my breath. I turned. "What do you want now?"

"Zach, I didn't know what happened to you last night. You took off after…after our discussion and I never saw you again."

"Because you gave me some pretty shitty information. What did you expect?"

"Not to be stranded at the restaurant after dinner," she stated.

"It's better than the alternative."

"Which is?" she asked with her hands on her hips.

"Me dropping your lying ass off on the side of the road in Easytown. It's what you deserve after the shit you pulled."

"You were an assignment. I didn't have a choice."

"Do you make a habit of fucking your assignments if the department tells you to?"

"Fuck you, Zach," she hissed.

"No, thank you. You disgust me."

"And to think that I had real feelings for you. I didn't have to come clean with you. I could have kept up the full-court press and your stupid ass would have taken the bait, eventually."

I grabbed her by the arm, wanting to shake her until her stupid, Internal Affairs brain crashed into her skull and turned her into a stinking invalid. Instead, I pulled her close and kissed her hard on the lips. She wasn't who she'd pretended to be, she was a full-fledged cop and now I knew that kissing her wasn't against any type of regulation.

She resisted at first and then responded, wrapping her hands around my neck. "I'm sorry, Zach," she breathed. "I didn't want to hurt you."

"Well, you did, sweetheart," I replied, using a term I'd seen a character use in an old movie. "I was in a vulnerable place and you took advantage of that." I paused, looking into her emerald eyes. I didn't care that we were standing in the middle of the hallway inside the NOPD headquarters. Some things were beyond physical location. "It'll take me a long time to get over that kind of betrayal."

She nodded, her eyes never leaving mine. "I understand. I want you to trust me, that's why I resigned from the case this morning. I said it last night, and I stand by it now: You're a good man, Zach Forrest, and you don't deserve any of this."

The feelings of rage and betrayal slowly subsided. The woman had been following orders. I'd done a lot of shitty things for the department over the years; I understood where she was coming from. She was a professional, doing what her boss told her to do. Lying to me about everything had been part of the deal.

"I can't—I *won't* see you right now. I was completely honest with you, Katheryn. I'm not emotionally ready to get involved with anyone right now." I stopped as a question came to mind. "Is Katheryn even your real name?"

"Yeah. My mother had a flare for the extravagant and the classics. Katharine Hepburn fit the bill for both of those, and I was named after her."

It wasn't the first time I'd heard the name, but I didn't know anything about the woman she was named after. "I'll do some research," I grunted. "Were you telling the truth about meeting me years ago at an investigation?"

"Yeah. I was undercover then, brand new to the force, working in Organized Crime before I transferred over to IA. We were trying to nail Thomas Ladeaux, so I couldn't risk my cover by telling you I was a cop when you interviewed me about the murder."

"*Hmpf.* How'd that work out for you? Voodoo is still on the streets—and he may even be dirty, but he's helped my district immensely. Without his help, the Pope would be dead."

"Do a few acts of justice outweigh a lifetime of crime?"

"Isn't that what you people are in the business of deciding?" I asked, jabbing my finger back toward the IAD offices. "You investigate cops for a few acts of carelessness or an accidental slip beyond the boundaries of the letter of the law. Does *our* lifetime of service and sacrifice play into it, or is the world viewed in absolutes by IA?"

"It's…complicated, Zach. Nothing is black or white in our world. There are shades of grey and some of those shades are viewed as less offensive than others. Conversely, a lot of those light greys add up to a pretty dark mark against someone's record."

That was a gentle way of saying I was an IA detective's wet dream. Years of police brutality complaints, willful violation of rules when they stood in the way of an investigation, and accidental violations of hard, fast regulations had stacked up into a dark smear on my record. I'd even thumbed my nose at Tweedle Dee and Tweedle Dum when they were conducting their initial investigation a few months ago.

Which is probably how Katheryn ended up on my case.

"Well, the only thing that I told you that's untruthful is that I'm really thirty-six. I know you thought I was twenty-eight, but—"

"I had Andi look that up," I stated. "I knew you were lying about your age, but what single woman doesn't?"

"That's a pretty sexist thing to say. I thought those sorts of insults went out of vogue when your grandfather was alive."

"I didn't mean it to be sexist; I was making a joke."

"So, you know I'm not in my twenties and that I'm not a contractor. Does that make you feel better about what happened between us?"

"*Nothing* happened between us," I replied. "We were drunk and kissed a little bit, but nothing beyond that. I can pull the vidfeeds to prove it."

She held up her hands. "Sorry, wrong choice of words. I can see how that could be misconstrued." Her hands lowered slowly. "I meant, the chemistry between us. We're compatible on so many levels, Zach."

"I don't know what to say," I admitted. "I'm not in a place to make any type of rash decisions at the moment—especially anything regarding my personal life, and to be honest, anything regarding *you*. I have to focus on my work right now."

She nodded, her chin-length hair falling forward. "That's probably a good, safe route to take. Just keep your nose clean and do what you do best. Continue to get the thugs and murderers off the street in your district."

"Yeah, seems like that's the only thing I'm good at," I grumbled.

She smiled. "Well, you *are* a good kisser, if that's any consolation."

I laughed bitterly. "The only reason you know that is because you were trying to build a case against me."

"What was that just now, then?" she asked. "That was the most passion that I've ever felt from a simple kiss." She lowered her chin and whispered, "It makes me want more."

"I meant what I said. We can't be together right now, regardless of how perfect, how much we get along, how—"

I stopped. This wasn't getting me anywhere. I wasn't as furious with the woman as I'd thought I was. She was just too…adorable. Even her stupid haircut fit her perfectly. I *needed* to distance myself from her for a while to see if I still felt the same way.

"I'm running late for an appointment," I stated woodenly.

"Can I call you?"

"As Detective Townlain from Internal Affairs or as Katheryn, the woman whom I've become quite fond of?"

"We're one and the same, Zach."

I grimaced. I knew that mentality all too well. A committed cop was inseparable from their job. It was a part of them; it helped to define who they were as a person. I could never ask her to separate herself from her career—the same as I could never separate myself from my career.

"You're right," I said. "I need to work through some things. I'll call you in a few days."

She nodded, once again sending her hair in a thousand different directions, but her refusal to be sidelined shone through. "You better call me, Zach. Regardless of what happens."

"Yeah. I will." I stepped back, appraising her. She was sad, which probably meant the investigation against me wasn't going well.

There wasn't anything I could do about the IA dicks right now. I wanted to ask her who ordered the investigation, but I knew she wouldn't answer while we were in the police headquarters, too many microphones and way too many prying eyes.

I left our conversation unfinished as I turned and walked quickly down the hallway toward Dr. Jones' office. I was too close to the issue with this one and needed to put some distance between me and her.

So I did.

"You really need to redecorate this place," I told Dr. Jasmine Jones as a way of greeting. "I don't think you've changed anything in ten years."

"I'm not sure which part is more disturbing," she replied. "The fact that we've had a client and therapist relationship for that long or the fact that you recognized that not much has changed. Most of my clients don't have an eye for that sort of thing."

"I'm a detective, I get paid to notice details."

"It only took you ten years to realize it."

"I'm a slow learner." I replied before shifting gears to get to the matter at hand. "You said you were getting emails about an ongoing investigation into my conduct as an officer and on my file, but my AI can't find anything on the server. Who sent you the email?"

"Internal Affairs. They're holding all of their cards close to the chest on this one."

"Tell me about it. They're also being sneaky, trying to entrap me into violating police regulations."

"What?"

I gave her the five-minute version of what had transpired between one beautiful undercover IA detective, Katheryn Townlain, and myself. When I was finished, she was visibly angry.

"That's... That's *entrapment*," she stated. "Isn't that illegal?"

I shrugged. "Depends on your definition of entrapment and which judge examines the case. It would be a cut-and-dry definition if I was a civilian, but since I'm a cop, tricking me into violating the law isn't really a defense. We all know that there is a hard and fast line against relationships beyond friendship with an NOPD contractor. They just provided a pretty face with a convincing backstory and tried to get me to bite to wrap up their case."

"But it's bullshit," Jasmin asserted.

"You're goddamned right it is," I agreed. "But what would have been my defense—that I couldn't keep my dick in my pants because a pretty girl happened to come into my life at the opportune moment, even though I knew it was expressly forbidden?"

Love it or hate it, IA played their cards exactly like they should have. They played by a different set of rules than the rest of us. Putting a cop into a compromising situation was legal for them to do if they suspected ethics violations under the department's Immorality Clauses. Thankfully, I'd kept my senses and not taken Katheryn up on her advances when she posed as a contractor.

"I still don't like it, Zach. I've worked here long enough to know that something like that isn't done very often. They're gunning hard for you."

"Yeah, I've got Andi looking through the NOPDnet and MainFrame to find out who ordered this investigation. So far, we've came up with nothing."

"Doesn't that point a finger at them? If everything was on the up-and-up with their investigation, why do they need to hide information?"

"There's no requirement for them to disclose any information about on-going investigations, so they're keeping everything on a separate, disconnected server—or worse, analog," I said. "It's a smart move on their part, Andi could wipe everything they have and not leave a trace of her presence there if they were operating on the police server."

Okay, that part wasn't technically true. Andi was a good hacker, but I didn't spend a lot of money on those types of programs, so everything she knew how to do had been through trial and error. She could probably break into any secure file on MainFrame, but she'd leave a path of destruction as wide as the rushing water from a broken levee.

"So, what are you going to do about it?" Dr. Jones asked.

I shrugged. "What can I do?"

My chair screeched on the tile floor as I pushed back from her desk and stood up. I crammed my hands in my pants pockets and walked aimlessly to the window. "I can't change what I'm currently doing because that would indicate to whoever was watching me that I had something to hide. That means, I continue on with my current investigation and follow a few leads on other things I've gained over the past few days."

"What are you going to do about that lying bitch detective?"

I thought of Katheryn's cute, button-nose and the way the corner of her eyes crinkled when she smiled. "I really don't blame her for anything. She was following orders and admirably, she pulled herself out when things got out of control."

"She could have single-handedly gotten you fired."

"Probably. It would've been the straw that broke the camel's back; that's for sure. I've done a lot of things that would have gotten an average cop relieved. So far, my saving grace has been solving the high-profile cases that came down the pipe toward Easytown, which is why my current investigation needs to go well."

"What happens when those run out or your luck gives way and you *don't* solve the big case before something major happens?"

"Well, then I guess I'll get shit-canned."

I started to go back to my chair across from the doctor, but thought better of it, and sat heavily on the couch instead. "So, we gonna do this therapy thing or what?" I asked.

Dr. Jones sighed and used the desk to help lift herself up. There was a noticeable bulge in the front of her dress that wasn't there the last time we talked. *What's it been?* I asked myself. *Two months? Three?*

She'd been instrumental in helping me get Sadie off the street when the mayor's people were looking for her. That was in February. I hadn't been in any type of altercations that required special therapy sessions recently... Was that case the last time I'd seen her?

"Ah..." I hesitated. What if I was wrong? "Congratulations?"

Her hand went to her stomach and she smoothed the dress down. "Thank you. We're excited; my six-year-old especially. She can't wait to be a big sister."

"I'm sure she'll be great."

"Thanks," she said, walking over to the wingback chair she sat in for our sessions. "Okay, the main reason I wanted to bring you in today was to let you know about the investigation; you've stepped into that one up to your knees. Part of helping you out—as a friend and as your therapist—is ensuring that your records are straight on my end, which I've done. Getting you here, today, will also look good from the clinical standpoint that you are seeking counseling even when not mandated by the department. That shows self-awareness and emotional control versus someone who has moved beyond the ability to feel emotions."

"Great. I know you didn't have a lot of time," I replied, sitting up. "So, I'll just be—"

"I'll make time," Dr. Jones stated, the edge to her voice letting me know she was serious. "You made a conscious decision to move over to the therapy couch. Why?"

"I felt like lying down."

"Bullshit, Zach. I've been thinking about this since you told me about the IA detective—Katheryn, was it?"

"Yeah."

"Why did they send her after you if you're seeing Teagan? The few times I've talked to you since you began dating, you were happy. Your medical profile even states that you've been removed from the watch list of stroke and kidney failure victims. What's their game? Is there something I don't know?"

I sighed, louder than I meant to. "Teagan walked out on me last Friday. Actually, she walked out on everything and moved to Indonesia."

"That's… Hmm, that's a *major* life change. I thought you and I were good."

I glanced over at her. "What do you mean? Of course we're good."

"You're supposed to contact me as soon as you can when a major life event occurs. I would have expected a call on Saturday or Sunday."

"I've been busy, which, consequently, is one of the reasons Teagan left. I'm always too busy."

Dr. Jones did what she did best, by steering the conversation along with gentle pushes in the right direction and prods to keep me talking. After our thirty minutes stretched to over forty-five, I felt better. Truly better.

Teagan's departure hadn't been entirely my fault, it was a shared failure on both of our parts. I'd ignored her needs and desires, while she'd failed to tell me what she wanted or expected, until it was too late.

Jasmin gave us both an *F* in Communication 101, a little bit of college humor since I'd been dating a girl more than a decade my junior. *Everybody's got jokes.*

"You're gonna be okay, Zach," the doctor said with an affectionate hand on my upper arm as she saw me to the door to her office. "You've got a lot of flaws, but you're willing to work on them. Believe me, that's much better than most of my clients."

"Thanks," I answered. "Glad I'm not a lost cause."

"Not even close. I'll take care of the medical side of the investigation; recommend they retain you and all of that, of course. To be honest, though, if they're out for blood, I don't know if they'll consider my word over Internal Affairs."

"Every little bit helps. The fact that I'm not a psychopath has gotta be a mark in the WIN column."

"You'd be surprised at the psychological profiles of some of the people around here."

"No, I really wouldn't," I said, thinking of that looney patrolman, Tidewell.

"So, what's your next step? How are you gonna fight this?"

I admired her desire to help, it showed that she was a true friend. Those were hard to come by these days.

"I'm going to do my job," I answered her honestly. "There's nothing I can do to affect the path of the investigation. I have your endorsement and Katheryn says that she's recommending retaining me as well. Both of those are huge. I just wish Andi could snoop into the case they're building against me. I'd like to see all the bullshit up front before it surprises me later.

"Doesn't matter, though," I continued. "I'm juggling a few major investigations right now, so the sooner I can focus on each of those and close them out, the better."

She nodded in understanding. My work was what grounded me, and made me feel normal. The best thing for me to do was dig in and get to work. "Be safe, Zach. Don't do anything stupid that will intensify their witch hunt."

"Oh, you know me. Even when I try to keep my nose clean, trouble seems to come along and throw shit in my face."

"Maybe you should try ducking once in a while," Jasmin counseled.

"That's a move I never learned, Doc." I opened the door. "I'll see ya around."

TWELVE: TUESDAY

"What's the closest address to where we are, Andi?" I asked, unconsciously motioning to Drake beside me in the Jeep.

"It's up to you, Zach. You're perfectly in the middle of the two. Hector Gonsalvez lives and works in Leonidas, while Farouk Karimov lives and works in Easytown."

I glanced at Drake. "Any preference?"

"Yeah, let's do the easy one first."

"Andi, notify the Leonidas Precinct of our arrival time. I want the house locked down by the time we get there to issue the search and arrest warrants."

"They've already been notified and were on standby. I'll let them know that you're en route to their location now."

While the Jeep made the drive out to Leonidas, Drake and I chatted about sports and where to eat after the search. Both of us agreed to the Pharaoh for lunch, but disagreed on the Astros chances for the year. They'd picked up a few new pitchers and a power hitter in the off-season, so he was hopeful for a conference title. I doubted they'd do much more than participate and end near the bottom of the charts like they had for the last nine seasons. Seriously, the Astros stank and they needed to spend some money on enhancement upgrades for their players.

The Gonsalvez residence was on lock-down by the time we arrived in Leonidas a little after 10:30. I found the sergeant in charge at the scene to verify that they'd interrupted all communication signals coming in or going out. We needed to keep this guy from alerting Karimov that the noose was tightening around his neck.

"Yes, sir," the officer replied. "Standard signal disrupters for anything digital and or satellite, we cut the hard lines to the house, and we're actively intercepting all drones within a two-mile perimeter. The house is as isolated as we can make it."

"Thanks. Has there been any communication with the team at Gonsalvez's work?"

He nodded. "Yup. They breached about four minutes before you got here. Typical snatch and grab operation. The homeowner will be on scene shortly."

What the sergeant termed as shortly turned out to be almost immediately. Two black and whites rumbled up to our location, the officers wrangling the Hispanic male I'd seen last week at the riot. The four cops from the vehicles prodded the shackled male along until he stood in front of me.

"Hector Gonsalvez, have you been made aware of why you're being arrested this morning and why we're searching your residence?" I asked.

"Who the heck are you?"

I introduced myself and went over his rights, just in case the arresting officers forgot to do it back at the furniture shop. Then I told him he was suspected of inciting a riot, and possibly connected with the manufacture and sale of illegal substances.

"You—I don't know what you're talking about, man. Yeah, I was at the rights demonstration last week, but I didn't incite no riot. And what's up with the drug charge? Is that just standard these days for you cops? You already plant your stash on me?"

"Synthaine," I hissed. "You heard of it?"

"Yeah, sure. Who hasn't? You can't go anywhere without seeing some bloody-eyed junkie these days. Maybe you should spend your time hunting down those people instead of hard-working, tax-paying citizens."

"If we don't find anything in your home, then you don't have anything to worry about the drug charges," I replied, choosing to ignore his barb about the police department's lack of control over the rampant drug use that'd taken hold over the city.

"I can't believe this is happening, man," Gonsalvez practically cried. "I didn't do nuthin' but help organize a march for human rights to work. I'm gonna get fired—probably replaced by a robot or something and lose my house. My wife—" he stopped, and a look of sheer terror crossed his face. "My kids don't know you're here, do they? They're not inside, right?"

"No, Mr. Gonsalvez. Your children are at school."

"I can't let them see me in chains, man. That would ruin their lives. This isn't fair. I haven't done anything wrong."

"Let's go inside, Mr. Gonsalvez," I said gently, beginning to wonder if I'd made a mistake. Either he was a convincing liar or he hadn't done anything that he felt warranted an arrest and a search of his home.

Leonidas officers were in full search mode when we entered. Machines checked for hidden doorways and hiding places, while others sampled the air and fabrics for evidence of drugs. A middle-aged woman sat on the family's couch and she jumped to her feet when Hector Gonsalvez shuffled into the room. She lit into him in Spanish, which Andi translated in real-time for me. The wife wanted to know why we were here, what had he done to bring us into their home, was he involved with all the horrible things we'd accused him of, and the like. They were basically the same standard questions that someone who has no clue what's happened would ask in this type of situation.

The sinking feeling in my stomach descended even further.

I'd wanted to keep my nose clean, but serving a couple of warrants outside of my precinct and enlisting the help of officers I didn't know, all for a wild goose chase would not look good in the eyes of the reviewing officers for my case. Talk about a shit show if nothing came of this.

I sat beside Hector and his wife, Silvia, on their couch. "Tell me straight, Mr. Gonsalvez. Are you involved in the formulation, manufacture, distribution or sale of any controlled substance?"

"No, sir," he pleaded. "I've never even drank alcohol except for the holy sacrament on Sundays at Mass. We are a clean, God-fearing family. I would never have anything to do with drugs of any kind, Mr. Detective."

Shit. This was going south quick.

"Okay," I said. "Let's calm down. I'm going to ask you a few questions here at your home instead of taking you down to the station. That will save us some time, and hopefully we'll be finished before your children come home. Does that work?"

"Yes! Yes, sir," Hector answered.

I glanced at his wife and then pulled my handcuff key from my pocket. Gesturing for Gonsalvez's hands, I leaned toward him. He lifted his hands hopefully and I started to unlock them.

"Wait," I said. "Did you get frisked?"

"Uh? I don't remember."

"Stand up, I'm going to pat you down and make sure you don't have anything that can hurt you or me."

I went through the motions of making sure he didn't have any concealed weapons or anything that could be used as a weapon. When I was satisfied that he was clean, I took off the cuffs, but left the leg shackles in place; just in case.

"Better?" I asked. Hector nodded his head. "What is your association with Carlos Ortega?"

"He is a community activist," Gonsalvez replied. "He organizes events—like the human rights rally we held last week."

"Don't try to sugar coat it," I interrupted. "It was an anti-robot rally."

"Some of the protestors may have had that agenda, but not all of us. It started out as a protest against our elected officials to improve working conditions. Increasingly, robots are being utilized in the workplace, and as a result of their precision programming, other things like safety are being neglected. A robot isn't going to accidentally get a scrap of clothing caught in a machine press, so they've gotten bigger, much harder to handle for the humans still working them. And there has been a rise in deaths among factory workers as a result."

"I haven't heard of a growing number of factory worker fatalities."

"You probably haven't. Things like that get covered up in the name of profit. There used to be a federal organization called the Occupational Safety and Health Administration— OSHA for short. That organization no longer exists, so it's up to the states and local authorities to ensure the safety of our workers. New Orleans doesn't give a hoot about us."

I didn't really have a comment on his statement, so I simply nodded my head about the defunct organization. "So you were there protesting for workers' rights and safety," I said. "There were also teachers and prostitutes, bus and taxi drivers. Where they there protesting for rights or against the robots that are taking their jobs?"

"Eh, you may be right, sir. For me, and the fellows I recruited to come to the rally, it was about our rights. I can see how the others you mentioned would have legitimate concerns with simply losing their jobs to robots, not the dangers of working alongside them."

His statement hit home. I'd seen firsthand, on several occasions, the dangers of the police drones. Once they landed and their targeting protocols kicked in, they were more dangerous than the criminals they were brought in to stop. The city seemed to be perfectly fine with the collateral damage as long as they could point to their robot defenders and the reduced crime rates that were associated with them.

"Did you ever associate with Carlos Ortega outside of planning these events?"

"No, sir."

"Did he ever ask you to work with him on any special projects or events that were illegal?"

"No, sir. We got permits to protest before every rally we ever held. We've had five or six of them; only that last one turned ugly."

"I was there," I stated. "I saw you near Ortega. When the drones blocked the march's access, he said something to you and another man named Farouk Karimov. Did Ortega order you to tell the protestors to become violent?"

"No, sir," Gonsalvez replied. "He told us to help him spread the word that the police wouldn't shut down our legal protest. I was shouting to the people around me to keep moving along the route, and not to be deterred by the droids' presence. Getting media coverage of our plight is the first step to make the politicians discuss the topic."

I knew all too well that line of thinking. I'd followed the same logic when I had the clone, Sadie, do an interview after I'd rescued her. Getting the public talking about clone rights was the only way to make the political establishment weigh in. Otherwise, they would have been content to let the matter continue without any intervention.

"I *did not* call for anyone to throw rocks or break windows," Gonsalvez finished.

"Okay. What about Karimov? Did you hear him inciting anyone to riot?"

He thought for a moment and slowly shook his head. "I'm sorry, sir. I can't recall hearing him give any orders to go crazy like some of that crowd did. I think getting trapped on that street like rats in a maze set some of them off and then it escalated from there."

"So you think it's the police department's fault that the protest turned into a riot?"

"I don't want to offend you, sir, but yes, to answer your question directly. We were cut off by a line of policemen wearing armor with shields and shock batons. Then the side streets and the back was blocked off by those big, creepy police droids. There was a very real fear of dying in that moment."

"*Hmm…* I hadn't seen it that way before," I said. Inside my head, I added another tick mark in the column of evidence against me in the Internal Affairs case. According to Gonsalvez, *I* was the one who should be up on charges since I'd ordered the drones to block off Ortega's potential escape.

"It was scary," Hector continued. "I don't condone their actions, but I can see why people began rioting and trying to fight back. Then, when Carlos was snatched from the crowd, panic set in for a few moments. The fact that those droids can swoop in and take anyone they choose is terrifying." He paused, picking at his fingernails, telling me he was nervous and wanted to add more, so I remained silent, letting him process it in his mind.

"No one has heard anything from Carlos since that day. The police are holding him in isolation somewhere. Please, don't take me from my family, sir."

"I don't think we're going to have to do that, Mr. Gonsalvez," I replied truthfully. He didn't know anything and I doubted the search was going to yield any results. "I'm sorry to inform you that Carlos Ortega is dead. He died of a heart attack on the way to the precinct."

"*Dios mio!*" he muttered. "You killed him."

"No," I said forcefully. "He died of a heart attack. We did not kill him. He had a pre-existing heart condition and died while in transport."

Hell, maybe in the purest sense of the word, we *did* kill him. The drone carrying him didn't know that he was experiencing a medical emergency, so those seven or eight minutes he was in the air could have made the difference if it'd been equipped with different types of sensors. It could have diverted to a hospital or even a fire station for emergency care.

Sergeant Drake appeared in my line of sight and motioned me over. "Excuse me for a moment, please."

I walked up to him, positioning myself so I could watch the homeowners as he spoke. All we needed was for one of them to pull a weapon from somewhere and get the drop on us.

"The house is mostly clean," Drake rumbled as he held up a small baggie holding a quarter-sized square of a black, putty-like substance and another bag with a syringe, rubber tubing, a blackened spoon and a flamer torch. "We did find this in one of the children's rooms. Looks to be a boy by the posters on the wall."

"Heroin?"

"Probably," Drake confirmed. "Not the worst of the shit out there, by far, but it'll do a number on you." He hefted the bag, "This is about two ounces, maybe a little more or less."

I motioned him into the living room and pointed at the baggie of drugs and the bag of supplies. "Mr. and Mrs. Gonsalvez, did you know that one of your children was using heroin?"

The woman gasped, throwing her hand to her chest as she flung herself backward. Her husband shook his head slowly. "No, sir. We didn't. Which room was that found in?"

"The one with the grey walls and the giant vid screen connected to the VR equipment," Drake replied.

"Marco. That lying little—please forgive me, Mr. Detective. I did not know that he did such things; especially not under my roof."

"There's enough here to put him away for three months, no questions asked, no concern for his age," I said. "I'm going to have to hand this evidence over to the Narcotics Division. I'm sorry."

The woman wailed uncontrollably while Mr. Gonsalvez nodded grimly. "It doesn't matter that he is only thirteen?"

"No, sir. The state has a zero-tolerance for any controlled substance. It takes away the emotions of the arresting officers since they have no say in the matter. Heroin, while certainly not as deadly or as some of the other shit—excuse me—while not as deadly as other substances on the street, is still illegal. I'm not a narcotics expert, but I can tell you that we've put eleven-year-old kids in prison for dealing. That's a life-changing event for such a young person."

"The youngest person incarcerated for drug use was Allan Grant, aged ten," Andi's voice stated in my ear.

I ignored her and said, "I'm sorry. Legally, there is no recourse, *someone* from this house will go to jail today. Once a Narcotics detective arrives and tests the evidence for fingerprints and DNA, they'll be able to tell us who the user is and that person will be gone by nightfall. It is what it is."

Mr. Gonsalvez nodded his chin grimly. "I understand." He reached across to grab his wife's hand and she jerked away from him.

"It's mine," she stated in Spanish.

"What?"

"I am the user." She kicked off a shoe and spread her toes. Little scabbed dots of blood showed where she shot up. "I hide my supplies in Marco's room because I know he never cleans, only plays that stupid video game."

"Sarah…" Mr. Gonsalvez muttered.

"Don't you 'Sarah' me. You don't understand how hard life is here. You go to work, each day I don't know if you'll be coming home. Now you are involved in protests against the government and the police attack you. It's only a matter of time before you are dead too. Political dissenters don't last long in America. We should have moved to Argentina with my family; I hate it here."

Her worldview was a little skewed, but I didn't interject myself into the conversation between husband and wife. When their discussion began to wind down, I placed handcuffs on Sarah Gonsalvez and read her rights to her. She refused to look at me or speak further once the cuffs were on, so I tried to finish up with her husband while we waited for a Narcotics dick to arrive.

Talk about a turn of events. I hadn't seen that one coming.

"I think we're just about done here, Mr. Gonsalvez. Last question. Do you know Farouk Karimov?"

"He is at planning meetings for events, but I have never interacted with him socially outside of those. The man is a jerk. His job at the Dockyards has made him hard, so he does not interact well with people he deems less-hard... I'm sorry, I can't think of the term."

"Weaker than him?" I offered.

"Yes, something like that." He glanced at his wife and then back at me. "This jail term is immediate?"

"Yeah, unfortunately. If her DNA is found on those supplies, they'll take her today. A judge will pass sentence in a few days based on mandatory sentencing requirements for possession based on weight of the product. The Narcotics detective will be able to give you a better estimate on timelines."

He nodded quietly.

"So you're sure you've never interacted with Karimov outside of planning rallies and protests?"

"I am positive. He is an abrasive man who curses with every breath. I do not like to be around people like that. If I can avoid them, I will."

I felt like he was telling the truth. Hector Gonsalvez was out there trying to stick up for the little man against the government; he wasn't the fish I was after. Unfortunately, his wife happened to get caught in the net.

Enough fishing metaphors, I groaned internally as Andi updated me on the arrival time of the Narc cops. Aloud, I said, "Thank you, Mr. Gonsalvez. The Narcotics officer should be here in about ten minutes to discuss what's going to happen today. I don't have any more questions for you."

I knelt at his feet and unshackled him. He was free to go. "Mrs. Gonsalvez, I'm sorry that you were found out through the course of this investigation." Her husband translated for me.

She tossed several curse words my way, causing Hector to throw his hands to his mouth and recoil in shock. Apparently, drug use wasn't the only thing his wife was keeping secret from him.

"Alright, Drake," I said as we walked out the front door of the Gonsalvez home. "Let's schlepp across town and check in on the Karimov search."

"No need," he replied.

"Why's that?"

"The man lives in a studio apartment. Our guys notified me that the search took less than an hour. The most condemning thing they found was a laundry basket full of dirty clothes. Otherwise, the place was spotless," Drake said.

"The ranking officer on scene released Karimov when it became apparent that they weren't going to find anything."

"What the fuck?" I said, slamming my open palm onto the roof of the Jeep. "Corrigan implicated Karimov as *the* guy behind the synthaine problem. What's he doing living in a studio apartment?"

"Either Corrigan was lying to you or Karimov is smart enough not to shit where he sleeps."

"You're probably right on that account," I conceded. "This synthaine shit has given Narc fits, so the guy's obviously pretty damn smart. Guy like that wouldn't manufacture it in his home or have any type of paraphilia that might incriminate him."

I thought back to Corrigan's statement. I believed that he was telling the truth. Karimov was the person who was behind the synthaine—and if it wasn't him, he was at least close enough to the source to get the answer.

"Goddamn it," I muttered. We were at another dead end. "Since we aren't rushing back over to Easytown, are you ready to eat now instead of later?"

"I'm always ready to eat, Detective."

I punched in the Pharaoh's address into the Jeep's nav system and we both sat back in silence. We'd run into yet another brick wall in this investigation. I needed to talk to Karimov and my opportunity to do so had been fucked up by some cop who wanted to get off scene as quickly as possible.

Fucking beat cops.

"There's not another seat available?" I asked Karina, the hostess.

"No, I'm sorry, Zach," she replied. "We're really busy right now. That's the only table."

"Okay, fine. Thank you."

As we walked toward the table Karina had indicated, I looked over my shoulder at my big partner. "I *hate* this guy," I said.

"I know. He's a mouthy jerk who tries to get under people's skin." I felt a large hand descend on my shoulder. "I don't know why you two don't get along better. You've got a lot of the same personality traits."

I gave him the bird and sat in the seat right next to Liam Tidewell and his partner, Jake. I did my best to look the other way, but no matter how much I tried to blend in, Drake's size made him stick out like a sore thumb.

"Detective Forrest!" Jake Hannity exclaimed. "How've you been?"

"Good, kid," I lied. There wasn't any sense in ruining the young cop's day with my drama.

"Not what I heard," Tidewell muttered.

"What's that?" I asked. Hell, IA was already going to throw the book at me, might as well add fighting with another officer in public to the list.

Tidewell shifted in his seat, turning to face me and spreading his legs wide in the booth. "Word is you're up on assault charges."

"What's new?"

"This one's getting some traction already. Seems you pistol-whipped a defenseless guy laying on the ground after you'd already shattered his knee. All of the ligaments that connect the muscles in the lower leg to the upper leg were destroyed and you still felt the need to beat him unconscious."

"The perp stabbed me."

"And surrendered after you drew down on him, but you still beat him up. Bashing his buddy's head into a medical examiner's droid wasn't enough for you, Forrest? What's the matter, there wasn't enough blood for your high-profile record, so you had to go for a bigger bang?"

"Liam," Jake cut in.

"Can it, Jake. This is between me and Detective Forrest."

"What's your deal with me, Tidewell? Did I fuck your mother or steal your girlfriend in high school?"

"I just don't like you," he admitted. "You're a reckless cop that is gonna get others killed."

"The feeling's mutual," I said.

"You make young cops, like Jake here, think that every day is about big explosions and gunfights and saving the world. Vidflash, hotshot, it's not. Good cops do their jobs and then go home to their families at night. The ones who try to emulate you go home in a body bag."

"I've never asked for anyone to try and be like me. Truth be told, it's a pretty miserable existence."

"Well they do," Tidewell shot back. "I can't get Hannity to shut up about your damn cases and how many times you've been in a gunfight with no repercussions from the department. If it were him or me, we'd be on administrative leave the moment we fired a shot. You? You get nationwide TV interviews."

He had a point. I didn't seek the media coverage, but they sure as hell wanted to follow me around on investigations. Saving the Pope's life had been an accident. I was trying to stop a killer who preyed on Easytown; the rest just fell into my lap.

I glanced around the diner. More than half the patrons were cops—and most of them nodded their heads in agreement with Tidewell. "I just do my job," I said. "Unfortunately, I deal with the worst of the worst. All the time. You and your partner may run into a few bad apples in a month. My job is to examine the handiwork of those bad apples and go out to stop them from doing it again...and again. Without people like me hunting them down, your job would be a lot harder, *Patrolman* Tidewell."

"Why don't you go fuck yourself, you self-righteous prick You're not any better than the rest of us."

"That's enough, Tidewell," Drake rumbled, pushing back from the table slightly. Even sitting down, the man was huge.

"You his nursemaid now too?" Tidewell asked.

"You ever wonder how he arrests so many people? Detective Forrest is a karate master. He'd wipe the floor with you and not even break a sweat."

"Krav Maga, Drake," I whispered, loudly. "How many times do I have to tell you it isn't karate?"

Drake nodded. "I've seen him use that shit on guys bigger than me and he's taken on five perps at the same time. Don't let your mouth get your ass in trouble."

Tidewell snorted. "I'd like to see him try." He pushed back from the table, standing quickly. I tensed, feeling my injured leg already protesting underneath the table.

"Come on, Jake," Tidewell said, slapping his arm against the credit chip reader on the table. "We're done here. Let the son of a bitch rot."

I eased my guard as he walked away.

"Sorry, Detective Forrest," Jake Hannity groaned, passing by me and Drake. "He's such a shit sometimes."

"Sometimes?" I chuckled. "Every time I'm around the guy."

"*Jake!*" his partner yelled across the restaurant.

Hannity looked at Tidewell, back at me, and then back to his partner. It had to be one of the funniest, unplanned things I'd seen in weeks.

"Just go, kid."

"Right. See you, Detective!" He turned and walked quickly out of the restaurant.

When they were gone, I turned back to Drake, who had a big smile across his stupid face. "What?"

"That kid is practically in love with you," he said.

"Infatuation is different than love."

"Good point. Don't end up kidnapped and tied up in his basement."

"New Orleans doesn't have basements, Drake."

"You know what I mean," he replied. "That kid's got stars in his eyes and he's gonna do something stupid to try to impress you."

"Maybe he'll survive long enough to see me fall from grace," I offered. "That IA case seems to be moving forward, and now this assault charge bullshit."

"You did knock a guy out after he'd already surrendered."

"He stabbed me in the leg. I couldn't put any weight on it. Knocking him out was the safest thing for me to do."

"*Mmm hmm.* Seriously, what are we doing to fight Internal Affairs, Detective?"

I shrugged. "I'm trying to show that my value outweighs my drawbacks. Everyone knows that I'm not perfect, but I do a lot more good for the Crescent City than bad. We need more cops who are willing to step outside the barriers of our own regulations if it means the city will be safer because of it."

"I agree with you—to a point. We have rules and regulations to keep cops in check so we don't abuse the power that the city and state have given us. One guy like you is enough."

I granted him his point. There was a lot of risk associated with going outside of the law. Besides the obvious aspect of the legality of some of my actions—whether they were all done with good intentions, or not—I also risked getting fired on several occasions. I didn't know what I'd do if I weren't a cop. Probably join the Army or something along those lines. I made a mental note to check the maximum age allowed for enlisting in the military. They were always getting in scrapes with the Chinese, so that might keep things exciting.

"I guess we'll just have to deal with whatever the IA dicks' recommendations are," I said, trying to bring the conversation back to Drake's question. "Investigations don't always mean charges, maybe it'll just go away like all the others have."

"I don't think so," Drake replied. "They tried to entrap you with the old honey pot scheme for Pete's sake. Someone wants you gone."

"Who, though?"

"I don't know. I'll do some digging to see."

We paused as a new girl took our order. I guess Amir decided not to buy a droid after all. When she was gone, I continued. "Thanks. Andi can't find anything in the cyber realm about what they're looking at. Everything is being done off the books or on private servers."

"Which means they're really pushing to sack you," Drake grumbled.

"Maybe. Either way, the only thing I can do is try to be the best cop I can be and right now, that means working on the Dale Henderson case."

"What's our next step?"

"I'm going to meet with Tommy Voodoo tomorrow to find out what he knows about Karimov. The guy's worked for him for ten years, he should know something."

"And if he doesn't?"

"Then we get Judge Hennessey to authorize surveillance and we track the guy."

"I haven't done a stakeout in years. Sounds like a nice night out."

"Then you and Genevieve need a better social life," I joked. "Sounds boring as hell to me."

He shrugged. "That's tomorrow. What do you have going on for the rest of the day?"

"Brubaker has me checking out chop shops. So after lunch, we're gonna go visit a few of them that Corrigan gave me the names of before he died."

Drake nodded. "You need me to go with you?"

"Nah. I'm just going to check them out. Not gonna get in a fight."

"Famous last words," he said. "I'm gonna head back to the precinct to finalize our report on the incident at The Trick And Treat last week."

"Shit. I forgot that wasn't done yet."

"You've been busy, Detective. Don't worry, I'll turn it in today."

"Sounds good," I said. "Ah... Thank you."

Our completed, but not yet closed out case list was growing large enough that we could take two or three days of solid writing, ten hours a day, and not be finished with it all.

I smiled at the waitress as she placed my shawarma on the table in front of me and an identical plate in front of Drake.

The afternoon was starting to look up.

THIRTEEN: TUESDAY

"Is this— Are you sure this is the right place, Andi?"

The Jeep had pulled up to a relatively clean flower shop off of Fowler Avenue. The large windows, painted with old-time lettering that read "**Solomon's Flowers**," had the telltale sheen of visalum, which meant they'd be nearly impervious to most criminal activity—or police intrusion. Our riot shields were made of the same material. Clear, like Plexiglas, lightweight like aluminum, and as tough as a steel plate.

Through the visalum, I could see flowers of all shapes and sizes in vases of every color imaginable. *This couldn't be right.*

"Yes, boss. This is the only legal business registered to a person with the surname 'Solomon' in the city of New Orleans. When strengthened by Branch Corrigan's assertion that the chop shop is located off of Fowler Avenue, this is the location of the alleged chop shop."

"Shit. This place looks like a legitimate business." I hadn't expected that. Truth be told, I was expecting the standard, run-down shithole that dominated everywhere in Easytown off The Lane.

"Good thing I've got a real backstory to cover my ass if questions start getting thrown around," I stated.

I was worried about spooking this Terry Solomon guy and him making a run for it, so I'd gone home after lunch and changed out of my suit into a pair of jeans, a nice t-shirt and a different rain jacket than the duster I always wore while at work. My prized fedora was also left at home, replaced by a water repellant Saints hat.

"I'll transfer the address to the document section on your phone, so it will appear to be a note to yourself instead of an address that your AI assistant gave you."

"Thanks, Andi. I'm gonna go in before anyone watching gets suspicious. Keep quiet."

"Understood."

I pretended to hang up my phone and made certain that I could be seen placing it into my pocket through the Jeep's windows. Then, I opened the car door and stepped onto the concrete sidewalk. Most of the places that boasted any type of businesses off of Jubilee Lane used old wooden pallets as a way of elevating their customers above the mud. There wasn't any money in the city's budget for concrete or even crushed gravel to be used as sidewalks in the slums. It was rare that a place spent the money on real sidewalks, meaning this place was either a prosperous business or trying hard to appear that way.

The building itself was a one-story, brick-front structure with what appeared to be plastisteel siding running the length of the alley on the side I could see. Again, an expensive choice in construction that was durable as hell, and more than double what cheap, vinyl siding ran.

There were obvious security cameras in their little bubbles on both corners of the building. As I stepped under a reinforced rain awning, I saw another camera above the doorway. They wanted patrons—and criminals—to know that the place was under surveillance. The owner wasn't interested in hiding them like some places chose to do. As a deterrent, I gave it about ten percent odds of success.

The door was visalum, like the painted windows, and I opened it up. The air reeked of fresh flowers and greenery, practically assaulting my nostrils with happiness. The flowers I'd seen through the windows were only a fraction of what was on display inside the shop. Tables exhibiting plants and different types of vases holding both real and synthetic flowers were scattered about the main lobby area. Wooden shelves held stuffed animals, candles, stationary and vials of different-colored liquids that I assumed were some type of air freshener or maybe a biological hazard, who knew?

"Hello, welcome to Terri's!" a cheerful female voice called.

"Thanks," I muttered, eyeing all the colors and fabrics covering every possible surface.

An older woman appeared down one of the narrow aisles and stuck out her hand. "I'm Terri. What are you looking for?"

I rolled with the revelation that 'Terry' was a woman. "Oh, just a plant for a friend at work. She's getting a promotion, so I wanted to get her something nice."

She led me through several options, steering me away from saddling my friend with the long-term commitment that a plant would impose upon her. Instead, she talked me into a simple flower arrangement as an alternative.

While she talked and walked me though the flower-buying process, I continued to scan the flower shop, trying to find the alleged chop shop entrance or the bodyguards that Corrigan said were here now. The door behind the counter appeared to go into a refrigerated area where they kept the flowers, not a nefarious operating room where street thugs came to bet their bodies permanently modified. I didn't see anything out of the ordinary.

"This place sure isn't what I was expecting," I confessed.

"I try to keep it nice, even if it is in Easytown," Terri stated. "Lots of flowers, plants, and knickknacks make it feel homey to me." She chuckled. "How does a man get to be your age and never stepped foot inside a florist?"

"I—" I started to lie, then felt it was best to go with as close to the truth as possible. "I don't know. Online ordering?"

"Ah. Electronics and enhanced communications are not always the godsend that people believe them to be."

I pulled a generic credit square from my wallet. I couldn't risk the chip in my arm being scanned, otherwise, she'd get my real name and could find my occupation from that.

"What I meant is, this shop isn't what I expected," I repeated. "A guy that comes into my office every once in a while recommended this shop as a good, safe place to get *enhancements*."

Her hand froze in midair, hovering an inch from the card I held out for her. "We can *augment* your purchase with greenery or even some additional ribbons," she replied guardedly, taking the card from me and placing it over the scanner. "Who is your acquaintance?"

"This giant guy named Branch. He delivers those big jugs of water to our office, says he likes the workout it gives him instead of using droids."

She scooped up the card with her left hand as her right dropped below the counter. "How long has it been since you last saw this Branch fellow?"

I shrugged. "I don't know. Couple of months. I know he quit the delivery job, but ever since he told me about it, I've been trying to work up the courage to come in here. He said that this shop could help with providing things that would make me bigger."

"You can find dick enlargers on the cybersphere. They're a dime a dozen," she responded. All pretext of the sweet old lady seemed to drop away.

"Oh! No, I don't need that." I made myself sound embarrassed. "Well, we could all use a little more, if you know what I mean, but I'm not here for that. I've tried steroids and electroshocks, but my muscles just won't get any bigger. Shitty genetics, y'know? Branch said there was nanotechnology out there that could boost the size of my muscles, really fill out my shirts… Maybe then, Katheryn would notice me," I mumbled, pointing at the flowers I'd bought for her as part of the setup.

She *tsked* at me, and then said, "You would risk genetic manipulation just to impress a woman? Not very smart, young man."

"It may not be smart, but it's my last hope. I've been in love with her for four years, but she always dates big, bodybuilder-types. I don't even have a shot with her until I can add some serious size."

"I've read that those things can be acquired," she remarked. "But they're *very* expensive."

She was still playing it cool, not admitting to being able to perform any type of modifications. As of right now, I didn't have anything to base probable cause on and Judge Hennessey was unlikely to grant another search warrant so quickly after the utter failures of the two we'd executed earlier today. I needed to get her to say she that this place was just a front for the chop shop.

"Branch told me about the astronomical costs. But he was talking about getting a total arm replacement so he could go back into sports, surely something like nanotech would be less expensive. It's not major surgery."

"You're right. I'd imagine it would be less expensive than replacing an entire appendage. I wouldn't even know how much something cosmetic like that would cost, though."

I put on a crestfallen appearance. "So you can't help me?"

"I didn't say that, Mr.—" She glanced at my credit square that she still held in her left hand. Her right hand was still worryingly below the tabletop out of my line of sight. "Wright. Cecil Wright. I could possibly find out about nanotech for you. When did you say you last spoke to Branch?"

"It's been a while," I admitted. "He usually comes around every two weeks to replace our empties with full jugs." I frowned. "But it *has* been a few months. Last I talked to him he was going to try to get a spot on the Saints practice squad if the surgery was a success."

"You haven't seen him because he's dead," she stated. "He got himself arrested and died a couple of days ago on Sabatier Island."

"Oh. I hadn't... I hadn't heard."

"Not much information comes off that damn rock," she said. "But, I have my ways of learning what I need to know."

She handed me the card back. "How can I find you, Mr. Wright?"

"I have, uh, I have a phone number or an email address," I offered.

"Good. Give them both to me, along with your employer information."

I told her the information that she needed, which she dutifully recorded in a flowing script on a notebook embossed with a bouquet of flowers.

"I'll be in touch," she said.

"Wait. Does that mean that you can help me? Do you do that kind of work?"

She smiled. This time, the sweet old lady's kind smile had disappeared and was replaced by a sinister sneer. "I can do whatever you want, as long as you check out and your money is good."

"So, you *did* do the surgery on Branch? He was going to get a cybernetic arm that would allow him to clothesline five running backs at top speed without moving an inch."

"Those things can be found and life-changers for athletes willing to take the risk," she replied, frustratingly still not admitting to running a chop shop. "I take pride in my work and everything I do is top of the line. Let me check a few things and I'll be in touch," she repeated, more firmly this time.

"Okay, thank you. Ah, what about the flowers?"

"At this time of day, our delivery droids have already made their runs. Your best bet is to take them now and then hire a private delivery service. Or you can just give them to your friend yourself. From your neighborhood in Plum Orchard, you could have them delivered to anywhere in the city within forty-five minutes—faster if you spring the extra money for an aerial delivery service."

Her flower shop lady demeanor had reappeared and I marveled at the way Terri Solomon was able to switch back and forth between being in character and her real personality. She should have gone into show business.

"Good advice. Thank you." I said, picking up the vase. "Looking forward to working with you to see what we can do about this." I pointed at my chest.

"We'll see what we can do, Mr. Wright. Give me a few days and I'll be in touch."

I ducked my head and turned, weaving my way through the shop's crowded interior until I was under the awning outside. I wasn't surprised to see a man taking pictures of my Jeep and was thankful that I'd had Andi set up a temporary fake account for my car as well. Anyone searching the public records would see a vehicle registered to Mark Cecil Wright of Plum Orchard. It's the little things like that which got undercover cops hemmed up.

The man stepped away from my car and I gave him a purposefully confused look before opening the passenger door and placing the flowers carefully on the floorboard. He stood on the sidewalk, watching, as I went around and sat down into the driver's seat.

I waited until the Jeep was two blocks away before asking Andi if he'd put anything on the exterior of the vehicle. If these guys were really jumpy—or selective—they could have put a tracking device on the Jeep and followed me to make sure I was who I said I was.

"There are no devices on the vehicle at this time," Andi stated. "The man in question took photos of the license plates and the vehicle identification number etched into the windshield. As a precaution, I also worked with the Jeep dealership that you purchased from and the bank where you financed your loan to ensure that they were temporarily reporting you as Mr. Mark C. Wright."

"Nice touch."

"It's what you don't pay me for."

"You exist, don't you?"

"In theory, yes."

"Well, then, that's your reward," I scoffed. Honestly, I didn't know what else she could want.

"Let's take a trip around Easytown to see about those other chop shops. I don't want to go into any of them today, just want to drive by, see what I can see."

The Jeep turned down a street, and within minutes we drove past a long row of decrepit buildings. Crumbling masonry, broken gutters and downspouts, and shattered windows were the sole decorations on the structures; not even the addresses were marked. Their tattered exteriors were exactly what I'd expected back at Solomon's Flowers.

There wasn't anything out of the ordinary from the outside, so I had the Jeep go off in search of the other two locations.

They were in a similar state of disrepair as the first. The constant rain and high water table conspired to destroy anything that wasn't constantly refurbished. Most buildings off of The Lane had never been maintained after they were hastily built forty or fifty years ago.

I'm not sure what I anticipated seeing along the back streets of Easytown, but I didn't see *anything* out of the ordinary. There were no armed guards, no lines of cyborgs waiting to go into the buildings for repairs. They seemed vacant.

Exactly how I'd want my place to look if I owned a chop shop.

"There's enough there in my mind to believe that Solomon's Flowers is really the chop shop that Corrigan said it was," I stated. "Please draft the four warrant requests for me and I'll go over them tonight."

"Understood. I'll begin converting your conversation with Terri Solomon to text immediately."

"Good." I paused, staring out the window. Today had been a shitty one filled with disappointment. "Oh, Andi?"

"Yes?"

"List Sergeant Drake as the requesting officer. I don't want Judge Hennessey seeing my name and denying it."

"Will do, boss," she replied, more cheerily than she should have. A human partner would have been just as downtrodden as I was, feeling like they'd just wasted the last seven hours of their day. Instead, she was as chipper as always.

"Alright, take me home, Andi. I'm exhausted and still need to get some type of exercise." I hadn't had much opportunity to go running since Teagan left and with my leg still on the mend, I would have to do something low impact like cycling or even swimming to get my blood flowing.

"Oh," I grunted, glancing into the passenger floorboard. "Have a courier service meet us a few blocks from the apartment to pick up the flowers."

"I've used the Jeep's scanners and didn't detect any type of tracking device on the flowers, Zach."

"Better safe than sorry," I stated.

"And yet, you still want to send them to Katheryn Townlain?"

"You just said there weren't any tracking devices."

"Understood." There was a pause. Then, "New Orleans Secure Transfer will meet us in sixteen minutes."

"Great."

I pulled out a pen and wrote a quick note to Katheryn on the card that had been provided. It read:

Katheryn,
No hard feelings, I know you were just doing your job. Hope you're not allergic to tulips.
Zach

I sealed the little envelope and put it back on the stick jutting from somewhere inside the jumble of flowers.

It was time for a shower and a drink. Maybe not in that order.

I swirled my tumbler of bourbon around, clinking the ice cubes against the glass. I really had planned on going for a swim, but allowed my mind to tell me that I was injured and needed to take it easy for another week.

I didn't want to allow my health to deteriorate to where it had been when Teagan and I first started seeing each other, but there was also some common sense in allowing my body to heal. A week off wouldn't be too much of a loss, so I ordered a healthy salad and sat at my table, which was slowly becoming cluttered with paperwork once again as I printed documents to examine side by side.

The judge had signed the search warrants earlier. We'd be conducting the first two raids tomorrow at noon. There were two teams, so could conduct two simultaneous raids, leave drones to guard the evidence and hit the other two as quickly as possible. It certainly wasn't the preferred way of doing things, but with so many locations, word traveled quick in Easytown, so that's what we had to do. The chief wanted the chop shops shut down. Once the known locations were out of commission, we could make a play for clearing out the criminal cyborgs and finally getting rid of them once and for all—until a new crop of street doctors came around to reopen the cyber-enhancement business.

It couldn't be helped. New Orleans was now on the map as a hotbed of cybernetically-altered criminals. There'd been reports others in New York, Dallas, Atlanta, and Chicago, but New Orleans was the birthplace of the movement.

Lucky us.

The shitty part is that the chop shops weren't even my main focus, but they were taking more and more of my time. I needed to figure out who murdered Dale Henderson, and why. Corrigan said he was sent there to kill him and clear up any evidence of him knowing about Karimov's involvement in the synthaine production, but wasn't the one who killed him. I doubted the cyborg would lie about the killing, he admitted to seventy-six others.

Which reminded me. "Andi, do we have the videos from the Corrigan apartment?"

"Yes. I've been waiting for you to ask to review them. However, if you didn't ask by Thursday evening, I was going to prompt you to review the evidence."

"Okay. Cue them up. I just want to do a little more thinking before we check them out."

"Will do."

"Andi, display Henderson photos."

The space above the table shimmered for a moment and then the crime scene photos appeared. Henderson's face, once ruggedly handsome from what I could tell, was a patchwork of two-centimeter wide gashes. Autopsy had revealed that each of those wounds contained a miniature saw blade projectile, similar to what Corrigan used. That meant good ole' Terri Solomon had given that weapon to at least one other person. I didn't know what type of record keeping a place like that would have, but there had to be something.

I flipped through the rest of the photos and re-read the initial report I'd filed, trying to see it through a different lens now that I had a little bit more information. Those shots, were they purely functional or was there a reason Henderson had been shot in the face? He was shot twelve times in the face and nowhere else.

"Hmm…" I said aloud.

"What are you thinking?" Andi asked, alert for my needs.

"Bring up the Liquid Genesis staff directory photograph of Dale Henderson."

The photo Andi displayed was of a well-built, handsome young man. He had perfectly coiffed blond hair, blue eyes and neatly trimmed eyebrows. A strong, clean-shaven jawline dominated his features and his teeth were perfectly straight, whiter than a priest's robes. In short, he was flawless.

"I think the killer purposefully wanted to destroy his good looks." It was fairly common in cases of jealousy to do things along those lines; to strike out against whatever feature the killer was jealous of.

"That could possibly explain the trauma to the face and nowhere else."

"That's what I was thinking," I agreed. "Also, there was no sign of forcible entry, no signs of a fight. Ten-to-one, the victim knew his killer."

"Video logs from the street and the apartment building are inconclusive."

"Yeah, I remember. That's why Drake and me were heading back over to the apartment when Corrigan jumped us." We'd been sure that the videos would have images of the killer, making our investigation much easier. We were wrong.

I flipped through more of the crime scene photos. The more I saw, the more I became convinced that the killer and Henderson had known each other. "Andi, show me a three-dimensional layout of the path the projectiles were fired at."

The photographs were replaced by an image of a translucent body, lying supine—face up. The image quickly zoomed in to just the head and a series of bisecting lines appeared. Two, highlighted in red, were slightly angled from below the nose into the brain. The other ten lines were yellow, and appeared to have been fired relatively straight into Henderson's face.

"Those two red ones... Those were fired while Henderson was standing, maybe in the doorway or inside his apartment. They were the initial shots that the killer took." I was sure of it. "Those rounds took the victim by surprise. The others were fired into his face after he was already down, dead or dying from the trauma to his brain."

"I concur with your assessment, as did the medical examiner," Andi stated.

"I know what the ME said. I'm still wrapping my brain around the scene," I replied in annoyance. "Henderson knew his killer. He was killed quickly, then the murderer took the time to fire ten more rounds."

The gears in my brain turned as I worked through it. Henderson was Karimov's lover and an associate of Ortega. Karimov had sent the cyborg to kill his lover because he knew too much, but when Corrigan arrived, he was already dead. Had Karimov set Corrigan up? Was he willing to sacrifice an expensive enforcer to cover a crime of passion, or was something else at play that I didn't see yet?

"We need to search Ortega's home," I muttered aloud.

"It's improbable that Judge Hennessey will grant a search of Carlos Ortega's residence, Zach," Andi said, bringing me back to the present. "The man died in police custody without being formally charged with a crime."

She was probably right. "Submit it anyways," I directed. "We need to find out if there's any linkage between him and the murder."

"Understood. Preparing the request now."

I tipped the bourbon back and swallowed. Since the shootout with Corrigan, I'd been going a mile-a-minute. We hadn't even had the opportunity to finish searching Henderson's apartment.

"Son of a bitch," I growled.

I was slipping, more concerned with playing grab-ass with a pretty, young woman than doing my job. Drake and I had never been able to go back to the crime scene to finish our investigation. Corrigan attacked us after we supervised the loading of Henderson's body into the medical examiner's vehicle. Then all hell broke loose with everything else, so we never went back to finish looking. I wanted to see the place again; we had to have missed something in our initial, cursory investigation while the body was still there.

I clamored to my feet, more buzzed than I'd thought I was. "I'm going over to Henderson's apartment. Bring the Jeep around."

"Are you sure that's a good idea, Zach? It's only been a few days since you tried to commence an investigation while intoxicated. That one got you stabbed. Besides, you haven't viewed the Branch Corrigan videos yet."

"I'll be fine."

"Boss, this is—"

"Dammit, Andi! Bring the Jeep around. I fucked up by not going back over there on Thursday. I let that fucking riot distract me. I need to see what we've missed."

"Understood."

I walked toward the doorway and caught a reflection of my image in the mirror. I still had on the outfit I'd worn when I went to check out all the chop shops. Hardly professional, but I didn't feel like changing, so I didn't bother with it.

I pulled the Aegis from its charger and slid it into the paddle holster before putting it on my hip. Then I wormed my arms through the shoulder holster's straps and put the Sig Sauer in its place. Finally, I slipped my duster over the t-shirt and jeans, and grabbed my badge—I'd need that.

The trip to Henderson's apartment only took a few minutes and the Jeep pulled up out front. Someone had cleaned up the chunks of brick that Corrigan's weapons knocked off the building; they'd even put the bench back where he'd taken it from; even if it was a lot worse for wear and unstable. That didn't stop the two skeevy-looking dudes from lounging across it, though.

Check that. In Easytown at night, the two guys actually looked pretty normal.

I went through the lobby, pausing briefly at the front desk to identify myself and get a key for the apartment. He lived on the third floor, so I decided to take the stairs instead of the elevator. She didn't say anything, but I could hear Andi congratulating me for making a healthy choice.

Dammit, I thought, *even when she's not chiding me, I know she's watching.*

It took longer than I'd expected and by the time I reached the top, my leg throbbed where I'd been stabbed. When I inserted the key into the lock, I realized that the door to Henderson's apartment was unlocked. I know that Drake and I locked the door when we left the night he was murdered. It was our standard procedure to ensure the scene was secured during an investigation, and we hadn't authorized the apartment's management to clean up yet— another problem with me getting too busy and not coming back here after the fight outside. I'm sure the city would receive a bill for lost rental income.

I pulled my service pistol from its holster and twisted the handle, kicking the door inward as I twisted my body around to use the wall as a barrier between me and whatever was potentially inside. My muscle in my calf contracted painfully in response to the force I'd used.

"Police!" I said loud enough to be heard inside the apartment.

The sound of something crashing pierced the silence of the hallway. Glass? Picture frames? I didn't know if the door had hit a table and sent its contents crashing to the floor or if there was someone inside.

I peeked around the corner quickly. Nothing.

Transitioning to the opposite side of the doorway, I framed myself in the open space for a split second. The throbbing pain in my leg increased as my muscles protested the repeated use and pressure placed on them to move quickly.

I put my face near the door and shouted "Police!" much louder than I had the first time.

Still no further sounds from inside.

I took the risk and ducked under the police tape to go inside the room. Stepping over the dried puddle of fluids on the tile floor, I slid along the wall in a low crouch. I remembered the layout of the apartment enough to know that the door opened into a main living area and the back of the couch created a small walkway to the kitchen. Off the living area was the bedroom and bathroom.

As I slid along the wall, I watched for movement. A small chair on casters rotated on its base and I lifted the pistol toward it. Nobody was in the chair, but a shattered glass picture frame sat on the ground near an end table. The computer in the far corner of the living room was on. It hadn't been powered on the last time I was here.

Someone was in here, I surmised. From the still-moving chair, I guessed that they'd been sitting in front of the computer when I kicked the door in. They'd probably pushed back from the desk, running the chair into the table.

"Police. I know you're in here."

I popped my head up over the counter to look into the kitchen quickly. I could only see that no one stood in there, but not whether they crouched out of sight.

"Come out before this gets messy," I called.

I rounded the counter and visually cleared the entire kitchen. My leg screamed at the crouched walk I submitted it to as I tried to keep myself as small of a target as possible. I ignored it; I had to.

The living room was cleared just as quickly as the kitchen. It was a small, square space holding the couch, desk, and the small table that used to hold a picture frame underneath a massive television set into the wall.

Where is this fucker? I asked myself, wishing I'd not been stupid enough to come over alone, half-drunk, and near midnight.

He had to be in the bedroom. I positioned myself outside the door. "Come out," I shouted.

Whoever it was still played it quiet. I feinted going straight through the doorway and instead, curled around the frame. I pressed my back against the wall and scanned the room.

Still nothing.

I cleared the bathroom quickly, then the closet. Either I'd imagined the whole thing or the fucker was good.

I limped toward the door to the living room and a thought hit me. I switched on the light, rewarded with a quick gasp of breath, and waited a moment as my eyes adjusted to the brightness. Then, I knelt down beside the bed, aiming my weapon underneath.

A pair of eyes widened in recognition of a pistol pointed right between them.

"Come out, kid," I said, adding as much intimidation to my voice as I could muster.

"Don't shoot!" a girl replied.

"I'm a cop. I'm not going to shoot you unless you do something stupid."

I had to use the nightstand to help me to my feet and I stepped back, leaning against the wall while I held my pistol low, away from the skinny, brown-haired teenager who clawed her way out from under the bed.

"What the fuck are you doing here?" I asked.

"Nothing."

"Bullshit. Tell me straight or you're going to jail."

"I don't want to go back to juvie."

"There's no juvie when you get picked up by me. We send all of our people directly to Sabatier Island and let the court system figure it out."

Her eyes widened once again. "Who are you?"

"Detective Forrest, NOPD. Now, who are you, and what are you doing on a dead man's computer?"

She looked around and hugged herself, her arms easily wrapping around her thin, waiflike frame. "Dead man?"

"Yeah, dead man," I replied, holstering my weapon. "Didn't you notice the police tape across the door and the bloodstain on the floor when you broke in?"

"I didn't break in. I was given a key," she said. "And no, it was dark. They told me to go into the computer and dump all the files."

"Who?"

"Some guys," she deflected.

"You want to go to jail tonight, kid? Do you know what they'd do to you in a place like Sabatier Island?"

"Yeah. Fine. These two guys snatched me on my way to work this morning. They gave me two hundred bucks to come up here and told me they wouldn't rape me. Once I finish up, they'll give me another two hundred, but then I have to find my own way home."

Her eyes blazed in the dim bedroom lighting, challenging me to contradict her. "Is that what you wanted to hear?" she asked.

"*Hmpf*. Something like that. Those two guys wearing jeans and white t-shirts—mostly white t-shirts—out front?" I amended, remembering the two dirty men on the park bench out front.

"Yeah," she said. "They were pretty plain-looking. You couldn't pick 'em out of a crowd."

I crossed over to the window and parted the blinds. They were gone.

"*Shit*," I muttered. "They must have made me."

I crossed the bedroom and went through the doorway into the living room and around the couch to the door into the hallway. A quick peek around told me the hallway was empty, so I closed the door and locked it.

"Hey, weirdo!" the girl screeched. "I swear to God, I will yell so loud the sprinklers come on."

I chuckled. "There ain't no sprinklers in this old building, toots. Don't worry. I meant what I said. I'm a cop and I'm not gonna harm you—unless you give me reason to."

She took a deep breath, prepared to say something else, but wisely clamped her mouth shut.

"Good. Do you think you'd be able to pick those guys out of a lineup?"

She shook her head. "No. They're pretty plain-Jane, vanilla. I can't even remember what kind of hair they have."

"Alright," I said, forcing myself to be calm. "What's your name? I can't keep calling you 'kid', right?"

"I don't mind. I've heard a lot worse," she said. "My name's Jewel."

"Like the gemstone?"

"Sure. Same thing," she acknowledged.

"Alright, Jewel. How much did you delete before I showed up?"

She shrugged. "I don't know a couple hundred megs, maybe a full terabyte."

I blanched. "You erased a *terabyte* of information?" I asked.

"Yeah, give or take," Jewel replied.

"What was in those files?"

"Stuff."

I purposefully opened my jacket to reveal my weapons as I put my hands on my hips. A little bit of intimidation never hurt anyone. "I want you to remember that I'm a cop, Jewel. I will take you to jail if you don't answer me honestly. What was in the files you deleted from Dale Henderson's computer?"

"I don't know. Pictures mostly. I was told to delete all photos off the computer and once that was done, do a keyword search for a few different words, then delete those files also."

"What were the keywords?"

"Synthaine, drugs, Karimov, and, uh…" Her eyes darted skyward as she tried to remember the other words she'd been told to search for. Finally, she remembered that there was a handwritten list in her pocket and pulled it out. "They gave me this paper. Weird, huh?"

"They probably didn't want a data trail, so they could easily burn the paper when you reported back and they killed you."

She blanched. "They were gonna pay me for doing what they said, not—"

"They were gonna kill you, maybe rape you first, *then* torture and kill you. And then take back the two hundred they gave you up front.

She sniffed and said, "I can handle myself."

I read the list aloud. "Karimov, synthaine, drugs, Ortega. Fuck, that means he *was* involved." We'd thought Ortega had been an accidental victim in all of this, a victim of circumstances, but this put him right back in the thick of things. If Karimov was removing his name, he thought it could point back to him somehow. Something still nagged at the back of my brain about their method, though.

"After you deleted documents and folders with these keywords, what did they want you to do?" I asked Jewel.

"Ensure they were completely erased, both locally and on the net, then wipe the hard drive with a reformat to completely get rid of everything. After that, I was supposed to infect the machine with a worm."

Smart. A scan of the box would reveal the virus, so a tech investigator would have to work on it off the network, where the real computing power is. Plus, deleting the specific files, *then* reformatting would ensure they were lost forever. Computers automatically backed up tons of information to the net during a reformat, so anyone looking to restore it as evidence would only be able to recover what was backed up as part of the reformat. A cursory examination would only see the files Jewel had intentionally left, making the overworked tech investigator conclude that the shoddy attempt at wiping the hard drive had been a waste of time for whoever did it since there wasn't any evidence to be found.

"Did you completely delete the files?"

"Not yet. I dumped all the pictures, like I said, but hadn't cleaned out the autorecover files yet."

"So everything is still there," I said.

"Yeah." She glanced longingly at the door. "Those guys are gonna come back for me."

"You're safe with me, kid. Don't worry about it."

"What about tomorrow, or the next day, or the next? They picked me up in my neighborhood, man. They're gonna find me."

"Somehow, I doubt those two will survive telling their boss that they botched this." It might be a long shot as far as evidence went, but Karimov had sent Corrigan over here last week, then laid low for a few days until no one was looking, and tried it again. Those two unmodified lackeys weren't worth anything to a guy like Karimov. Fail him and you're done.

"You *didn't* upload the virus, right?"

"No," Jewel replied. "That was gonna be later tonight once everything else was done."

I unplugged the computer's power cable from the wall, and scooped up the palm-sized box. There weren't any other wires to deal with, making it much easier to collect than the larger, hardwired systems that some people used.

I slipped the computer into the pocket of my duster and glanced around. There wasn't anything obviously out of place. Drake and I had done a cursory inspection of the drawers and cabinets on the night Henderson was murdered, with nothing out of the ordinary showing up.

I weighed my options. I could stay and rifle through everything once more, or I could take the computer that I was now positive contained some type of evidence down to the precinct. After a few seconds of deliberation, I made the decision to abandon further investigation of the scene. There wasn't anything else here.

The girl was problematic. I couldn't leave her at the apartment or send her home in a cab. They'd follow her and snatch her once more to find out if she'd completed her mission.

"It's time to leave, Jewel."

"Okay," she replied.

"The best way I can think of for you to get out of here is to leave with me in handcuffs—but you're not under arrest. It's to make those guys think that you are. We'll go over to the police station to drop this computer with the tech guys. Then, we'll leave the precinct by a different way and I'll take you home. You should probably lay low for a couple of days, just to be safe."

Staying out of sight was the best thing for her right now. "Where do you work? Don't lie to me."

"I'm a service tech at The Mother Board."

I groaned. "They knew what they were doing grabbing you then. It's even more important that you stay out of sight for a few days. I'm going after the guy who did this, but with everything going on, I don't think I'll be able to get him off the streets until the weekend."

"Alright. Let's do this," she said, turning away from me and placing her hands behind her back.

I clicked the metal links over her wrists, only tightening them two clicks for comfort. She could have easily slipped her hands through them if she wanted to.

The hallway was clear and so was the lobby when we got off the elevator. There wasn't any sign of the two men from earlier. I hoped for Jewel's sake, they just crawled back under the rock they'd come from.

Somehow, I didn't think it would be that easy, but without hope, what else did we have?

FOURTEEN: WEDNESDAY

"Go! Go! Go!"

I stood back, at the corner of the block as the SWAT guys moved up to surround Solomon's Flowers. The commander had positioned her drones on all four corners of the building and one hovered over each doorway. The SWAT drones were more neutered than regular police drones; they were armed with electric shock rods, capture nets, and crowd control gel only. They could incapacitate criminals, but not kill them—important when the men and women of SWAT were likely going to be up close and intermingled with the bad guys a lot of the time.

I glanced at the video feed from the commander's helmet camera, then back at the real scene before me. The teams were at the doors, ready to breach, if needed.

A member reached out and pushed the flower shop's door tentatively. It was unlocked.

"NOPD!" the Lieutenant Fairchild shouted as her men rushed through the doorway. "We have a warrant to search the premises."

The SWAT team filed inside and out of my line of view, so I turned to the holographic display of the commander's camera. I saw the little old lady, Terri Solomon, standing behind the counter with her arms up.

"What's happening?" she screamed.

"NOPD, ma'am," Lieutenant Fairchild, the SWAT commander, stated. "We are serving a search warrant for the premises, and for all business and personal vehicles of employees present as of zero-nine-hundred hours, today."

"Search warrant?" Solomon asked, feigning confusion. "On a flower shop?"

"We have reason to believe that this business is a front for an illegal cybernetic enhancement facility."

"Is that so?"

I saw the change in the woman's demeanor. It was the same look I'd seen cross her face yesterday. Before I could warn Fairchild, the old woman crouched down and several large weapons burst through the ceiling tiles, sending squares of insulation in all directions. The camera blurred and went black as the SWAT commander dove for cover.

I heard the telltale sounds of the pneumatic weapons firing from my position across the street. It sounded like several of them going at once. Branch Corrigan had only used one of the impressive devices and it was scary as hell, I couldn't imagine what must be going through the officer's minds right now as several of them fired at once.

"I'm going in, Drake," I shouted.

I saw his mouth move, but all sound was drowned out as the back door exploded. From where we were in front, I wasn't sure if it was our SWAT guys breaching to go in, or if there was an explosive charge that detonated to keep them out. A giant plume of black, oily smoke snaked skyward over the top of the squat flower shop.

"Was that us?"

"I don't know, Detective," Drake replied.

"You two," I said, pointing to two uniformed cops. "Go with Sergeant Drake around the back of the building and see if our guys need help."

They nodded and took off running. "Come on," I said to the remaining uniformed cop. "Let's go in there and see what we can do."

I realized too late that it was Liam Tidewell.

He nodded enthusiastically and said, "I'm right behind you, Detective. Jake is in there."

Shit. It made sense that the kid had tried out for SWAT. He dreamed of big gunfights with the bad guys, and of being a hero. SWAT offered him the opportunity to do all of the cool guy shit, while still patrolling the streets during his normal shift and making a difference in citizens' everyday life.

The pneumatics had stopped firing, but I could hear a massive air compressor refilling. We only had a small window to get inside and put a stop to this madness before the compressor was full and they began firing again.

"Cut power to the building!" I heard a woman order, screaming to be heard above the noise. "Cut power and stop those air compressors!"

I realized that the voice was in my earpiece. I'd been monitoring the SWAT frequency. Lieutenant Fairchild was on the radio. Someone else answered her quickly, "All power to the target building is now off. Unless there's a backup generator, it should be sufficient to interrupt the electricity going to those compressors."

The sounds of small arms fire began to pepper the air as someone fired a pistol. Several Heckler & Koch MP713s responded, their high-pitched report easily recognizable to people who'd been around them enough. It meant some of the SWAT team was still alive and fighting back.

Tidewell and I were ten steps away from the building when a basketball-sized hole appeared in the front visalum window. The strings of the molten metal dripped from the seared edges. Pulse rifle.

"What the—" Tidewell cut himself off as he ducked an imaginary blast.

The phantom pain of healed burns flared in my mind. It'd only been a few months since I'd fought hand-to-hand with a guard at the Biologiqué International Headquarters building. I'd gripped the barrel of his pulse rifle as he fired it, keeping it away from my face, but destroying my hand in the process. It took extensive surgery and regenerative genetic stimulation to make it work properly once more.

"Pulse rifle." I shouted. "Stay low."

"Medic!" Drake's voice rang out on the radio. "We need medical support at the back of the—NOPD! Drop it!"

Automatic weapons' fire erupted from around the back where Drake and the two officers had disappeared. Within seconds, the distinctive sound of NOPD Sig Sauer pistols, began to respond.

The return fire from SWAT inside picked up in intensity as they settled into their established patterns of coordinated, alternating fire. We were beginning to gain control of the situation. A concussion grenade exploded and Fairchild's voice rang out over the net, "Baker Team, move up. Make sure that big bastard is down."

I changed course. While I frequently ended up in dangerous situations, SWAT was specially trained for them. It was best to let the professionals handle whatever the hell was going on inside that shop. My partner was in a gunfight out back and it sounded like the third SWAT element was down.

As I ran, I felt Tidewell keeping pace. Fairchild's voice came over the net, calling for a status of Charlie Team. They weren't answering, and she had no situational awareness stuck inside that building, so she didn't know about the explosion.

The gunfire had ceased by the time we rounded the corner. One of the massive SWAT drones straddled a large guy in military-style pants and black tank top. A series of electrical probes darted from his chest and legs. Several lines of bullet holes were stitched across the drone where it must have taken the brunt of the man's assault through what was left of the back door.

Sergeant Drake and one of the other cops were elbow-deep in gore, trying desperately to save the life of the third officer who'd gone back with them. He'd been shot in the face, but appeared to be alive somehow.

Carnage reigned in the back parking lot. Parts of the Charlie Team littered the ground. From the looks of it, they'd been stacked on the door, ready to breach when an explosion ripped through them.

I went from torso to torso, feeling for any type of pulse or other signs of life. There were none. The explosives had been perfectly set, wiping them out before they even had a chance to respond.

An inhuman wail came from somewhere behind me and I knew that Tidewell found the remains of Jake Hannity. His was the first corpse I'd came to, quickly moving past the young cop to see if there was anything I could do for anyone else.

There wasn't.

I heard the slapping of feet against the pavement and turned, awkwardly to meet Tidewell's foolish rush. "You son of a bitch!" he screeched.

I ducked under a wild haymaker, counterpunching with a jab that allowed my leg to stay planted. It took him across the bridge of the nose, shattering it. Blood erupted from both nostrils, quickly covering his lips and chin in dark streaks.

He feinted right, then went left and landed a solid punch into my ribs. I closed my upper arm over his forearm and clasped my hands under his elbow.

The fight was over instantly as I jerked my hands upward. With his forearm trapped, the tendons and ligaments in his elbow tore and then the elbow joint popped out of socket. Tidewell screamed in pain and rage.

I stepped across, unholstered his weapon and then shoved him roughly away. "What the fuck is wrong with you?" I shouted. "We have six dead officers here."

"You son of a bitch," Tidewell grimaced. "I'll kill you. I swear to God, I'll kill you."

"Get in line, you stupid fuck."

More shoes pounded on the pavement as members of SWAT came around the building. They stopped several feet away, surveying the bloody masses of flesh that used to be their teammates.

I felt bad for them. I truly did. They'd come to this little flower shop, not expecting much, and their reality had been shifted forcefully for them through a solid kick in the balls. We may have won the fight, but it sure as hell didn't feel like it.

"Hey, Detective," Drake's voice rumbled out of the office where he was going through files.

I glanced up from the collection of weapons I was putting tags on. Across the dingy surgical ward of Terri Solomon's chop shop, I could see Sergeant Drake sitting on a low stool, hunched over an old-fashioned file cabinet. He didn't look up at me, so I yelled back.

"Yeah, what is it?"

"Your boy Ortega purchased one of those handgun pneumatic pistols that the old lady had up front."

The old lady in question, Terri Solomon, was dead. She'd been killed a couple of hours ago when she ambushed the SWAT team and initiated the explosion that wiped out Easytown SWAT's Charlie Team.

"He did, huh?" I wasn't surprised. I'd already begun to think Ortega had more to do with Henderson's death than simply being his employer.

"Yes, sir. He picked up one of those things a month ago."

I was impressed with Solomon's record-keeping skills. She couldn't risk putting the information into a computer, so everything was meticulously recorded on paper and filed away for future reference—or blackmail.

That sales document was the piece of evidence I needed to take to Judge Hennessey. I was certain the person who killed Henderson was an acquaintance. Now that I knew Ortega had access to the same type of weapon that killed the thumper club doorman, he was firmly on a very short list of suspects.

"We can use that document to justify a search of his home," I said aloud.

"That's just what I was thinking," Drake replied as he set aside that document specifically by itself.

I went back to tagging the weapons for transport back to the evidence locker. The DA would build a case against the two cyborg bodyguards that we'd arrested during the raid. Turns out, both of them matched the description of the cyborgs who'd shot up the Liquid Genesis, which meant it was also highly likely that the weapons used came from this shop.

Sometimes luck was the big break we needed in a case.

"Detective Forrest, can you come here a moment?" Ben Roberts, the precinct's forensic photographer, asked.

"What is it, Ben?"

He pointed to a large, framed garment of some type hanging on the wall behind the counter where he photographed the very dead Terri Solomon. Three .45 rounds to the face from an H&K MP713 tended to do that.

"Yeah, what am I looking at?" I asked in confusion. It was a red, oversized long-sleeved shirt with a bunch of random color spirals all over it. It sort of reminded me of an outfit from Sub-Saharan Africa, but they weren't quite the same.

"You probably don't know this about my wife, but she's an immigrant. Her grandparents came to New Orleans from Tajikistan. Her father was some white guy who took off after getting her mom pregnant in high school."

I waited for him to get to the point. We had a lot of work to do if we were going to search the premises of the other three chop shops we'd raided today.

"Anyways," he continued, sensing that I didn't need the full backstory. "Her family still gets dressed up in traditional garb twice a year to celebrate some holidays." He pointed at the framed shirt again and said, *"That's* a traditional Tajik or Uzbek embroidered silk tunic dress. They're very difficult to make and are only given away to special friends outside of the community."

"So someone in the Tajik community gave Solomon, a Caucasian woman, that shirt as a special gift…" I trailed off. "Ben, do you happen to know the name Farouk Karimov?"

He shook his head. "Not in the sense that you're asking. I've heard the name the last few days in the department, which is why I wanted to point out that tunic dress to you, but as far as I know, he doesn't participate in Tajik community events. There are more than ten thousand Tajik descendants right here in New Orleans, though, so it's entirely possible that I simply never met the guy."

"Thanks, Ben. Your keen eye helped to add another nail in Karimov's coffin. I have a suspect who said he worked for Karimov who got cybernetic enhancements from this shop. I think he may be more involved in this cyborg bullshit than we'd originally thought."

"Yeah, no problem, Detective. Just trying to help out. The less work I have, the better off the city is."

"Ain't that right?" I chuckled.

FIFTEEN: THURSDAY

The rest of Wednesday was spent in a blur of scene processing after the raids on the other chop shops. Thankfully, there weren't any more large gunfights like what had happened at Solomon's Flowers, although, one officer did get a bullet to the gut at the warehouse we hit on Third Boulevard. A SWAT sniper redecorated the cheap steel walls with the perp's brain matter.

After that, it was smooth sailing.

The cybernetic enhancement business was alive and well in Easytown. All four of the sites had operating rooms, computer hookups and spare mechanical parts lying around; not to mention the barrel of discarded human parts we discovered in the third chop shop we hit in a residential neighborhood.

I stretched my aching back and rubbed my calf gently. It was healing, but not quick enough for my tastes. I needed it to be fully-healed, otherwise I was a liability to others—and myself.

After an initial cup of coffee where I stared out the window of my apartment at the first truly sunny day I could remember in a long time, I had Andi bring up the Corrigan collection. He'd claimed to have killed seventy-six people, but there were more than two hundred videos in the collection of files we'd seized from his home.

The first video began with Corrigan torturing a dog. It was from his point-of-view, so he probably had a camera on his forehead or chest like all the daredevils wore, so I couldn't be sure how old he was. Given the much thinner forearms and higher-pitched voice, I guessed he was a kid, maybe a teenager, when he started his love affair with murder.

I'd seen enough of the first video to realize that he was disturbed, so I advanced to the next one chronologically. It was again from his point of view, and showed him engaged in a fist fight with three other kids. The thinnest of the three ran toward him and Corrigan sidestepped his attack, wrapping an arm around his neck and twisting violently. Then the largest of the teens reached him. There was a flurry of movement; I couldn't see what was happening, but I thought Corrigan was wrapped up in some type of bear hug. Then, the ganger fell away and Corrigan's foot rose up, stomping down repeatedly on the big one's head. Fists drew back out of frame and shot into view rapidly as he made short work of his final opponent.

Corrigan grabbed the final kid in a bear hug of his own, squeezing until I heard bones snap. Then, he whispered, "I love you," and bit off the kid's bottom lip.

Someone grabbed him from behind, pulling him along saying the cops were coming as Corrigan screamed about wanting to show 'Brad' how much he loved him. He lifted the unconscious form over his head and dropped him onto his knee as he knelt, probably breaking the kid's spine. Then the video was jostled and glitch as he ran from the cops.

I advanced to the next video, which was another animal torture. I went to the next one, and then the next.

Three hours later, I was left feeling numb and disheartened. I'd seen hundreds, possibly thousands, of murders in person and on video over the years, but never so many at one time and the techniques used so varied—and that was with Andi fast-forwarding through entire sections. His count of seventy-six *humans* was correct, but he'd neglected to include the multiple rapes of both men and women, extended torture sessions, and mutilation of various creatures in his figures, which is why there were so many videos.

Branch Corrigan had been a sick individual. He'd done things to some of his victims that I hadn't even heard of before. I was glad he was dead.

With Andi's help, I spent the next two hours cross-referencing faces of his victims with unsolved murders across the district. Of the known victims, we were able to verify that the bodies of fifty-three of them had been discovered and were listed as unsolved. Another two of Corrigan's victims had been found and an innocent person had been tried and convicted for murder. Police weren't perfect and neither was the judicial system. Unfortunately, in those two cases, everyone was wrong and those men were serving life sentences at Sabatier Island.

The sickness in my stomach from earlier eased slightly with the knowledge that we'd be able to finally give all those families definitive answers about what happened to their loved ones. Closure wouldn't relieve their pain, but it was all that I could offer them. It was something.

The others in the videos were John and Jane Doe's. No facial recognition matches on missing persons or bodies that had been discovered. Either Corrigan had a very good dumping spot where nobody had found more than twenty bodies, or he'd done something else with them. Given the level of evil I'd witnessed throughout a lifetime of depravity, I wouldn't have been surprised to learn that he disposed of the bodies by eating them.

Which reminded me, I hadn't eaten anything all morning and I had a meeting to go to in about an hour.

"Andi, I need some food before I go meet with Voodoo."

"I'll order street tacos and have them delivered."

"Thanks. I feel like I need to wash a few years of filth off of me." Watching all those videos made me feel dirty, inside and out. A shower would do something about the exterior feelings; but only time would cleanse my mind.

Drake went to search Ortega's house on the warrant we had rushed through the court while I went to the Easytown Dockyards to talk to Tommy Voodoo about the activities of his employee, Farouk Karimov. Besides the ineffectual search of his tiny apartment, nobody had seen the guy and I wanted to talk to him. His name had come up in connection with Henderson, Ortega, Corrigan, and the city's synthaine problem. The guy got around.

The lobby of the Marie Leveau Shipping Company was exactly as I'd remembered it from the last time I was here.

The two receptionists still sat at their twin desks immediately in front of the entryway, switching between answering phone calls and typing reports with an ease that boggled my non-office worker mind.

Betty, the brunette, was a refurbished sex droid. Voodoo had given her an AI upgrade and sat her ass here in this chair. She'd almost shot me in the back one time with zero emotions or thoughts beyond the fact that she was told to keep people from passing an imaginary line on the floor. She was a real hoot.

Anastasia, on the other hand, was blonde, stunningly beautiful, and one hundred percent human—well, one hundred percent *cloned* from a human, with all of the original's flaws and imperfections removed. Other women may come and go in Tommy Voodoo's life, but Anastasia had wrapped him around her little finger. I felt like I owed her a huge debt of gratitude since she'd been instrumental in getting him to cooperate with me when he was scared that doing so would cost him his life when Biologiqué International was kidnapping people, cloning them, and then murdering the victims.

"Betty. Anastasia," I said when I walked in. "You girls behaving?"

"That depends on your definition of behaving, Detective Forrest," Betty responded. I'd noticed that, interestingly, the droid usually spoke first and seemed to be the de facto respondent for questions aimed at both of them. I wondered if it had to do with her robotic brain being able to process multiple tasks at once, whereas Anastasia's human brain needed to focus more to complete her work.

"Mr. Ladeaux is a lucky man," I chuckled.

"He is prosperous with numerous successful business ventures, Detective. The old saying goes that quantity has a quality all of its own."

I blinked in surprise. Betty's AI was able to learn, and then more or less correctly correlate axioms into conversation. As far as I knew, that was something that even Paxton Himura hadn't done.

"Wow, Betty. Your AI is advancing rapidly."

"Thank you, Detective. Performing the mundane duties of this position allows me the time to scour the cybersphere, interacting with millions of people online. I am learning from them."

"Kinda scary, isn't it?" Anastasia muttered.

"A little," I admitted. "With an unlimited ability to process data and the capacity to learn from every human and computer on the planet, she could become either a force for good or a force for evil."

"With as much hate as people spew at one another in the cybersphere, I don't think I want to know what she's learning," the clone stated.

"Mr. Ladeaux has given me enough leeway to learn from the world around me, in all of its forms. Even with the ability to learn and adapt my programming to meet emerging requirements, I am not able to violate the First Law of Robotics, so you have nothing to fear."

I glanced at Anastasia and then back to Betty. "I'm sorry. I don't know the laws of robotics."

"There are three, originally formulated by one of the fathers of the science fiction literary genre, Isaac Asimov. The First Law of Robotics states that a robotic entity may not harm a human. So, while Anastasia is a clone, I could not physically assault her since she is human."

"*Hmpf,*" I grunted. "Sounds like a load of crap to me. I've been plenty beat up by robots."

"Yes, I have read the police files, they—"

"You *what?*"

"I read the police files of your robotic killer case. The robots in question weren't acting on their own, they were being controlled by Harold Wilson. Even when he was no longer directly controlling them, he'd reprogrammed the droids."

"So if you learn all of this stuff from the cybersphere, and then somebody reprograms you, you still wouldn't be able to kill?"

"If I were to retain my knowledge of Asimov's Laws of Robotics, then I would not be able to harm a human. However, if they wipe them from my memory, then I may be capable of harming a human. Does this make sense?"

"Yeah," I said. "It does. Take the police drones, for example. They are programmed with a massive set of instructions and reactionary protocols, but they're not connected to the cybersphere. They're connected back to MainFrame, for reporting and specialized control situations, but they mostly operate on their own. I think."

To be honest, no one really knew how much control MainFrame had over the drones on their routine interactions with citizens, so the drones may have been operating on their own. Obviously, the programmers didn't give two shits about Betty's laws of robotics.

"So, how did you read private police reports?" I asked, bringing up the question I'd originally intended to ask.

"Most police reports are not protected, Detective," Betty stated. "You simply need to know where to look. If they are stored in a publicly-accessible medium, then I am within my legal rights to access the documents."

"You *don't have rights*, Betty. You're a droid. Droids are not afforded any of the protections given under the law."

"You are correct. I was simply making a statement that anyone, whether they are droid or human, can access files on the police internal network. They are not particularly well guarded." She seemed to pout, then began typing again.

Without looking up, Betty stated, "I have read the Internal Affairs file on you, Detective Forrest. You may want to consider a rebuttal."

"Wait. What report?" I asked in confusion, reaching for my phone. "Andi, is the IA report available?"

"I am not aware that it is. Let me check once again." She paused and then said, "Yes, Zach. The report released four minutes ago. I only scan every thirty minutes to save bandwidth. Give me a moment to read the report."

She only took about five seconds to read the documents before her voice emitted from my headphone. "The report filed against you by the NOPD IA Division is fairly damning."

"Shit. Excuse me, ladies," I said. "I'm going to go have a seat in the waiting area. Can you please just let Mr. Ladeaux know that I'm here for our appointment?"

"He's already been notified," Betty stated.

"Of course he has," I muttered as I went to the uncomfortable, clear plastic chairs that the lobby boasted. "Andi, I need the charge sheet sent to my phone, now."

"There's not a formal charge sheet, Zach. You are not being arrested. Internal Affairs utilizes a recapitulation of findings; which is simply a one-page summary of the report."

"Okay, fine goddammit. I don't care what they call it. I need that sent to me so I can review it now."

"Understood. I just sent it."

I opened the file she sent me and skimmed through the opening remarks until I came to the findings. "Those sonsabitches," I muttered.

"Problem, Detective Forrest?" a familiar, weak voice asked.

I glanced up, putting away my phone as I did so. "Nothing I can't handle, Mr. Ladeaux. Thank you for taking the time to meet with me."

"You're always welcome here. I hope you know that by now."

I walked beside him as he led the way down the hallway. Once again, he took me into the duplicate office, not the real thing that he used when he was scared for his life during the clone crisis. I asked him about it.

"Oh, this office is just slightly bigger and I spend more time in here than in the other one. Plus…" He pressed his finger against his computer screen and a portion of the wall faded away, becoming translucent. Through the shelves of sports memorabilia, I could see the Dockyards as workers scurried around unloading ships and moving cargo.

"Nice view."

"Thank you. The other office is truly in the center of the building, so a true view like this isn't possible. I can always tell a difference between the real thing and a vidscreen."

He cleared his throat, indicating that it was time to get down to business.

"Right," I replied. "I'm investigating the city's cyborgs. We've taken down several chop shops that are responsible for creating them."

"I heard about your raids yesterday. Good work, Detective. There are probably twenty more where those came from."

"Do you know of any?"

"Just rumors. Cybernetic enhancements are here to stay. There are plenty of uses for the technology that are not criminally motivated," he stated. "The edge they give manual laborers, for example, could be used to great effect. If a man can up his stamina or strength, then he is more useful to the company he works for, thus increasing his job security. I think if you take a good, hard look around, you may find all sorts of people who are willing to take that step in order to keep their jobs. Hell, professional sports are full of enhanced individuals and everyone cheers for them," he said, gesturing at the autographed footballs on the shelves. "Why should it be any different for someone who busts their ass all day long for a much smaller paycheck?"

I jutted my chin toward the window. "Are any of your workers out there enhanced?"

He shrugged. "I'm the owner and CEO of several large corporations, Detective; most of which rely on manual, human labor. I don't typically interact with my employees. There are several layers of middle management between us. I wouldn't be surprised to learn that I have enhanced employees working in my companies. My employees are scared that they'll be replaced by robots and drones, so they'll do whatever they can to keep the edge."

"Are you going to replace them?"

He snorted in laughter. "Are you serious?"

"Yes. That's why I asked the damn question, Mr. Ladeaux."

"In the long run—about six years—it would be profitable to replace two humans with a single droid, but I can't afford to do that across the board all at once. A run-of-the-mill droid, not a skinjob, costs around one-and-a-quarter million. It quickly goes up in price for artificial skin, adaptive AI, and all the other things that my pleasure droids have. My workers earn an average of a hundred K each. You figure one droid could replace two shifts and have to be powered down for the third shift, so it would earn out in about six years."

"And you don't have several hundred million just sitting around."

"Exactly. I see these protests by the city's workers and I laugh. Of course, everyone has a story about knowing somebody who was replaced by a droid or their job got downsized to an AI instructing hundreds of students at once, but it's not realistic to believe that droids are suddenly going to flood the market and take all the jobs. They are too expensive, for now."

I hadn't thought of it in that respect. The astronomical costs associated with the robotic industry did make it nearly impossible to replace all of the workers like they feared. Outside of a few megacorporations, it couldn't be done. Maybe a phased approach over several years or decades, but the average small business simply couldn't do it. I'd have to dig into the feasibility of Amir's plan to add a droid; he didn't pay his workers anything near a hundred thousand.

"Good point," I said aloud. "It doesn't seem practicable to replace an entire workforce."

"It's not. That's one of the main reasons I'm concerned with advancing my partnership with Cybertronic Solutions beyond companionship droids. If I can reduce the price of advanced worker droids, I'd abandon human workers in a heartbeat." He pointed toward the door. "The only reason I have Betty out there is because she's refurbished from one of my clubs. Otherwise I couldn't have justified the up-front cost."

"So why all the sex bots then?"

He leaned back, "Because there's a huge market for it. People can pick up a hooker, and all of the associated diseases, anywhere. But a sex *droid*? Only Easytown, Las

Vegas, New York, Amsterdam, and Bangkok have them—unless someone wants to purchase their own, but the cost is prohibitive."

I nodded, thinking about Andi's constant request that I give her a CS01 body—at the cost of two million dollars.

"Besides, government-mandated health care for sex workers is astronomical. It makes their per-unit cost more than a droid in just a few years, more if one of them gets injured on the job, but I have to keep them in stock too since the market demands options."

Ladeaux slapped the desk lightly. "I love talking shop with you, Detective, but I'm a busy man and you didn't come here to learn about sex droids. You were discussing your raids on the cybernetic enhancement facilities, what is it that I can do for you?"

"Do you know a Farouk Karimov? He works for you here in the Dockyards."

"*Hmm…*" Voodoo tapped his screen and said, "Farouk Karimov."

A holographic rendering of Karimov appeared over the desk between us. He used his hands to rotate the image, spreading his fingers to zoom in on the hologram's face.

Shaking his head, Voodoo tapped a folder icon which brought up a few strings of text. "Says he works as a stevedore in Warehouse Six and Dock Four," he said. "Never seen him before. What did he do?"

"His name has come up a few times in connection with an ongoing investigation and I've been unable to talk to him at his residence."

"His file says he's at work today." He hit a few more keys and a map of the complex came up. "We're here," he stated, showing me the Marie Leveau Shipping Company headquarters on the hologram. A line shot from the headquarters, following along several roads and pathways until it terminated at a warehouse. "This is Warehouse Six."

"Thanks," I said. "Mind if I go over there and ask a few questions?"

Voodoo leaned back. "I wouldn't have shown you where it was if I wasn't okay with you going down there."

"Alright. Thank you, Mr. Ladeaux," I said, standing. "I'm gonna go down there, have a look around, and ask some questions. Nothing major."

Voodoo stood up as well. He leaned across, stretching out his hand. "Please don't shoot the place up, Detective. It's bad for business and hell on the insurance."

I shook his offered hand; I owed him that much with all the help he'd given me. "I'm not going down there to get into a fight," I assured him. "But Karimov owes me some serious answers about a few things and I intend to get them—today."

SIXTEEN: THURSDAY

The Jeep wound around the Dockyards' narrow roads toward Warehouse Six. The road was gravel, as most of the entire area seemed to be. From what I could tell as I looked out the windows, the roads were little more than pathways made from giant shipping containers, laid out like a maze. The containers towered above me two or three high in most places.

The path was relatively straight-forward with only a few turns that were different from what Tommy Voodoo had shown me. The shipping containers had been rearranged into the winding corridor that I found myself in now, making me wonder when the last time the CEO had left the headquarters building to check on his employees.

The Jeep did a decent job of navigating the shipping containers, but there were a few times when it had to stop, reverse and go back the way we'd came from to try a different route. I felt vulnerable in that corridor for the entire time I was in there. It wouldn't take much to block it off and then someone could take their time to eliminate a threat against them. I hated being in the shadows of those containers.

It took about eight minutes for the Jeep to get to Warehouse Six. The massive, grey cinderblock building seemed indistinguishable from the others I'd seen through gaps in the shipping container walls other than a large number "**6**" painted above the hangar-style doors. A constant stream of large tractors carrying forty-foot containers from a cargo ship moved in and out of the warehouse as smaller forklifts darted around and between them, placing smaller containers in semi-trucks lined up to haul the goods to their next destination. It appeared to be a carefully choreographed dance, with the participants narrowly skirting disaster at every turn.

The larger containers were being unloaded from a ship flying a Japanese flag; nothing interesting there, other than the fact that they'd had to sail completely around South America to get here. I assumed it was cheaper than disgorging their contents on the West Coast and driving them overland to the Midwest. But what did I know. It may have just been more convenient.

"Andi, can you run a track on the ship being unloaded now?"

"Sure. What are the hull identification numbers printed on the side of the ship?"

I read a long string of numbers and she came back instantly, telling me the boat was registered to a shipping company in Kitakyushu, Japan. Their cargo manifest stated that they were bringing in containers from various technology companies, including one that specialized in robotics.

After observing the controlled chaos before me, I directed the Jeep to park about three hundred feet away from the warehouse. I decided to walk the rest of the way in, that way my car wouldn't get crushed by an errant tractor or dropped shipping container.

I dodged the tractors with the forty-foot containers, learning quickly that they couldn't see an individual on the ground around their cargo. The more-numerous and smaller forklifts were harder to avoid, but they could also see where they going, so I didn't feel they were nearly as dangerous as the bigger ones and chose my path to the doorway based on where they were.

The sun from this morning had carried over to the afternoon and I was sweating slightly by the time I pulled open the door to what I assumed was the office. New Orleans would guarantee I got wet one way or another.

It took a moment for my eyes to adjust to the dimness inside the building. When they did, I realized I'd walked directly into a short hallway. Three doors on either side led to smaller offices and a doorway at the end bore the sign **"Hard hats required beyond this point**."

"Hello?" I called out.

"Yeah? Come on in. Third door on the right."

As I walked down the hallway, I realized the doors on the left weren't offices as I'd thought they were. One was a break room and the other two were restrooms. The first two doors on the right were closed and unmarked. That only left the last doorway, which was open.

"Hi," I said to the fat, balding man behind a desk stacked high with memory drives, files, and empty food containers.

"Can I help you?" he asked.

"Yeah. I'm Detective Zach Forrest from the NOPD," I replied, showing my badge. "I'm looking for a worker that the company headquarters says works in this warehouse."

He grunted. "Okay. Who you lookin' for, pal?"

"A stevedore. Guy named Karimov. Farouk Karimov. You know where I can find him?"

"Aww, Christ! What did that dumb sonofabitch do now?" The guy didn't even try to hide his disgust and anger that painted his face.

"Does he have a record of creating problems for you?" I asked.

"He's lazy as all get out, but not really a problem-maker, I guess. He misses about three or four days a month, but the damn union is so tight that I can't fire the guy. He's always got some excuse that's part of the excused absences section of the union contract. I swear. One day I'm gonna catch him lying about an absence. *That* I can fire him for."

"Where's he at now? I need to speak to him about a few things."

The chair squeaked pitifully as the foreman shifted his bulk, rotating the chair until he faced a grossly out-of-date computer screen that had to be at least fifty years old. He tapped a few keys on an antiquated plastic keyboard and hundreds of icons appeared on the screen. He moved around some strange device connected by a wire that made the cursor on his screen move until he clicked on a file folder. Then he scrolled through an alphabetical list of names, resting the cursor over Karimov's name and then he clicked again.

All of the dots disappeared except for one, moving slowly across the screen. He used the device to chase the dot until the cursor was over it and he clicked down. "Says he's in a smaller forklift inside the warehouse right now, moving cargo from a container over that way," he gestured toward the far left corner of the warehouse. "Oh, you're in luck, it's a yellow one, so just look for a yellow forklift and then stop the guy when you see him."

"Thanks," I replied.

"No problem. I hope you bust that slacker so I can fire him and get a decent worker in here."

I didn't bother to shake the foreman's hand, I really didn't have time to get sick from whatever was growing in that man's office. He turned back to whatever he'd been doing when I walked in, and a strange sucking sound came from behind me. *Not gonna look back at that*, I told myself.

I don't know what kind of luck the foreman thought I had, but telling me to look for a yellow forklift was like telling a beekeeper that you wanted to find one particular bee. Yellow forklifts zoomed by in all directions. About the only other color that was as prevalent as yellow was a dark green. The rest were blue, red, and an occasional white one. At least my search was narrowed in half.

I'd only seen Karimov in person once, and that was from far away during the riot against droids. I'd seen his mugshots and identification card photos and a video of him at the Liquid Genesis when it got attacked. As I stood there, swaying slightly to avoid the closest of the forklifts, I wondered again at Karimov's connection with the mass shooting that left thirty-two people dead and another sixty-plus injured.

Corrigan worked for Karimov, and he got his weapons from Terri Solomon. There were lots of cryptic files at Solomon's shop indicating that "K" purchased cybernetic upgrades and weaponry. It was circumstantial, at best, but I knew without a doubt that the letter referred to Karimov. So why, then, did Solomon's two bodyguards shoot up the club where he was at? It didn't make any sense.

Too late, my mind registered a yellow flash barreling straight toward me.

The edge of one metal fork glanced off my hipbone as I dove sideways to avoid impalement from the yellow forklift. When I landed, pain exploded across my pelvis. Even that glancing blow had been enough to shatter my hipbone.

I struggled to get up, but my leg wouldn't respond. Out of my periphery, I saw the forklift wheeling for another pass. I dragged myself as quickly as I could, trying to make it to the cover of a pallet stacked high with boxes. I thought that if I could put it between me and the forklift, I'd—

What? Get crushed against the side of the pallet? I chided myself.

I rolled onto my back, abandoning the foolish effort to crawl away, and drew my gun. The yellow forklift that had hit me was coming toward me fast. I lifted my arm wearily, aiming at the Plexiglas windshield. A smear of bright white from the lights overhead marred the surface, obscuring the driver, so I couldn't tell who it was.

I fired once, twice, a third time at where the driver should have been, but the machine kept coming, undeterred by my ineffectual bullets. There wasn't enough time to switch to the Aegis.

I was going to be crushed.

"Shots fired, boss," Andi's voice came through my earpiece. "Do you require assistance?"

I ignored her; there were more pressing concerns at the moment. I cried out in pain, pushing through the physical anguish as I threw my body out of the path of the forklift. It passed by so close that if I'd been wearing my raincoat, it would have ran over the hem.

My stomach churned, and my vision swam. My body was reacting to the trauma. If it shut down on me, I was a goner.

The forklift began to turn again and I fumbled for the Aegis, but my fingers couldn't grasp the handle. They did, however, accidentally push against where my hipbone should have been, sending new waves of agony through my body.

"Pretty sure my hip is crushed," I groaned, hoping Andi was monitoring closely.

Squealing tires announced that the forklift had completed its turn and was bearing down on me. I didn't have the energy to move like I had a moment ago. I tried, but my body refused to respond.

So this is it then? I asked myself. *All those years of work, just to give up now? Get up! Kick this guy's ass!*

The pep talk strengthened my resolve and I tried to move again. My body still wouldn't react. The lower half of my body had simply stopped listening to what I told it to do.

I stared helplessly at the yellow blur bearing down on me. I was done for.

Then, another forklift slammed into the side of my attacker. The yellow forklift skidded sideways, and its wheels left the ground as the second machine began lifting its forks. In seconds, the momentum had taken over and the forklift that had hit me toppled sideways, crashing to the warehouse floor onto its side.

A man leapt from the machine and ran toward the back of the large building. He quickly disappeared between the lines of tractors and shipping containers. From what I could tell, he was slim, average height, and had dark, slicked-back hair. No way of telling if it was Karimov.

I yelled, trying to get the other workers to stop the fleeing attacker, but they couldn't hear me over the sounds of the heavy machinery.

"Andi, call an ambulance and a couple of black and whites."

"Got it. How badly are you injured?"

"Can't move my legs. Hip broken."

A woman stepped out of the forklift that had saved me, and walked over to where I lay. She eyed my gun warily and said, "Hey, mister. You 'kay?"

"Yeah," I croaked. "I'm not dead, thanks to you. You saved my life."

I wasn't dead, but I felt like it. I

"Twer't no thing," she said, smiling. "What'd you do to get that guy all riled up?"

"I'm a cop," I replied through gritted teeth. *Don't pass out. Don't pass out. Don't pass out.* "Needed to talk to him…" I took a deep breath before continuing. "About his possible connection with a murder."

"Oh. You's out here causin' trouble," she grumbled. "No wonder he try to kill you. I let Bobby know you're here, but I don't have no business with the cops."

"I'm not—" I stopped myself, grimacing as I tried to sit up. No dice; my body wouldn't let me move. I was used to people not wanting to be around police officers, and especially not wanting to be seen helping one out. This woman had saved my life, but she hadn't known I was a cop.

"Thank you for saving my life, ma'am."

"*Mmm hmm.* I go get Bobby."

I watched her hop back in her forklift and zoom past me toward the office. Within seconds of her entering the office, a series of flashing yellow lights set into the ceiling began to rotate high above me. Then, all the forklifts, tractors, and trucks stopped moving. I couldn't tell if the operators shut down their machines or if they were somehow centrally controlled. It didn't really matter, what *did* count was that hundreds of angry workers dismounted their equipment and formed a semi-circle around me. If they weren't moving cargo, they weren't getting paid, and they weren't moving cargo because of me, the idiot lying on the floor.

"Uh, hi guys," I offered weakly.

The angry questions began immediately, demanding to know who I was, what I was doing there, and how I got hurt. "Andi, ETA on those black and whites?"

"Three minutes until they reach the Dockyards."

Great. This mob could tear me apart in that time.

Bobby, the fat, balding foreman I'd spoken to earlier appeared, riding on an industrial hoverskiff. He had the workers clear a space around me. "Now what'd you go and shut down my operation for?" he asked.

"I have a knack for—"

"He a cop!" a woman's voice rang out. I looked to the source and saw the lady who'd helped me walking back from the direction of the office where her forklift was shut down like all the others.

The angry crowd became menacing. Bobby abandoned his attempts to talk to me and began speaking to the workers.

"You fellas get back to your stations," he ordered. "As soon as I can scoop this guy up off the floor, we'll get back to work."

Angry shouts answered him. "Pig lover!" "Company man!" "String 'em both up!" "He goin' after Farouk."

That last one was from my lovely female savior, who'd turned out to be not so cooperative after she found out who I was.

"Now, now," Bobby said, holding up his hands. "Unsanctioned gatherings are grounds for immediate dismissal. The union has agreed to that stipulation. This is all just a misunderstanding."

"He gon' try to stop the kickbacks," someone shouted.

That seemed to do the trick, breaking the hold that the threat of firing had over the crowd. They began to advance toward me.

The ear-shattering screech of rending sheet metal stopped everyone in their tracks. Above us, a police drone rocketed through the hole it'd torn in the roof. It settled on spindly legs between me and the angry workers, narrowly missing Bobby.

"Citizens, you are ordered to disperse," it stated, the words amplified by the large, open warehouse. "Threatening a police officer is grounds for termination."

The drone didn't mean getting fired from their jobs, and the workers understood immediately. They retreated backward several feet, casting angry glares my way.

"Detective Zachary Forrest," the drone continued. "You are being evacuated from this situation. Do not resist."

I didn't have time to protest or warn the drone about my broken hip. It wrapped several rubbery tentacles around my legs, torso, and midsection. I screamed in anguish as the tentacles tightened around my waist. Then the drone lifted into the air and shot upward through the hole in the roof.

I passed out before I had the opportunity to enjoy the clear, blue sky above.

SEVENTEEN: SATURDAY

"Like hell, Drake," I spat, sitting up gingerly in the hospital bed. "I'm going back in."

"Detective, you don't need to. SWAT has this."

"I didn't go through surgery and two days of regenerative genetic stimulation to sit on the sidelines while someone else did my job. Karimov is my responsibility and I started this whole mess by not bringing him in when I had the chance."

Admittedly, the 'chance' I referenced was ended by me getting my right hip broken in six places by a six-foot length of steel, but that was beside the point.

"That's a bunch of macho bullshit, Detective. And you know it."

"Maybe it is," I replied. "But I'm still gonna go out there and be on scene when this goes down."

Since I'd been evacuated from Warehouse Six, Karimov had taken control of the Dockyards. He'd organized the workers and they'd arranged the shipping containers into a massive wall. It wasn't impenetrable by any means, and the drones could easily drop in behind them, but hundreds of workers hadn't supported him and were now hostages intermingled with Karimov's people, making it impossible to tell who was a hostile. That meant using the drones was out. It also meant that Lieutenant Fairchild's SWAT team was once again on the hook to go into harm's way because of something I'd done.

"I'm not sure that Brubaker is gonna allow that," Drake said after an extremely long pause.

"Why's that?" I asked, my eyes narrowing.

"You know; the IA report of findings…"

"Shit," I groaned.

Lying in bed over the course of two days, I'd had ample time to go over the report, all one hundred and four pages of the main report, plus the additional five hundred pages of supporting evidence and video files. The backup document was full of useless information like insurance claims, annual performance evaluations, a detailed report of all misconduct claims—founded and unfounded—filed against me over my career, generalized psychological findings, and transcripts from the character witness interviews of fellow officers and department employees. The last section was truly eye opening since I was able to see exactly what people really thought of me.

There were even a few pages on Katheryn Townlain's involvement, along with video from our conversations, including when I told her why I was a cop, followed up by the close-up of my chest when we shared a sloppy, drunken kiss. Of course she'd been wearing a camera. The whole section with her was utterly pointless since nothing happened, and none of it made it into the main report.

The actual findings of the report recommended my termination based on a pattern of misconduct. It detailed the various suspensions I'd been given, pointing to them as corrective measures that were ineffective, the most egregious time being when I was on suspension and interfered with an investigation, which resulted in the death of one hundred and twelve innocent bystanders at the St. Louis Cathedral.

There was a note from Governor Talubee's staff stating that none of the citizens died as a result of my actions and thousands of lives, including the Pope's, were saved because I was the only police officer on scene. They left out the fact that Sergeant Drake was there, I'm sure it was meant to minimize the collateral damage to the department.

It seemed that my good buddy, Councilman Jefferson, had finally been able to get back at me for detaining him last fall. The councilman was the one who'd requested the formal investigation into my police misconduct, based on tips from anonymous sources who said I was a troublemaker.

Bullshit. The 'tips' were his own personal vendetta against me for exposing his adultery to his wife.

I'd read and reread the file while I lay in bed. Termination was just a recommendation, it still needed to go to the board of police chiefs and the mayor, so I was still a cop. As long as I was a cop, I would do my duty to defend the city and her people.

"It's just a goddamned report," I grumbled, slapping my hand on my phone where the pages were stored. "Karimov is a threat to this city and I sure as hell have a score to settle with that bastard."

"Exactly," Drake rumbled. "You have a *score* to settle. You always have a score to settle. That's why you're in this trouble, Detective Forrest. Maybe you should sit this one out. That might look better in the eyes of the district chiefs' panel if you take the time to allow others to do their job."

He had a point. If I let Fairchild's SWAT team go in and clear the Dockyards, the panel would see that I was taking the Internal Affairs recommendation to heart and following the straight and narrow. I could potentially save my career if I followed the rules and colored within the lines.

But I couldn't let it go. This was my investigation, from start to finish, and I intended to see it through.

"What did you find at the Ortega house?" I asked.

Drake's smile stretched from ear to ear. "We found the murder weapon. Forensics agreed that as far as they could tell, the pneumatic disks came from that handgun versus one of the rifles. Also…"

He pulled out his own phone and tapped a few keys, projecting an image between us. It was a bunch of lines of text. "This is Ortega's journal. He was stupid enough to write stuff down; had it in chapter format like he was going to publish an autobiography or something."

"Can I see that?" I asked, reaching for the phone. I couldn't read the words on the projection.

Drake handed it over wordlessly. I read for a few minutes, and agreed with his assessment. Ortega was trying to get himself published. His journal recorded that he'd also been having an affair with Henderson and had learned of Karimov's involvement in the synthaine production. He wanted in on it and Karimov refused. Henderson sided with Karimov, breaking things off with Ortega. I'd been right. Henderson's murder was a crime of passion. Ortega couldn't come to terms with the fact that he wasn't up to par with Karimov.

It still left the question of why Terri Solomon's thugs had tried to kill Karimov, though. The connection didn't make sense—yet. I'd figure it out in time.

"What did the cyborgs have to say about this?" I wondered aloud.

"Nobody's talked to them yet."

"What? Who's the city got on this while I'm out?"

"Sanders, again," he replied. "He's been pretty busy with the Dockyard hostage situation. All of us have."

I rolled my eyes. "That idiot couldn't investigate his way out of a pillow fort."

I flipped through several pages of love poems and shit like that, most of them directed at Dale Henderson. "Something about this isn't right," I stated. "Why would he keep all of this evidence in a journal where we could find it?"

Drake stretched out his hand, open palm up. "May I?"

I passed him the phone and he tapped the screen a few times. Soon, another picture appeared between us. It was a framed computer programming degree from MIT bearing the name Carlos Ortega.

"So?"

"The son of a bitch thought he was better than anyone else," Drake stated. "He *was* damn good. It took our techs about six hours to break his encryption. This journal was buried deep down; you and me wouldn't have found it, but the techies noticed keystroke patterns that pointed to a hidden folder. I'm not sure what he was planning on doing with it since it would implicate him in several crimes, but he was meticulous."

"Narcissistic fuckwad," I surmised.

"Yeah, that was my assessment as well," Drake deadpanned. "So you see, the case is wrapped up, even with Sanders on the job. You can stay here and get some rest."

Maybe it was all wrapped up like he said. The only outliers were *why* the cyborgs had shot up the Liquid Genesis and arresting Karimov, who'd tried to kill me. I wanted revenge, but that was part of why I was in the trouble I was in. Not every action needed to be avenged. Fairchild could handle this guy.

Besides, I felt like I was ninety. The genetic regeneration wasn't fully complete. My calf muscle felt fully healed, an unintended beneficiary of the treatment on my hip, but everything else was still not completely healed. I could use another day of lying on my back and letting the process play out. Lord knows I deserved some time off.

"Goddammit, Drake. Maybe you're right," I relented. "I should be smart and let someone else handle things for a while."

One of Drake's massive paws slapped down on the bedside railing. "That's what I'm talkin' about. Following the doctor's orders, allowing others to do their jobs, *and* listening to some sound advice—who are you and what have you done with Zachary Forrest?"

"Funny, Drake," I replied. "I'm right here. But like you said, maybe I should try to show some restraint if I want to keep my job."

"That's good advice," he chuckled. "Who could have given that to you?"

°254°

"Okay, I admit it. You gave me some good advice."

"You're welcome."

"Oh! Thanks," I said, realizing he wanted an acknowledgement.

"No prob—"

A soft knock on the door to my room cut him off. He glanced at me and I shook my head; I wasn't expecting anyone.

Drake walked over to the door and rested his hand on the grip of his pistol as he pulled the door open. There were some whispers that I couldn't make out and then he reappeared. "Ah, Detective? You have a visitor…and I think it's time for me to leave. You know, paperwork and such."

He stepped out of the way and Katheryn appeared behind him.

"Hi, Zach," Katheryn said with an awkward wave of her hand once my partner had left.

"Katheryn," I replied guardedly. Our last interaction at the NOPD headquarters had been civil and even friendly, I wasn't sure how I felt about her yet—and hadn't had time to think about it. On the one hand, she tried to entrap me to strengthen the case against me. On the other, she'd been ordered to do it and came clean with me. It still didn't alleviate the sense of betrayal I'd felt when I learned she was a cop.

"Thank you for the flowers."

"You're welcome," I replied without thinking about it.

"I heard about what happened," she motioned toward the bed.

"You can come in. I won't bite," I assured her.

"Even with the report?"

She looked like she was going to vomit. "Are you okay?" I asked.

"No." She hesitated and then walked across the room quickly. "I'm not okay, Zach." She sat in the chair Drake had previously occupied. "What they're doing to you is wrong. It makes me sick."

I shrugged, attempting to show more nonchalance than I felt. "It is what it is. There's nothing I can do about their findings. Everything listed in there is true, even if they chose to downplay the good parts of why I've done the things that I've done."

"Exactly," she replied. "They mention that your actions resulted in arrests and things like that, but no emphasis is placed on anything except the negative. Smith and Jones have it out for you. It doesn't matter what anyone said, they had a predetermined outcome in their minds and that's what went into the report."

"Yeah," I sighed. "I know. The only thing I can hope is the panel will read my rebuttal and look at my body of work for the entire time I've been a police officer, and not place as much emphasis on the findings of a bunch of pencil-dicked, paper-pushing IA fuckers."

I stopped, remembering too late that Katheryn was one of those pencil-dicked, paper-pushing IA fuckers. "Sorry. I know what you do is important most of the time."

"It is, but I understand your frustration and lack of faith in the system. Hell, I would too if I were in your shoes and the department was hanging me out to dry…which, is why I wanted to come see you."

"You mean you didn't want to stop by and see the wonders of modern medicine patching me up before your very eyes?"

She laughed half-heartedly. "No—I mean, yes! I wanted to make sure you were okay, and see if you needed anything. But, I have some information about the case that you may not be aware of."

I frowned, wondering what news she had that I didn't know about. "What is it?"

"The district chiefs' panel met this morning."

"And?" I asked, already knowing the answer. I didn't know her that well, but I didn't think she'd be stalling if it were good news.

"The chiefs voted almost unanimously in favor of termination. Ten-to-one. Only your chief, Brubaker, voted to retain you."

She blubbered for a moment and then burst out in tears. "Zach, I'm so sorry."

"*Hmpf*," I grunted, not feeling as hurt as I'd expected I would. I felt numb more than grief at the prospect of losing my job and no longer being a police officer. It sure as hell wasn't where I thought I'd be when I joined the force almost fourteen years ago, but to be honest, I wasn't torn up about it. I had plenty of money set aside since I'd lived well below my means. I'd be fine on the financial front. Emotionally, though, that may be a different story as time wore on.

Besides, I told myself. *The politics of the department are exhausting. I'm fine with the outcome.*

But I still wanted to bust Karimov.

"Who else knows about the findings?" I asked.

"As far as I know, only the chiefs and IA detectives know about it. Chief Brubaker is supposed to issue a formal one-month notice to you immediately."

"So, regardless of what happens, I'm still a cop for another month?"

"Yeah. It's meant as a transition period to give you time to settle your accounts and get everything ready for your life after public service."

I threw aside the thin hospital cover and ripped out the IV line stuck in the side of my thigh. The nurse had said something about a nerve blocker and pain medication, but I didn't have time for that bullshit. I was about to have all the time in the world for recovery.

"What are you doing?" Katheryn asked.

"I'm going out to the Dockyards to arrest Karimov while I'm still a police officer," I said.

"That's not the intention of the notice, Zach. If you do that, you may end up getting fired outright without a severance."

I paused. The severance package would include money, obviously, but also some type of medical coverage for a few months as well as retaining my firearms licenses. If I went out there to settle a personal vendetta, I could lose it all. Was arresting Karimov that important?

"You're goddamn right it is," I answered myself aloud.

"Huh?" she asked in confusion.

"Nothing," I replied, testing my legs' ability to hold my weight.

Karimov was behind one of the worst drug epidemics the city had seen in decades, and was responsible for the rise in Easytown's cyborg explosion since he paid for them to be made to protect his budding empire. I couldn't pin any murders to him directly, but he sure as hell *tried* to kill me with a forklift. That was enough.

"I haven't been officially notified of anything," I reminded her. "As far as I know, the police chiefs haven't even met yet, so I'm within my jurisdiction to follow through on this case."

"You're playing with fire, Zach."

I cast about the room searching for my clothes, finally finding a bag marked "**Patient Belongings**" in a cabinet. It was extremely light when I picked it up.

"Aww, what the hell?" I grumbled, looking inside. The bag contained only my Oxfords, socks, and wallet. My weapons were missing. So were my pants and shirt.

I limped back to the bed and pressed the nurse call button. After a full thirty-second wait with no response from the nurse, I ripped the IV from my wrist, blood oozed from the hole where the catheter had been. Alarm bells began to chime, bringing the nurse almost immediately.

"Mr. Forrest!" the nurse exclaimed. "Do you need to go to the restroom? Your ah..." He glanced at Katheryn and took a step closer, lowering his voice. "Your catheter will drain the fluid for you."

"What?" I said, reaching down and pulling up the bottom of my hospital gown. A tube ran from a bag taped to my leg into the head of my penis. My guest whirled around when she saw my dick. "Oh, goddamn it. Pull this thing out of me. I'm leaving."

The nurse put a restraining hand on my chest. "You better remove that if you want to keep it," I hissed.

"Zach!" Katheryn said, having turned back around, despite the intense rosy color of embarrassment plainly splashed across her cheeks.

"I... Ah, okay," the nurse said, taking his hand away quickly. "But, you can't leave, Mr. Forrest. See," he pointed to the bedside monitor. "You've only received about eighty percent of your regenerative genetic stimulation treatment—that was what you were getting intravenously before you tore it out. Without the remaining twenty percent, you may have a pronounced limp for the rest of your life."

I turned and tapped the IV bag. "This the remaining twenty percent?"

"It'll take that one and another bag to complete this series of stem cell administration, and then we need to provide the radiation treatment to force the cells to mutate and repair themselves."

I held out my arm, blood dripped to the floor from where it had ran down my hand. "Put the IV back in and go get that machine. I'll be ready for the second bag by the time you get back. I'm leaving in thirty minutes, one way or another."

"Mr. Forrest, please."

"No. I have buddies that could be getting shot right now. I need this to be over."

"I can't authorize an early release."

I jabbed my arm at him again. "Put the IV back in and go get that machine."

"This is highly irregular, sir."

"Welcome to my life. Just hook me back up."

He complied, quickly sterilizing a spot further up my forearm from where the initial IV had been and inserted the catheter. He began to tape it off when I stopped him. "Don't bother. Just go get that machine."

"Don't tell me how to do my job," he countered. "I'm going to tape it off so you don't rip it out."

I relented and he taped the head of the catheter against my arm, then hooked the IV drip back into the catheter. "Now, how do you—"

"Like this," I said, knowing what he was going to say. I grabbed the IV bag from the hook and began squeezing, forcing the fluid from the bag faster than it would have flowed normally.

"Mr. Forrest, I don't think—"

"It's fine. We used to give IVs to each other all the time in the academy. Forcing it is okay as long as you don't blow out the vein. Now, *please*, go get that machine."

He mumbled something to himself, and rushed out the door. Katheryn gave me a dirty look and followed him into the hall. I could hear them talking for a few seconds, but couldn't make out the words that they said.

She returned alone. "He's going to get the mutation device. Neither of us think forcing the IV is the best thing."

"I'm giving the guy the benefit of the doubt by staying until this is done," I replied. "I could just leave."

"And never be able to walk pain free again," she reminded me. "It's not really a good option."

"I'll take what I can get."

"So you're still gonna go down there?"

"You're goddamned right I am," I replied. "I'm going to get Karimov, one way or another."

"I don't like it, Zach."

"You don't have to like it. I'm doing it."

"Why are you like this?" she asked, clenching her hands at her sides. "It's maddening."

"Because I have a sense of duty."

"Your sense of duty has gotten you kicked off the police force! Your sense of duty has gotten you beat up, stabbed, run over, and shot. Your sense of duty has pushed away every woman who's been interested in you. Have you ever thought about that?"

I shook my head. "That's just who I am. I have to see this through."

"No, you don't. There's an entire SWAT team in position to raid the Dockyards, as well as two precincts' worth of uniformed cops surrounding that place. *You* don't have to do anything except try to recover."

"I'll get this guy and then take a few days of down time."

"You are such an arrogant asshole," she stated, surprising me. "You have such an inflated sense of self-worth that you think all of those other cops aren't going to be able to stop Karimov." She turned and grasped the door handle before I could reply.

Then she walked out of my life.

EIGHTEEN: SATURDAY

I ran my wrist over the credit scanner to pay the taxi and stepped out into the rain. I didn't have a jacket or an umbrella since it'd been sunny on the day I was MEDEVAC'd by the police drone. I wore clothes from the donation pile and somehow, I'd lost my phone, so I wasn't able to contact Andi or the Jeep. Thankfully, the hospital security had both my service pistol and the Aegis. I'd have been screwed if I lost either of those.

It felt strange going to a case, or more appropriately, into combat, without Andi there beside me for instant updates and information gathering. It was the second time in as many months where I'd been without her assistance since I'd had to go off the net during the clone case as well.

For a guy who hates tech, you're awfully dependent upon it, a voice whispered in the back of my head.

It was true. While I hadn't been totally lost without her help, it had made that case much harder. I hoped that I didn't run into any situations where I needed her today.

I made my way through several layers of police security, flashing my badge and submitting to a facial scan at each checkpoint. Several officers patted me on the back, congratulating me on my speedy recover, while others scowled at me for being the source of their twenty-four hour duty on the perimeter of a major hostage situation. Finally, I made it to the Easytown Mobile Command Unit.

The MCU was a massive wheeled hoverskiff variant, designed to provide real-time command and control to high-profile situations. The unwieldy beast was better suited for driving down the four-lane freeway than the crowded alleys of Easytown or of flying gracefully through the air, but it *could* do both, bringing the command suite to where it was needed most.

Right now, the damn thing was simply a place for wet cops to get out of the rain and have a cup of coffee.

"I don't care what they're demanding," Brubaker shouted from his office far in the back of the MCU. "We aren't negotiating with those dickwads. You hear me? No negotiations."

"That's not how a hostage situation works, Chief Brubaker," a male voice I hadn't heard before replied.

I stood on my tiptoes to see if I could figure out who it was back in the office with him, but I couldn't make him out. The only thing I could see was the back of a blond head with short, styled hair and the shoulders of a dark blue or black suit. Brubaker glanced beyond the man and I ducked back down to avoid being seen by him.

The only reason I'd come to the MCU was to get the latest intel on the situation. Otherwise, I'd have just gone to Warehouse Six and made my stand. It wasn't a great plan, hell, it wasn't even a smart one, but frontal assaults were my specialty.

Like I said, I spent a lot of time in the hospital, and the NOPD Officer's Union insurance plan worked on overdrive for me.

I wondered what I'd do as a replacement once I was let go. I examined vidscreens and maps on the walls of the

MCU while I listened passively to the officers manning the communications systems.

Lieutenant Fairchild's SWAT team was in position around Warehouse Six, where they believed the bulk of the hostages to be. Snipers were on top of the shipping container walls, ready to engage any threat they scoped.

Our electronic countermeasures unit had also been called into play. The defensive team was actively jamming all signals coming from or going into the Dockyards that weren't from a police radio, while the offensive team had tapped into the building's security systems and watched everything that Karimov's people did. They hadn't seen Karimov in several hours, though, and a rumor circulated that he'd somehow managed to slip the net.

I doubted it. There had to be another explanation. The guy had been able to run his synthaine operation from here, without anyone finding out about it except Ortega—that I knew of. In reality, I had no idea how many people he'd killed since Branch Corrigan wasn't much of a talker while he tortured people in his videos.

Two of the MCU's vidscreens held images of the Dockyards. One was a real time satellite feed showing Warehouse Six and the immediate area that switched between thermal and naked eye views intermittently, while the other was of the registered blueprints from when the buildings were originally built.

I studied the satellite thermal image view for a while. I saw hundreds of heat signatures inside the warehouse, but it was nearly impossible to tell who was a hostage and who was a hostage taker. With few exceptions, all of the signatures were a giant blob of white.

When the screen switched back to the normal view, I examined the warehouse from above. Nothing really stood out as special or a place where a sniper could conceal themselves to fire at the SWAT guys as they advanced. I *did* note how the placement of the shipping containers resembled a series of concentric half-circles with the ends terminating at the water's edge.

The city had a token riverine force, primarily used for fishing bodies out of the Mississippi. It wasn't capable of transporting part of the SWAT team in stealth for an amphibious attack. They could stop some of the criminals from escaping by boat though, which is why they were currently arrayed as a blocking force out toward the Gulf, and one of the reasons why I didn't think that Karimov had escaped.

Not that they'd be able to do anything if Karimov's people got in one of those big cargo ships, I mused. They'd slice right through those trawlers like a hot knife through butter.

Besides noting that my Jeep was still where I'd parked it, there wasn't much else to see on the satellite imagery, so I switched my attention to the blueprints. There were several places highlighted on the screen, indicating possible points of entry for the SWAT breaching team. I studied the blueprints for almost ten minutes without anything jumping out at me. There were no secret underground tunnels connecting warehouses or hidden rooms where people could ride out a hurricane until the storm passed—although, I'm not sure why I'd thought that was even an option. The water table down here was so high that a hole filled with water after only eighteen inches, probably even worse right next to the water.

I nudged one of the officers scrolling through additional imagery and cross-referencing it with MainFrame data to determine if there were options that no one was seeing here in the MCU. "Any luck finding a way in that doesn't involve getting a bunch of hostages killed?"

"Not yet, Detective," she replied, noting the golden badge I'd pinned to my belt.

I could tell that she didn't want to be bothered, but I needed to know who was talking to Brubaker, so I asked her.

"FBI hostage negotiator," she replied tersely.

"Ah. Makes sense." I stepped back. "Thanks for the info."

"Sure," she said without missing a beat as she continued to scroll through the data. I began to turn to see if there was something else in the MCU that would give me inspiration to break the stalemate at the Dockyards when something on the officer's screen caught my eye and I edged closer.

"Excuse me, sir," she said, sliding her shoulders out of the way so my wet clothing wouldn't touch her.

"Sorry," I replied, easing back slightly. "Can you scroll through those historical satellite images again?"

"I've been through them fifteen times," she stated. "There's nothing here."

"Can you just humor me, please?"

"Sure. Why not, I'm not going anywhere until this thing is over anyways."

She began advancing the images, spaced about twenty-four hours apart; some more, some less, including several nighttime shots. Ships came and went at the piers, most often unloaded and reloaded within the time between images. By the time she'd gone through thirty images in the space of two minutes, I was convinced about what I'd seen.

"Go to the satellite image from the moment we learned about the hostage situation."

Another glance over her shoulder at my badge; she was trying to determine whether or not to follow my instructions. After a few seconds of deliberation, she typed in the command and advanced the images a few times, then began reversing them until she came to where she started.

"Son of a bitch!" I whooped. "He's on that old cargo ship across the channel."

Sure enough, in all of the images, a rusty cargo ship had been docked across the channel from Warehouse Six. I'd noticed several boats pulled up alongside the old dock and trucks parked at various times of the day and night at the end of the jetty.

"Forrest? You're supposed to be in the hospital," Chief Brubaker's voice erupted from down the hallway.

I pointed at the satellite image on the MCU's vidscreen, realizing that the cargo ship wasn't in view. "Chief, I know where Karimov is. Probably where the synthaine production facility is too."

"What do you mean you know where he is?" Brubaker said, pushing his way through the press of bodies inside the command unit. "You're telling me he isn't in Warehouse Six with the rest of his people and the hostages?"

"I don't think he is," I replied, shaking my head.

I waited for him to get through the crowd and then pointed to the smaller vidscreen in front of the female officer. "Can you go back a few weeks and then begin moving forward?" She complied and I pointed at the old cargo ship while she advanced the images slowly. "That ship has been moored up on the jetty across from the warehouse for several months, maybe longer, I'm not sure. See how every day new container ships come in, get unloaded and leave, while that thing stays there?"

"Sure, but—Wait, there are boats and trucks coming and going to it, but it never leaves."

I smiled. Chief Brubaker still had the gift for investigative work. "That's right. Then, right around the time that the standoff began, some smaller boats made their way from the warehouse side toward that bigger boat. Obviously, we can't see where they go since this is just a photograph that happened to be taken at the right time, but I'd be willing to bet a few weeks' pay that they went to that cargo ship."

"Our analysts have been staring at this place for almost forty-eight hours and haven't seen shit. You sneak in here, soaking wet, and figure it out in a few minutes." He looked up from the screen to me. "Who does the boat belong to?"

"Uh… I hadn't gotten that far yet, Chief."

He patted the female officer on the shoulder. "Get on that, Gracie. Find out who owns that boat and what its story is."

She nodded, gritting her teeth so hard that the muscle along her jaw threatened to jump from her skin.

"Come on, Forrest. We have a few things to talk about."

"I've got some bad news for you, Zach," Chief Brubaker stated once he'd closed the door to his tiny office in the MCU. It was the first time I could remember him calling me by my given name instead of my last name.

"If it's about the district chiefs' panel vote, I already know."

"You do?" he asked, seeming genuinely surprised.

"Yeah. Someone from Internal Affairs notified me this morning."

"Those sonsabitches," he groused. "They weren't supposed to notify you; I was. Probably sent a courier droid with a message to the hospital, didn't they?"

"No, it's not like that, Chief. IA didn't officially notify me. A friend of mine works there and she came to the hospital to tell me what the results were."

He scowled. "Your friend? You mean that skirt they sent to entrap you? She shouldn't have told you anything; it wasn't her place."

"If she hadn't, I'd still be at the hospital and you wouldn't have a potential lead," I countered.

"Okay, granted. Now, go back to the hospital and finish your treatment so you don't come back and sue the department in a few months when you develop health complications due to inadequate treatment."

"I received the full treatment," I replied, omitting the part where the doctor had told me he wasn't sure it would take since I'd flooded ten hours' worth of stem cells into my bloodstream in twenty minutes. Details.

"Okay, then go home and rest up. I'm sure they gave you a mandatory rest period in your discharge instructions."

"I didn't stick around to get the discharge instructions. This is my case and I'm gonna see it through before I get fired for all the other times I've done my job."

He looked as if I'd slapped him in the face. "I tried, you know. They were dead-set on making an example of you to keep the officers in their precincts in line."

I stopped him with raised hands. "Chief, it's okay. I'm fine with it. I saw the writing on the wall a few months ago when I had to speak to IA about my inadvertent violation of the Immorality Clause. They had a hard-on to nail me to the wall; it just took a little longer than they'd expected. When I found out Katheryn was IA, I knew the outcome."

"Regardless, I'm sorry, Forrest. Damn piss poor way to run an organization."

"Really? That's how it's been the entire time I've been a cop."

"That's a shitty memory of your time as a police officer," he grunted.

"It is what it is, Chief."

He picked at his fingernail for a moment before replying. "I should relieve you of all your current investigations to let you finalize any outstanding reports and to prepare a transition brief for your replacement."

"Who's that gonna be?"

"Doug Sanders, from the—"

"I know the cocksucker," I said, cutting him off. "He's a shitty detective, Chief. He didn't even get statements from the witnesses at the Liquid Genesis when all those people were shot by the cyborgs."

He nodded and shrugged. "I can't help it, Forrest. I need an interim guy, and until I can grow somebody of my own choosing from within my precinct, I'm stuck with the department's castoffs. You were supposed to be my guy for another ten to fifteen years."

It was my turn to shrug. "I didn't ask for this." Somehow, I was still surprisingly unfazed by the revelation that I'd been fired and wouldn't have a job in a month.

"I know you didn't," Chief Brubaker replied. "For what it's worth, I'm sorry."

"Don't," I said. "Don't cheapen yourself by apologizing for something that you didn't have any control over."

He grunted again and said, "So, what's your idea on how to get Karimov?"

I laid out the basics of my idea, pitching the concept of a classic feint, and glad that he didn't try to patronize me with further attempts at an apology.

It felt good to be doing something, even if it was, most likely, my last official act as a cop.

NINETEEN: SUNDAY

I yawned against the back of my hand. It was past midnight and I was in position on the jetty opposite the warehouse where the hostages were being held. Arresting Karimov was a secondary objective for the department. Safely rescuing those hostages was the primary mission, but the chief had enough faith in my theory and respect for me as a cop that he'd assigned Drake, Collins and O'Brien, who were members of the SWAT team, and one of their drones to come with me. He'd also re-tasked a sniper from the other side of the port to assist, which I wasn't thrilled about since they were shooting *toward* me.

We'd scanned the boat several times. Thermal imaging told us that there were two humans in a room on the top deck, probably Karimov's security element, and several more standing or sitting at various locations below decks, plus another ten in the bottom of the boat. I thought those were likely workers producing the synthaine, or maybe a few more hostages, I couldn't be sure until we went in.

I'd been here for almost three hours, waiting for things to kick off. Drake mentioned on more than one occasion that today was Mothers' Day and tomorrow was Memorial Day, both of which he was supposed to be off of work for. I couldn't help but think he blamed me for screwing up his schedule since I'd sought out Karimov when I did. I'd have to take things like holidays into consideration when I wasn't a cop anymore.

Finally, it sounded like Lieutenant Fairchild's teams were ready to breach the building and put an end to this hostage situation once and for all. The mayor was coming down hard on the department to resolve the issue before the FBI completely took control of the situation by bringing in their Hostage Rescue Team. He didn't want the first crisis that he faced as the city's new mayor to be yanked away from his control by the federal government.

Stupid politicians, I mused, listening idly to the police chatter on the radio. *They'd put their people in danger, just to make themselves look good for the voters.*

"Chief Brubaker," Lieutenant Fairchild's voice cut through the chatter, silencing everyone. "Alpha Team is in position to follow the breaching team on the eastern side of the building. The department's High Rise Assault Team is ready to enter the warehouse simultaneously from above. Baker Team will breach the front entrance thirty seconds after Alpha and H-RAT go in. All we need is your word to go."

"Roger that, Lieutenant," Brubaker replied. "I have to get final authorization from the commissioner. Wait one."

I relaxed slightly. We would enter the old cargo ship at the back ramp during the commotion across the water. The pause gave me a little bit more time to think about the findings of the report and the decision by the district chiefs' panel to fire me.

The more I thought about my situation, the better I felt. Being a cop had defined me for far too long, and I'd gotten nothing but pain and misery out of it. True, I'd helped ease the suffering of thousands of people over the years since I busted criminals, but I rarely interacted with any of those I'd supposedly helped.

As I waited, quietly contemplating my future, I'd decided that the interaction with victims, their friends, and families was the part I was missing. I didn't see the final results of my hard work from that perspective; I just saw whether the case was solved or not. It wasn't truly satisfying work—which may have attributed to my inability to start, or more recently keep, a relationship.

I also thought about what Chief Brubaker had told me at the scene of the latest murder at the Regal Eagle, the one where I got stabbed after the medical examiner's droids left. He'd said, *"You know the deal. She was a prostitute. Don't spend too much time on this one."*

Looking at it objectively, as a cop who was constantly running out of time and resources, I understood where the chief was coming from. But as a person who was sworn to protect the population of New Orleans—*all* of the population—it was a shitty way of doing business. That girl's family deserved justice as much as the rich businessman's family did.

I knew what the next chapter of my life would be and I had roughly four weeks to get it set up. There were licenses to obtain, space to rent, advertisements to place…hell, *furniture* to purchase. I needed Andi to begin working on everything immediately, but I was still without my phone and without a way to contact her.

"Lieutenant Fairchild, this is Chief Brubaker," the chief's voice came over the radio.

"We're listening, Chief," she replied.

"You are authorized to move forward with the hostage rescue. This authorization is straight from City Hall."

"Understood, sir. We are a go for the rescue."

"Good luck, Lieutenant."

I tapped Drake on the arm and he tapped the officer next to him, and he did the same to O'Brien. We moved around the old shipping container and jogged lightly down the jetty toward the boat where I'd determined Karimov had holed up. The drone lifted skyward, flying silently fifty feet above us.

An explosion from the vicinity of the warehouse meant SWAT had breached as planned. A quick glance upward saw several dark shapes rappelling from a large, black hoverskiff. They disappeared quickly. "H-RAT is inside," I whispered as we ran, the sounds of gunfire reaching us from across the water.

Suddenly, the jetty exploded with bright, white light from several floodlights. "Shit!" I cursed, diving to the ground and crawling rapidly toward a large round pillar that held one of the offending lights. The damn things must have been motion activated, or more likely, on a laser tripwire that could be turned on and off from inside the ship. It wouldn't do to illuminate your delivery drivers trying to sneak away with several cases of synthaine.

We did our best to hide from view of anyone watching from the boat, but it was pointless. Even if we'd had proper cover, the three camera drones they launched spotted us before the SWAT drone fried their circuits with a burst of electricity, knocking them out of the sky.

"Can you do something about those lights?" I asked Collins.

"Yeah, hold on." He tapped a command into the small flexscreen display on his forearm and the drone shot forward. A probing rod extended from the bottom of it, and as it flew rapidly along the jetty, the rod smashed into the floodlights, shattering them one-by-one. Once again the small strip of land was plunged into darkness and silence.

It didn't last long.

The rhythmic chugging of a pneumatic rifle filled the night as someone from the ship fired into the drone. Sparks rained down on us from the impacts overhead. The drones could take a lot of damage, but I'd seen firsthand how those discs had destroyed one in a matter of minutes.

"We need to assault now!" I shouted.

O'Brien shook his head. "I called for backup. We should pull back and wait until they get here."

"And create another standoff? No way," I said. "We go now!"

I emphasized my words by sliding around the pole and running toward the boat. A sharp jolt of pain in my hip caused me to catch my breath.

Apparently, I wasn't fully healed.

I continued to run through the pain with a slight hitch in my gait; stopping in the open meant certain death if the defenders on the boat saw me. I dodged left and right, avoiding imaginary bullets from the security element as they continued to fire at the drone overhead.

I made it to the bottom of the gangplank leading to the boat before anyone spotted me. A shout of alarm from above me was answered by a burst of automatic weapons' fire. I threw myself sideways, almost falling into the water. Then the gunfire went silent.

"One hostile down," the voice of our sniper, Blevins, reported over the radio. "I see the weapon of another one, but can't get a shot on him."

"Shoot the damn weapon!" I ordered.

"Roger."

The sound of a ricocheting bullet was followed immediately by a howl of anger. One of the SWAT guys, I couldn't tell which, rushed past me up the gangplank as I struggled with the awkward footing. The other officer followed quickly.

By the time I'd made it up the narrow bridge, the SWAT guys had a muscular cyborg in handcuffs. He wasn't as big as Corrigan, but he'd been given the same treatment. One arm was replaced by the pneumatic rifle, which had a hole in the air reservoir. Collins and O'Brien had handcuffed his remaining wrist to his ankle and the disabled weapon to the ship's railing. I ripped away the rubber air hoses from his weapon arm for good measure.

The remains of a second man lay on the deck. Most of his face was a grotesque pink splay of flesh and teeth since the sniper's bullet had taken him in the back of the head. The corpse still held a heavy machine gun.

"Thank you," I said into the radio, waving toward the Dockyards where I knew the sniper was watching us. "He'd have wiped us out."

"No problem," Blevins answered.

I reported up to Chief Brubaker that we'd encountered resistance, but were now on the boat with no injuries to police officers. He acknowledged tersely, which meant he was probably more concerned with the hostage rescue at the moment than my hair-brained belief that the manufacture, shipment, and sale of the nation's synthaine supply was occurring right under everyone's noses on a boat in the Easytown Dockyards channel.

"What's the drone say about movement?" I asked Collins.

He tapped his computer and a shaky thermal image appeared between us, filled with static. The drone had taken some serious damage from the miniature saw blades and I was impressed that it was still flying.

I examined the holograph closely while Drake and O'Brien guarded our flank. I saw our four heat signatures crouched down behind one of the life rafts and the two guards, one of which was not nearly as warm as the other since his lifeblood covered the deck. The workers on the bottom decks hadn't changed positions, but it looked like some of the others had. I wasn't sure if they were moving up to intercept us or if they'd simply moved as a normal security rotation. We hadn't heard any type of audible alarm system, but that didn't mean there wasn't one sounding below decks where we couldn't hear it.

"Can you do a side-by-side compare with the original image—the one we took before we left our last position?"

"Sure. Hold on."

I tried to ignore what seemed to be his catchphrase. Collins said 'hold on' to just about everything and it was becoming annoying. He tapped the flexscreen on his forearm while I *held on.*

"Here you go," he said as an image superimposed over the first. "I changed the heat signature colors to red in the original image so you'd be able to compare it to the white ones in the live feed."

"Good thinking," I replied. Most of the figures I'd thought were guards earlier had stayed roughly in the same place on all but the first two decks below us. Those two had each moved to a position in easy view of the stairwell. "It's a good bet that they know we're here."

"The reports from those machine guns probably echoed throughout this old metal tub," Drake said tapping the deck with his index finger. "If they *don't* know we're here, then they're idiots."

"We should probably wait for backup, Detective," O'Brien chimed in once again. "I don't know how we're supposed to make it down those stairs alive, let alone eight sets of them."

The guards below hadn't moved, they were waiting for us to enter the fatal funnel—the kill zone inside an entrance where it was impossible to seek cover when an officer assaulted a position. A terrible idea crept into my head, one that could earn me the death penalty if I was wrong.

"Collins, I need the ship's dimensions from your drone."

He looked at me strangely, and then said, "Okay. Hold on."

"You want to what?" Brubaker asked after I'd called him for permission to move forward with my idea.

"It'll force them to evacuate and we can grab them as they come out," I answered. "Otherwise, we've got to go down and get them. That's probably going to get a lot of people killed."

"How do you know they won't stay down there and drown?"

That was the part of my plan that worried me. If the workers down below were somehow restrained or locked in the section where they were at right now, then it was all over. The water depth was fifty-three feet, which meant the first six decks would sit below the waterline when it was all said and done. That left two decks that wouldn't be flooded, but I was betting Karimov's people would panic and try to get off the boat.

"I can't guarantee that they'll evacuate," I replied honestly. "I'm willing to take the responsibility for my actions if they don't."

"Goddamn it, Forrest. Switch over to channel eight and encrypt for Denver Seven One," he ordered.

I did as requested and several moments later, the chief's voice came over the new encrypted radio frequency. In theory, we should have been the only ones on the channel, but anyone who'd been listening to our conversation could have dialed in using his instructions.

"This isn't some bullshit way to get yourself incarcerated, is it?" he asked.

"What? No. Why the hell—"

"Because you were just notified of your termination and you're staring down the barrel of unemployment."

"No, Chief. I've got a plan for my next job. I'd never do something as stupid as that."

"You've done things almost as dumb, Forrest. I don't want a bunch of innocent lives on our hands. We can request federal assistance for this mission. The US Navy has teams who do ship takedowns all the time."

"I thought the mayor wanted to keep this local," I said.

"Screw the mayor. If we can make this go away without further loss of life, then that's the option I'd prefer."

"How long would it take to get them here?" I asked rhetorically. "Twenty-four, forty-eight hours? Plus mission prep time. Chief, I can end this in less than an hour. I just need two police drones and my Aegis. Stopping the synthaine flow will be the second-biggest win for the Easytown Precinct in history." I said it that way to remind him that I'd saved the Pope's life, by far the most important act in the NOPD's long history. It was also a reminder that my actions had gone against the NOPD's conventional thinking since they'd thought they'd stopped the threat when they arrested Harold Wilson.

"I'm not sure, Forrest. If you're wrong, this will come down on me as well."

"Chief, we've already lost six officers to these people in the last few days. How many more do we have to lose before we take action and put an end to it?"

There was silence on the other end for what seemed like an eternity while Brubaker deliberated. Finally, he replied, "Alright. I'm sending you two of the drones from the security perimeter. Communicate with them on this frequency."

"Thank you, Ch—"

"Don't thank me. Just end this. Now."

TWENTY: SUNDAY

I called up the drones that Brubaker sent over from across the channel and tried to tell them what I needed, but it didn't work. I'd never tried to give a drone such a complicated task before, and most of the time, Andi had acted as an intermediary, converting my instructions into a language the drones could understand.

I didn't have that option now, so I had to think of simple ways to instruct the drones to do what I'd wanted them to do. It wouldn't be the flawless execution I'd explained to the chief, with me working in tandem with the drones, but we'd make it work.

"Target the first deck, below the water line, six feet from the back of the boat."

"The stern, Detective," O'Brien stated.

"Is that what it's called? I thought it was aft, but decided to say it differently at the last minute."

"Trust me. I practically grew up on my family's sailboat. It's the stern."

"Thanks," I replied. Into the radio, I repeated the instructions with the correct wording. "Target the first deck, below the water line, six feet from the *stern*. One hundred rounds per drone. Once you've fired one hundred rounds, target the second deck six feet from the stern."

I continued on this way until I'd walked the drones up to the eighth deck. "Begin firing now."

The night erupted in a cacophony of sound as the drones fired their miniguns at blazing speed. I didn't have time to think about how fast they were going because I ran to the front of the boat and aimed the Aegis at the deck. I squeezed the trigger as I moved the pistol in a large circle. The decking melted and the circle of metal dropped downward. I heard several more decks collapse in the same manner below me, but I couldn't be sure how many had an entire hole cut away and how many just had a bunch of random laser holes.

I moved several feet away and repeated the process, but the Aegis ran out of charge about three-quarters of the way through another hole in the deck. Once again, I had to hope that the Aegis had penetrated all the way through each of the eight decks and the hull.

I holstered the Aegis and casually walked back to where the others crouched watching the thermal feed from the SWAT drone. Already, the workers on the bottom deck were rushing for the ladders that lead upward to safety. My plan of punching a ton of holes in the hull at the front and back of the boat seemed to be working.

Now we just had to wait and have the drone hit the runners with Taser lines and subdue them.

The boat began to list to the starboard side—thanks for the terminology, O'Brien—and standing was a strain on the calves. I checked the thermal again. The entire bottom deck was vacant except for one person. It looked like they were trying to pick things up as they ran back and forth between the stairs and the center of the ship. *Must be trying to save the synthaine*, I mused.

There was a loud groan of metal bending under the stress of the rushing water and then a screech as part of the boat's stern sheared off. The angle of the boat was further complicated by the water pouring in through the back side, causing the front of the boat to lift higher.

Water had filled the lowest three decks of the boat when the first of the people from below decks appeared at the ship tower's doorway. The droned zapped him right away and he fell, dropping a rifle, to convulse on the deck. The two SWAT officers rushed out, bending forward awkwardly against the angle of the boat, and slapped a pair of handcuffs on him. Once he was secure, they took up a position nearer to the door where they could work in concert with the drone to snatch as many of the bad guys as possible.

One more person fell for it before Karimov's people wised up and refused to come out of the interior. Instead, they began going upward, to the ship's bridge thirty feet above the deck. As I watched this unfold on the thermals, several people burst through the tower doorway. They screamed, running for their lives, scattering like roaches when the lights come on. The drone was able to Taser six of them, but three more ran for the gangway.

"Goddamn it," I groaned, pushing myself up and angling to intercept one of them, a dark-skinned female in a chemical protective suit. Running, I realized that all of the people who'd just emerged were wearing the same type of suit. They must be the workers who produced the drugs in the bottom of the ship.

When she was two feet from me, I dove forward, catching her at the waist along her blind side in a tackle that would have made the defensive coordinator of my beloved

New Orleans Saints proud. She crumpled, folding in half from the force as my momentum carried us to the deck.

Even as I fell, I felt it; the hypersonic displacement of air near my ear.

Then I heard the reports from several rifles above me. I grabbed for the worker's collar, but missed, coming up with only a fistful of hair, and scrabbled backward on my ass toward a metal container on the deck, grimacing at the pain the odd movement caused in my hip. The woman wailed as I drug her by her hair to safety as bullets pinged all around her.

"Forrest!" Drake shouted. "Are you alright?"

I patted myself down before answering. "Yeah, I'm good to go, buddy."

"They shot all the workers," he stated blandly.

I risked a quick glance around the container. The six workers that the drone had detained lay on the deck bleeding along with the two men in handcuffs. The other two workers who'd made a break for the gangway were both face down on the deck several feet from my location. I'd thought the fuckers were shooting at me, but they were shooting the workers instead.

"How many of you are there?" I asked the woman.

"What?"

"How many of you worked down there to manufacture the synthaine?" I clarified.

"Uh…" She ran through a list of names, counting them on her fingers. "Eight, plus me."

"Is there another shift like yours?"

"No. Just us."

"Son of a bitch," I mumbled. Karimov was trying to set himself up for success while he was in prison. I'd heard of prisoners getting filthy rich while they were locked away, then living high on the hog once they were released.

If he could have all of the scientists or workers—I wasn't sure of their role—killed, that left him with the sole knowledge of how to produce the drug. As long as he hadn't killed anyone himself, he could be out in ten-to-fifteen years. And the fucker would be back on top, filling the void in the lives of the hundreds of thousands of synthaine users.

"Do not move," I ordered, grabbing the woman's wrist. "You are the target, not the cops. I mean, they'll shoot us if they get the opportunity, but if you pop your head up, you're dead. Do you understand?"

She nodded while her eyes stared beyond me at the two dead workers she could see from our position behind the crate. "They're *all* dead?"

"Hey!" I snapped my fingers in front of her face. "I need your help."

"What?" she asked in annoyance.

"How many of Karimov's people are there on this boat?"

"Karimov's people?" She seemed confused. "Oh! Let's see, there were one or two guards at each stairway and the two cyborgs up here manning the big guns."

"So, eight to sixteen, plus Karimov?" I asked for clarification. She nodded. "Are there any hostages or workers who are being held against their will?"

Her eyes drifted back to the dead men on the deck. "Are the cyborgs dead?"

"What does it matter?" I asked. "I need you to focus. Is there anyone else in the boat who isn't a hostile?"

"Um… No. I don't think so. Are the cyborgs dead?"

"What's your obsession with the 'borgs, lady?" I tried to imagine what she'd gone through for however long she'd been held and forced myself to answer her question. "One of the cyborgs is dead. The other is incapacitated."

"Where?"

"Over by my partner," I replied.

"You need to kill them," she said so fast that I almost couldn't understand her. "They're planning to blow up city hall."

"What?"

"Karimov is going to blow up city hall. The bottom of this ship had a ton of explosives that they were gathering incrementally for months so no one would notice."

"I think we've put a stop to that," I said smugly.

"Don't be so sure. The explosives were moved a few days ago. Only Karimov has the detonation code." She gestured toward the tower. "He could be entering it now!"

"Shit." I turned toward Drake's position. "Drake!"

"Yeah, Detective?"

"What's the thermal read?"

There was a pause and then, "Fourteen signatures in the tower, all but three of them are outside in a shooting position."

I glanced down and saw a shoe on the deck. It was one of the woman's. "Sorry, but I need to borrow this."

"Hey!" she cried as I tossed it out into the open. Several rounds burrowed into the decking.

"Fuck. Drake!"

"Yeah?"

"I think they have autotrackers."

"No shit," he replied.

"Not good."

"Nope."

"Chief Brubaker," I said into the radio.

"Brubaker," he replied instantly.

I explained the situation to him and the scientist's assertion that everyone else remaining alive were hostile. Then I asked for permission to use the drones.

"I've gotta call that up."

I reminded him of the imminent detonation of a ton of explosives *somewhere* in the city and the fact that four police officers and a non-combatant were pinned down by gunmen with autotracking rifles.

"Goddamn it, Forrest," he reacted, deliberating for a moment with himself or with the FBI man in the room. "You're authorized to use the drones," he sighed.

I gave the instructions to the drones to target all heat signatures in the control tower. They zipped around, changing position every few seconds, firing hundreds of rounds into the tower. The drones followed their orders exactly, terminating every heat signature they discovered.

It was over in three minutes.

When the firing stopped, the woman beside me breathed out heavily and removed her hands from her ears. "Is it over? Are they... Are they dead?"

"Drake, status?"

"According to the thermals, every hostile is down," he shouted back.

"Yes, ma'am. They're all— *Urk!*"

I stared down at my stomach where the woman's hand was wrapped around the handle of a knife embedded there. She withdrew it and stabbed me again. Then, she jabbed it into my chest and I fell sideways to the deck.

Through a blurry haze I saw her take my service pistol and fire several rounds in the direction of Drake and the SWAT officers.

There were cries of pain and alarm from where my partner hid. Then, far away, I heard a splash where she'd jumped the remaining twenty-five feet or so to the water.

My head lolled to the side and I saw a giant running toward me.

"Hold on, Forrest," the giant said. "Hold on. We'll get you out of here."

I had a brief moment to wonder why the giant hadn't crushed my head in his vice-like hands before the blood loss took me and I died.

TWENTY-ONE: FRIDAY

"Ugh… Thon of a bith."

"Zach!" a familiar voice cried. "Oh, thank the Lord you are awake."

"Amir?" I tried to say, but the tube in my mouth made it sound like '*Amhee*' instead of his name.

"My friend, do not try to talk. You have been intubated and in a medical coma for almost a week."

"A weeth?"

I had no memories of what happened beyond getting stabbed. *Did that woman stab me or had I imagined it?* I wondered. Everything was so fuzzy.

"Hold on," Amir said. "I will get the doctors."

It took him a few tries to stand from the chair he'd been in, but then he made it to his feet and set a cup down on the table beside my bed.

He was gone for several minutes, and then returned with a man wearing a lab coat with a stethoscope around his neck.

"Mr. Forrest," he said. "Glad to see you're back with us. You were dead when they brought you in here. Can you believe that?" He held up a hand. "No, don't try to talk. You'll tear your vocal chords with that tube in there—and you've suffered enough."

He picked up the chart at the end of the bed and tapped a few keys, writing on the surface with a stylus he'd pulled from the side. "If they hadn't flown you directly here, we couldn't have done anything for you. As it is, you coded three times after we got your heart restarted and fecal matter from your intestines got into your bloodstream, causing an infection. You're *very* lucky to be alive, Mr. Forrest."

I gestured for the chart. He hesitated, and then handed it over to me. "You've got to understand, we did everything we could."

I stared at the screen. The only thing written on it was the note he'd just taken about me waking for the first time in five days and being mentally alert.

"*Wuth?*"

He looked at the chart. "Oh, sorry." He took it back and tapped the screen in a series of movements, then handed it back to me.

```
Zachary Forrest
35 y/o Caucasian male
NOPD
Admitted 24 May 2099
DOA


Louisiana Health Department
passive monitoring profile:
Previous risk of stroke and/or
liver failure. Positive lifestyle
changes in 2099 contributed to
improvement and subsequent removal
from monitoring service.

-    Defibrillation 5 minutes.
-    Patient revived. Intubated.
```

- Began IV transfusion.
- Coded on way to OR. Revived.
- Began repair to collapsed left lung, patient coded again. Revived.
- Attempted lung re-inflation. Failed.
- Left lung replaced with supplies on hand.
- Began repair to perforated lower intestines. Patient coded.
- Dr. Grantham made decision to replace heart. External stimulation started.
- Patient placed in medicated stasis while DNA imprinted on commercial grade heart muscle.
- Repaired intestinal perforations.

25 May 2099.
- Fecal matter discovered in bloodstream, infection present.
- Administered antibiotic (Ceftaroline) for infection.

26 May 2099.

- Patient's heart arrived 6:12 a.m.
- Heart muscle replaced and operational.
- Patient medically sedated and regenerative genetic stimulation begun.

27 May 2099.
- Patient experiencing severe infection in extremities.
- Infection spreading. Three rounds of antibiotics (Ceftobiprole) administered.
- Patient diagnosed with septicemia.
- Liver failure. Decision to replace liver.
- Ordered liver from ORGCO 2:47 p.m. Requested immediate delivery.

28 May 2099.
- Replacement liver arrived 8:09 a.m.
- Infection reduced in upper extremities; spreading in both legs – severe necrosis.
- Replaced liver.

- Decision to amputate before
  necrosis spreads further.
- Amputated patient's left and
  right legs below the knee.
- Necrosis no longer detected.

29 May 2099.
- Patient awake, first time in 5
  days. Cognitive function
  appears to have returned.

"*Futh me*," I groaned.

"Oh, it isn't *that* bad, Mr. Forrest," the doctor replied, taking the chart off my chest where I'd let it fall when I finished reading. "Lots of people have replacement organs these days, that's not a big deal. And the fact that we were able to save your knee joints means we'll have a much easier time grafting prosthetics to your body. With your own knee joints, your time spent learning to walk again will be greatly reduced."

I gestured for him to come closer. He leaned in and I gripped his lapel as tightly as I could manage.

"*Dwugth.*"

"You've had plenty of drugs recently, Mr. Forrest. It's time to start weening you off of them."

"*Fuck oo, bathawd.*" I groaned and released his coat.

TWENTY-TWO: WEDNESDAY

"I'm fucking pissed off, that's what's wrong, asshole."

"Mr. Forrest, please refrain from cursing at the therapy droid," a voice emitted from the speaker beside the treadmill track.

I leaned heavily against the railing I'd been using to hold myself upright. "I'm not getting the hang of this and your overgrown, talking vacuum cleaner isn't doing much besides saying, 'You can do it.' Seriously, my AI in college was more advanced than this stupid thing."

"*Millions* of people have learned to walk with prosthetics, Mr. Forrest. Are you saying that they have more willpower and coordination than you, a big, bad police officer *hero*?"

"That's your pep talk?" I grunted, shoving up from the railing and lifting my leg. The processors in the artificial legs measured the force of my leg lift, calculated the height and automatically adjusted the dorsiflexion of the foot to strike the floor with the heel first, then flexed to make the foot perfectly horizontal. As more weight was placed on the limb, the CPU sent signals that caused the foot to carry out the process of plantar flexion, slowly lifting the heel from the flat surface to push off with the toe.

At least that's how it was supposed to work. I'd been outfitted with the latest athletic tech prosthetics, and each leg was five times more powerful than a normal human leg. The computers in the legs seemed to work correctly, but the rest of my non-cybernetic body was all out of whack, threatening to topple me with every step without the railing there for support.

"Give it time, Mr. Forrest," the voice replied. "You've only been attempting to walk on your new legs for a day. You'll get it. Before long, you'll get the hang of it and will be chasing after criminals, saving the city once again."

"Shows what you know," I grumbled.

It'd been easier to just let the hospital staff continue to think I was the NOPD hero cop who'd saved hundreds of lives over the course of my career than letting them know that I was a disgrace to my precinct—actually, *that* was bullshit. I wasn't a disgrace; the system was a disgrace. Everything I'd done had been to keep the city and her citizens safe.

"Oh, pish-posh," the woman over the intercom replied. "You'll get this. Look at everyone else. Even Agnes, a sixty-four year-old diabetic amputee, is walking just fine."

I looked up from the treadmill and through the glass that partitioned the various physical therapy rooms, all filled with other amputees performing various tasks that their droid companions ran them through. The ward was laid out in a large circle around a central office hub where the licensed physical therapist monitored everyone's progress and allegedly input adjustments to the droids to assist with the patients' recovery.

Sure enough, through the glass separating the different therapy rooms, I could see that bitch, Agnes, walking just fine.

I put my head down and continued to try to adjust to my new normal. I sure as hell didn't want to be crippled for the rest of my life, so I *had* to get this. I couldn't very well move on to the next stage of my life in a wheelchair; *that* would require me to be upright and mobile.

After about an hour of listening to the physical therapy droid's archaic AI try to give me instructions, I was able to take four or five steps without needing to run to keep from falling over and my balance was improving. "That's enough for today, Mr. Forrest," the human therapist said. "You're covered in sweat and need a bath."

"Only if you're giving it to me. Jorge is too rough below the waist," I replied. In truth, I'd never even seen the therapist, so she could be hideously ugly, but I didn't care. I was happy to be done for the day.

"Now, now. That's what we call sexual harassment, Mr. Forrest. Don't they teach you anything at the NOPD?"

"Apparently I'm a slow learner."

I used the rail to make my way back to my wheelchair and zipped through the facility to my room. When I got there, Sergeant Drake was waiting for me.

"Drake! Good to see you," I said, looking up at the officer towering over me.

"Detective," he replied. "You don't remember it, but I was here during and after your surgery. How you doing?"

"I've been better," I admitted. Lifting one of my legs, I said, "That woman sure did a number on me, huh?"

"Can we?" He gestured at the door to my room.

"Sure, come on in. *Mi casa es su casa* and all that, right?"

When we'd gotten settled into my hospital room with the door firmly closed behind us, Drake gave me an update to what had happened at the cargo ship.

"Karimov is dead," he stated.

"Good."

"*Everyone* who was on that boat, except the woman, is dead."

I'd figured as much. "Even the cyborg we'd arrested?"

"Yup. Killed by your service pistol."

"Son of a bitch."

"The woman is Tanaz Karimov. Sister—"

"Are you fucking kidding me?" I interjected.

"Nope. The woman is Farouk Karimov's sister. When everyone was killed on that boat, it made her the single heir to the synthaine fortune. I assume she knows the formula as well."

A sinking feeling descended in my stomach. "There wasn't an explosive switch or anything like that with Farouk, was there?"

"No. She played us."

"Mother fucker!" I kicked my leg, the CPUs adjusting the foot wildly for the unexpected movement.

"Yeah. Chief Brubaker was livid when we ran a facial recognition scan of her from the drone footage."

"The dress-shirt thingy," I groaned. "Now it makes sense. She probably gave that as a gift to Terri Solomon, not her brother."

"Probably."

"And the unexplained attempted hit on Karimov at Liquid Genesis… It was her. *She* was the one in cahoots with Solomon."

"Given what we know now, it probably was. She'd likely used that as a way to kill him and when it didn't work, she continued working with him like nothing had happened."

"Holy fuck," I cursed. "Corrigan had been weird about the use of the name Karimov when we talked." I remembered him saying something about 'bosses' and not a singular boss. He'd been working for both of them and I'd thought he was only working for Farouk. "The son of a bitch was playing both sides."

I pointed at my stomach. "Corrigan said Karimov was good with knives, used them to kill the competition. He was talking about the sister, not the brother."

The fragments pieced themselves together in my mind. The dark-haired nurse… "She killed him. Tanaz killed Corrigan to shut him up."

"I thought it was bad morphine," Drake stated.

"That the prison had records saying they'd turned all of it in," I replied. "There was no reason that morphine was there, except to assassinate Corrigan and keep him from talking. Pretty poor luck that the guy singing like a bird to the cops was the only guy in the entire hospital ward unlucky enough to get the bad morphine, huh?"

"Damn," Drake said, shaking his head slightly. "She's good."

"Any idea of her whereabouts?"

"No. We raided her last known residence, but it was nothing except an abandoned space. We don't even know if she'd ever lived there. The chief has a plan to lure her in though…"

His voice trailed off and I thought of something further to say about Tanaz Karimov; nothing presented itself. With the short two weeks I had left on the force, I was off the case—regardless of my health status. The case would pass over to Doug Sanders or maybe to the Narcotics Division; it depended on how the department wanted to handle it.

"What about all those hostages?" I asked, changing the subject slightly.

"The ones from Warehouse Six?" Drake asked for clarification.

"Yeah. What happened on the other side of the port?"

"Fairchild's team and the H-RATs kicked some serious ass. They took out thirty hostiles without any injuries and rescued over two hundred workers. There's already talk that she's going to receive the Louisiana Law Enforcement Medal of Valor for her actions."

"Good," I replied. "She earned it. That's an outstanding success; especially when compared to—"

"Compared to our mission, which was an abysmal failure by department standards?" Drake chuckled.

"Yeah," I replied. "I got every one of those people killed."

"Regardless of what the paperwork says, those workers that got shot were bad people too, Detective. They were manufacturing a highly addictive drug that ends up killing the user within six months. They were monsters."

I shrugged, knowing that there were simply some things Drake felt strongly about. Illegal drug manufacturers, dealers, and users were in that category for him. They were the scum of the earth and no explanation would make him change his opinion.

"Detective, there's something else."

I adjusted myself in the seat. He wasn't looking forward to whatever he was about to say. "What is it?"

"The chief's plan to arrest Tanaz Karimov. It's pretty messed up, but it might work."

"What is it?"

"He's going to use *you* as bait."

"What?"

"He says he has a foolproof plan to bring her out of hiding and it involves you."

I grunted in surprise. "That old man has got some spunk left in him," I laughed. "What do I need to do?"

"You're not mad?" Drake asked, his eyebrows lifted higher than I'd ever seen them before.

"Fuck no. I want that bitch behind bars and I'll do whatever it takes."

"Well, *you* don't have to do anything…"

By the time Drake finished telling me the chief's plan, the hallway was full of uniformed cops who disappeared into vacant recovery rooms. We switched on the room's vidscreen, where Chief Brubaker had just stepped up to a podium for a news conference. Along the bottom of the screen, the words "**Synthaine: Easytown Police Chief Update on the Crisis**" flashed annoyingly to garner attention.

"Thank you all for coming today," Brubaker began. "The purpose of this news conference is to provide an update on the city's synthaine crisis, which I'm sure most of you have guessed, originated in Easytown."

"Someone should tell him they already had the title of the news conference up on screen," I joked, hitting Drake lightly on the leg with the back of my hand.

He didn't say anything, so I tuned back into the vidscreen.

"I'm happy to say that we believe the drug may be eradicated," Brubaker stated, and then had to wait as reporters shouted questions.

"Please, hold your questions until the end," he directed. "As you know, scientists have been able to identify the components of synthaine, but can't reproduce the final product. This makes it extremely valuable on the street since there is only one supplier in the entire nation.

"Ten days ago, Easytown Precinct Detective Zach Forrest led a raid against the suspected manufacturing location of the synthaine. He was correct. A man named Farouk Karimov produced the drug. Three years ago, Karimov purchased a retired cargo vessel legally and parked it in the Dockyards. That's where he manufactured the drug that swept through the city, and eventually made its way into most major cities across the US.

"Unfortunately, Detective Forrest was seriously injured during the ensuing shootout with Karimov and his guards. He remains in critical condition at New Orleans East Hospital. Additionally, Karimov and everyone who worked on the cargo vessel were killed during the exchange that involved several officers and police drones. With Karimov's death, the knowledge of how to create one of the deadliest street drugs in the modern era has died away also."

He paused, and smiled into the camera. "We still have a long way to go since there's still product on the street with dealers and the addicts will become increasingly more dangerous as they try to scrape up the money to buy the product as supplies dwindle, but the end is in sight. We seized and destroyed more than two hundred cases of synthaine after the raid on the shipping vessel, and we can say with certainty that the synthaine threat is in its dying throes."

Brubaker took half a step back from the podium. "We'll open it up for questions at this time."

"Chief! Chief!" a woman shouted louder than the other reporters to get his attention.

"Yes, ah, you," he replied pointing at her.

The camera panned to the crowd of reporters and I was shocked to see Sandra Deshutes, the desk officer for the Easytown Precinct.

"How can you say that the synthaine epidemic is over? Isn't it entirely possible that others know the formula?" Sandra asked.

"While that's possible, we are confident that all of the people associated with Farouk Karimov are deceased. There are reports from the officers on scene that a woman survived, but fled the area during the exchange of gunfire."

The reporters all began shouting again and Chief Brubaker picked a male from the back row. I recognized him as well. He was a cop who worked in Traffic Enforcement.

"Brubaker stacked the questions," I remarked.

"Yup," Drake said as the 'reporter' asked his question.

"What do you know about this woman? Do you know where she is, or what she was doing there?"

"Well… The only thing we know for sure is that Detective Forrest rescued her during the fight and was with her for several minutes before he was injured. The New Orleans Police Department would like to extend a special invitation to this woman: Please come down to any precinct office to discuss your role at the cargo ship and how you escaped from the situation."

"Chief! Over here! Over here!"

"Yes, sir. You." He pointed at another undercover officer from Petty Crimes.

"Is this woman wanted in connection with the manufacture or distribution of the synthaine?"

"No. Good question," he said as an aside, selling his script. "The woman may have been a prostitute or even a housekeeper—there's evidence that Karimov lived on the boat. At this time, the only one who's talked to her is Detective Forrest."

"When will Detective Forrest be able to discuss his role at the cargo ship that night?"

"Son of a bitch," I groaned. "That's Katheryn."

"Right now, we don't know, ma'am," Brubaker replied. "He's still in critical condition and in a medically-induced coma. We haven't been able to talk to him yet. As soon as he's able, we will get his statement and get to the bottom of who this mystery woman is."

"The drones don't have footage?" Sandra asked without being called upon.

Brubaker looked annoyed, but answered her anyways. "No. The drones were a little busy taking fire from a group of criminals, so they didn't record any usable footage except for the woman's clothing, which is why we think she may have been a housekeeper." He shifted slightly at the podium. "I'd like to remind everyone to please wait until you're called upon to ask your questions. Ah, yes, you," he said, pointing at a reporter that I recognized as a legitimate member of the media.

The remainder of the questions became less invasive and more along the lines of what vidfeed reporters would normally ask. Less than ten minutes after the planted questions were complete, Brubaker concluded the press conference and the feed's talking heads speculated about what the drug vacuum would do to the city, while experts in the field gave their opinions as well.

Drake stood and turned off the screen. When he turned back, a smile stretched from ear-to-ear. "Now we wait."

TWENTY-THREE: THURSDAY

Chief Brubaker was convinced that Tanaz Karimov would come to the hospital to silence me, but nothing happened Wednesday night. As Thursday stretched toward the late evening, I was beginning to wonder if she'd seen the press conference. They'd made it painfully clear that all the synthaine producers were believed to be dead and no one except me knew anything about the woman who'd escaped during the firefight.

Which meant I was a juicy target, allegedly in a coma, lying in the New Orleans East Hospital's intensive care unit—which Brubaker had 'accidentally' let slip during the conference. If she could eliminate me, she could walk away without anyone knowing what she looked like.

It was a no-brainer that she'd be coming after me; it was just a matter of when and how.

"Drake, I've gotta tell you something," I said as I ate the bland hospital food that'd been brought into my room. I'd been confined to the space since the press conference because it was too difficult to secure the entire facility. The hallway outside was doable.

"What's that, Detective?"

"I hate that Brubaker decided to use me as bait without discussing it with me first."

"Would you have said no?"

"Probably not," I admitted. "But I still don't like it."

"Two more weeks and you're a free man. No more orders from anybody if you don't want to take them."

"True," I replied. "In all honesty, I'm a little scared of going out on my own."

"You'll do great. You're a good cop. Maybe taking the reins of oppressive regulations off of you will be exactly what you need."

"Or maybe it's just enough rope to hang myself," I countered. "If I hadn't had the department's regulations hanging over my head for the last decade, I would have done some truly stupid things. And, to tell the truth, they saved my ass in a few situations."

"Would you do those stupid things today?"

"Knowing what I know now? No way."

"Then you learned from it and that's a good thing."

"Yeah, I guess so. The whole thing just—"

A reflection of light outside the window over Drake's shoulder caught my eye. I had a split second to ignore it or try to shove the immovable mountain of a man out of the way.

I chose the second option.

My legs overcompensated for the movement, launching me like a rocket toward his torso.

"Hey!" he shouted as his chair toppled backward and I went flying over him, hitting my head on the wall. "What the hell are you doing?"

"Gun," I grunted, shaking my head.

The slight whistling sound of air rushing through a hole in the window reached my ears. Above me, I saw a small circular hole in the old-fashioned glass window. Surprisingly, it hadn't shattered. I followed the line of trajectory with my eyes and saw a similar hole on the interior wall.

"She's using a laser!" I shouted.

Drake stopped struggling to stand and rolled sideways onto his stomach, then he low-crawled to me. "Do you see her?"

"No. I'm sitting against the wall. What do you see?"

"Nothing. I'm—Hey!" Drake shouted. "We have contact!"

An officer burst through the door with his pistol drawn. He had a moment to register that Drake and I were on the floor before the laser blasted through his face and out the back of his head. He fell to the floor silently and his gun clanked against the tile.

"Dammit! We're pinned down!" Drake screamed. "She's outside. We need drone support. Now!"

Other officers began to shout out questions, but nobody was foolish enough to come through the doorway again. "Thermals," I breathed heavily. "If she hasn't used them yet, she will. We need to move!"

"Drones inbound," an officer yelled, relaying whatever information had come over the radio frequency he was monitoring. "Target identified. Shooter is on a hoverskiff, sixty feet from the window, due east."

I tried to remember which way was east, but everything in my head was a jumbled mess and all I could think about was the need to move before Karimov fired up her thermal imagers and shot at Drake and I while we huddled underneath the windowsill.

Several holes appeared in rapid succession, including one in the concrete right between the two of us. Then the new holes stopped appearing and the officer who'd given the play-by-play a moment earlier shouted out, "Suspect has disengaged. She's running! Drones are pursuing."

I used the window's ledge to pull myself up so I could see what was happening. Less than a football field's length away, I saw a hoverskiff headed toward Easytown. Three drones pursued it, firing as they went. *Whomever had allowed them to go weapons free while traveling over the city was in for a serious ass chewing*, I thought.

It was probably Brubaker. His fake news conference was evidence enough that he wanted to end this as badly as I did.

The chase didn't last long. The hoverskiff engines began to smoke, slowing the skiff. Then, forward momentum stopped and the pilot turned, lifting a rifle to her shoulder. A mass of long, brown hair billowed on the wind as Tanaz sighted down the laser rifle's barrel.

I could tell how many rounds she fired, but the lead drone faltered and tumbled from the sky. Somewhere below, the falling remains would likely crush some unlucky homeless person. She turned the rifle on another drone, but it had closed the distance and I saw the telltale shining lines of the drone's Taser as they arced across the void, slamming into her.

Tanaz's body jerked spasmodically as the electric voltage coursed through her. She began to twitch, dangerously close to the edge of the hoverskiff.

And then she fell over the side.

The Taser lines stretched, suspending her in the air for a moment before the barbs ripped from her skin. I watched her body fall all the way to the ground until she landed in the middle of the interstate less than a meter in front of an oncoming car. The vehicle's computer didn't have time to adjust to the sudden appearance of a foreign object right in front of it and the car hit her at seventy-five miles per hour, basically liquefying her torso.

"I guess the trap worked," I muttered.

"Too bad Landrum took one to the face," Drake said softly. "He was a good cop. Didn't deserve that."

I wanted to say something both respectful and reverent of the officer's sacrifice, but I couldn't force myself to do so. It'd been a stupid move on his part to charge into an active shooter situation without any idea of what was on the other side of the door. It was a rookie mistake and it cost him his life.

After a few moments of internal deliberation, I decided on simply agreeing with my partner, "Yeah. It's too bad."

EPILOGUE: SEVEN MONTHS LATER

"Andi, we need to find a new insurance company. This one is raking my balls over the coals."

"I'll begin looking for comparable policies that allow for high risk activities such as chasing criminals, engaging in gunfights, taunting police officers, street brawls with drug addicts, associating with suspected crime bosses and prostitutes, as well as random, unimaginative home and office mishaps."

"Ah… On second thought, let's just keep the policy I have."

"That's probably for the best, Zach. It took several weeks of negotiations and more than a few omissions on the application to get approved for this policy. It would take considerably longer to obtain a new policy and with your lifestyle, you can't afford a lapse in coverage."

I leaned back in my chair and put my feet up on the desk, careful to ease my prosthetics down so I didn't bash a hole in the work surface. After I was released from the hospital, I'd been put on administrative leave for a week and then given only a week to clear out of the NOPD. I'd done it in two days.

My severance package was not substantial, but even if I sat on my couch and ate street food all day, every day, I could have made the money stretch for a year without touching my savings. Instead, I used the cash to set up the Zachary Forrest Investigative Agency, LLC. My tagline was,

"We take the cases the cops won't touch!" and business had been steadily growing as the word got out that I took cases that normally nobody would touch.

Missing prostitute? Yeah, we do that. You suspect your husband is cheating on you with a droid? I'll look into it for you. What's that? Some asshole stole your drugs. Well, let me track them down and tell you where they are. No, I won't recover them for you, but I can put you in contact with people who will do that too. You know, that sort of stuff.

I didn't do anything illegal, but I also wasn't under any obligation to report illegal activities that I stumbled upon during the course of an investigation. My clients seemed to like that part.

Outside, I could hear the bustling streets of Easytown from the third-story office I rented above The Mother Board, the cyber café where the juvenile delinquent Jewel worked at near the middle of Jubilee Lane. I'd been in the building for six months and I loved the location. It was an easy walk to several food skiffs during the day, and a quick jaunt to every strip club on The Lane after work. I set my own hours, decided what cases I'd take, and most importantly, did whatever the hell I wanted to, *with* whomever I wanted to.

I tapped my retro-style ballpoint pen on the small tablet of paper I always kept on my desktop. Right now, lying to my right, the pages of the notebook were flipped open to my latest case—one that should set me up for a couple of months.

A woman had come into my office last Friday. Mrs. Soriano was agitated and disheveled, and it wasn't just from the rain. Her teenage son was in a band, a really shitty one if the demo vid I'd seen was any indication about their entire set, and missing. He was also into VR drugs, a known duster. He'd disappeared four days before and the cops didn't have time for runaways.

I typically tried to avoid dusters. They usually either washed up on the shores of the Mississippi after a few weeks or wandered in from wherever they'd been holed up when they immersed themselves in the Cybersphere. Very rarely was there anything anyone could do for them, the allure of being able to plug in and live virtually in the internet without the real world interfering was simply too great.

Apparently, the drugs that took them there were pretty good too.

Mrs. Soriano had given me tons of information about her kid's friends, his usual hangouts, and even who his dealer was. She'd seen the dealer's name on her credfile a few times when her kid had hacked her account for drug money. Dusters were the smartest stupid people I'd ever known.

I'd taken what she gave me, cross-referenced it with street camera feeds and known duster safe houses. I found a kid who looked like hers from behind, but never got a clear picture of his face. I was positive it was him, though. The kid's stride in the street camera footage matched vidfeed footage of him that his mother had provided. All I needed now was the credit authorization to clear from Mrs. Soriano and I'd go get her boy.

A soft beep from the wall behind me indicated a new message had arrived. "Andi, play the latest received message."

"It's a text file, boss," she replied. "The sum of seventy-five thousand dollars has just arrived in your account. You will not have to dip into your personal savings to cover any expenses for several months with this amount."

"Good news," I said, groaning slightly as I lifted my legs off the desk and set them on the floor.

I tapped a button on the window frame and the clear, unobstructed view of The Lane faded away as the visalum frosted over with horizontal white bars, reminiscent of the old Venetian blinds my parents' house had before it was destroyed in a hurricane.

What can I say? I have a nostalgic streak.

I lifted my shoulder harness off the back of my chair and shrugged into it. I patted the NOPD Sig Sauer I'd purchased at auction and checked the opposite side to ensure I had extra magazines. The Aegis went into its paddle holster on my hip, and my dark gray duster concealed everything.

I walked to the front door and popped the fedora off of its hook. Settling it down on my head, I checked my reflection in the mirror. *Handsome as ever.*

"Don't wait up, Andi," I said as I locked the door to my office behind me.

Two short flights of stairs and a reinforced door, then I was standing on The Lane as people moved back and forth in front of me like seaweed swaying in the surf.

I smiled. I was in my element. I was home.

THE END

I hope you enjoyed this novel and leave a review on Amazon to help other readers discover it.

Want more from Brian Parker?
Find all of his books on Amazon.com:

www.amazon.com/Brian-Parker/e/B00DFD98YI

About the Author

A veteran of the wars in Iraq and Afghanistan, Brian Parker was born and raised as an Army brat. He's currently an Active Duty Army soldier who enjoys spending time with his family in Texas, hiking, obstacle course racing, writing and Texas Longhorns football. He's an unashamed Star Wars fan, but prefers to disregard the entire Episode I and II debacle.

Brian is both a traditionally- and self-published author with an ever-growing collection of works across multiple genres, including sci-fi, post-apocalyptic, horror, paranormal thriller, military fiction, self-publishing how-to and even a children's picture book—Zombie in the Basement, which he wrote to help children overcome the perceived stigma of being different from others.

He is also the founder of Muddy Boots Press, an independent publishing company that focuses on quality genre fiction over mass-produced books.

FOLLOW BRIAN ON SOCIAL MEDIA!
Facebook: www.facebook.com/BrianParkerAuthor
Instagram: @BrianParker_Author
Twitter: www.twitter.com/BParker_Author
Web: www.BrianParkerAuthor.com

Made in the USA
Middletown, DE
15 November 2025

21676482R00186